The Glare of Truth

Max Anderson Mysteries, Volume 3

Hayden Trenholm

Published by House of Straw Press, 2023.

THE GLARE OF TRUTH

First edition. September 1, 2023.

ISBN: 978-1927881668

Written by Hayden Trenholm.

Also by Hayden Trenholm

Max Anderson Mysteries
In the Shadow of Versailles
By Dawn's Early Light
The Glare of Truth

Standalone
Let Me Gather My Thoughts

Watch for more at https://www.haydentrenholm.com/.

This book is dedicated to the **East Block Irregulars**, one of the finest writing groups in the known world!

Chapter 1 Tuesday, September 20, 1921

Max had been dreaming about bees. When he woke, the buzzing remained.

"Jacqui, you're snoring." *No, she isn't*, thought Max, *she's in Marseilles visiting her sick cousin.* The buzzing started again. Max turned on the bed-side light. According to his alarm clock, it was after three.

The buzzing was coming from the other room.

It was the telephone.

The air was cold against his bare skin as he staggered from his bed to the room that served as living space and kitchen of his small apartment on Rue Lepic. Henri had warned him about having a telephone installed. "It is nothing but an invasion of privacy."

The black box vibrated again. Max lifted the receiver. The Bakelite felt cold against his swollen ear, a souvenir of the bout at O'Brien's gym the previous day.

"Max Anderson."

"Max, Max is that you?" The voice was slurred; the words were in English. "It's Erich."

Erich Harvey, part-time investigative reporter, full-time lush. Max had used him as a "researcher" in a few cases. His work was good as long as you got him early in the day. Unfortunately, three in the morning was not early for Harvey, it was very late.

"Can't this wait?"

"No," said Harvey, his voice suddenly sobered. "I don't think it can. I... I may have killed a man."

"Where are you?"

1

"At Le Salon de Chêne, on St. Germaine."

Max was surprised. Only the better bars in the Latin Quarter had phones; de Chêne didn't qualify.

"Stay there; I'll come as soon as I can."

Max pulled on his clothes and wondered why he was bothering. He'd known Harvey for about a year but they were hardly close. *I guess I'm a sucker for hard luck cases.* And Harvey certainly fit the bill. He was an old timer, stationed in Paris since before the war. Max didn't know if the war had broken Harvey – he didn't talk about it – but something had. Now he eked out what living he could writing freelance pieces for the papers back home. Life hadn't gotten any easier with the influx of Americans that flooded the city after the devaluation of the franc last year. They all needed to supplement their allowances and they all thought journalism was the best way to do it.

Max wondered if Harvey had killed one of those; he'd certainly threatened to do so often enough.

The Metro wouldn't open for another two hours and taxis were few and far between at this time of night even in Pigalle, where the bars never closed and the prostitutes and their customers never seemed to sleep. He rummaged through his cupboard and found a day-old brioche. He smeared it with butter and apricot jam, flavoured with vanilla and rum. Coffee would have to wait but he couldn't face Harvey on an empty stomach.

Max finished dressing and added a quilted jacket; fall nights could be cold in Paris. Almost as an afterthought, he shoved his five-shot Kolb in the jacket pocket.

Max's luck held steady; there wasn't a taxi in sight, either at the café across the street or the length of Clichy as far as he could see. Gare de L'Est was only ten minutes away so Max pulled his jacket tighter and headed down Clichy past the bars, the girls and the small clusters of drunken tourists that populated the City of Light when the lights should properly be off.

Ten minutes on foot and another ten by cab brought him to the front door of Le Salon de Chêne. The bars in the Latin Quarter kept more sedate hours, though you could always find one that catered to the late-night crowd. The windows were shuttered but a small light glimmered over the front door. Max knocked softly on the glass and a few moments later the blind was pulled aside and a single bloodshot eye glared out at him. Max flashed a fifty franc note and the door swung open.

Le Salon de Chêne was a typical St. Germaine establishment. A half dozen tables scattered in the small space that surrounded the long zinc-topped bar. Three ex-soldiers – judging by their pinned-up sleeves and pant legs – sat together on stools at one end of the bar. Harvey was seated at a table in the back corner, nursing a beer and looking miserable.

"Who did you kill, Erich?" said Max, as he slipped into the chair opposite the newsman. Harvey had shrunk in the last few months; his suit, frayed at cuffs and collar and smudged with dirt, draped his narrow shoulders like a discarded army tent. His hair had now gone completely grey except a single streak of pure white that ran through his long bangs like a badge.

"A guy named Réjean. Can't remember his last name. He works for Le Grand Parisien." A daily known more for its inflammatory headlines than the accuracy of its stories. "And I only might have killed him."

"What happened?"

"We were having a drink. He said a few things about America and Americans that I didn't care for. I let it go for a while because he was buying. Finally, I told him where he could shove his opinions. I may have said something about his parentage. He was unmoved until I brought the church into it. Then he pulled a knife."

"A religious zealot, eh?' said Max. "I know the type."

"The bartender was getting a bit pissed so we took it outside. I happened to have brought a bottle with me so I hit him with it. He went down and I left. An hour later, so I'm told, he was pulled out of the Seine. Not breathing."

"Where was this? The fight I mean."

"At a place over on Rue Jacob."

"Jacob is two blocks from the Seine. How did he get in the river?"

Harvey frowned and looked down into his beer glass, which was almost empty. Max signalled the waiter and ordered another beer for Harvey and an espresso for himself.

"Were you drinking, Erich?"

"I'd had a bottle of wine and a couple of pastis. Not much."

Max raised his eyebrow and Harvey shrugged.

"I've been drinking every day for nearly forty years, Max. I was as sober as I ever am. I've spent the last three hours trying to rectify that sad fact. Hard to do it on a budget." He gestured at an empty brandy glass so Max added a pastis to his order.

Harvey had enough brandy in him already that his hand didn't shake when he raised the glass to his lips, not so much that he didn't drink half of it on the first gulp. The brandy seemed to help; Harvey's leonine head lifted and the focus in his rheumy eyes sharpened slightly.

"Did you and this Réjean have a history?"

"I used to borrow his copy for the Paris Herald. He was a cleaner writer than most in the city. His work was easy to translate. He kept trying to present me with a bill for it and I kept tearing it up. We got along fine."

"Until tonight?"

"Yeah." Harvey's gaze drifted past Max's shoulder as if there was something more interesting on the wall behind him than a faded poster from the Great Exhibition. Max thought Harvey had something more to say on the subject of Réjean, but wasn't ready to say it yet.

"Who told you Réjean was in the Seine?"

Harvey's brow furrowed as if he were trying to recall ancient history rather than the events of a few hours before. "Who? Pierre Delacroix, a funny little fellow who writes for Le Journal. He came into Le Dôme with a couple of pirettes on his arm, right before closing time. Came right up to me and said 'they just pulled Réjean LaFoie' – that's the name – 'out of the river. I'd make myself scarce if I were you.'"

"Did he say why?"

Harvey shook his head mournfully. "Gave me the good news and left. Took both of the girls with him."

"He came all the way to Le Dôme to tell you that? How did he know you were there?"

"I... I don't know."

If Harvey had anything else to say, Max was going to have to wait to hear it. The glass door rattled as a heavy fist pounded on the frame.

"Open in the name of the Sureté."

MAX RODE DOWN TO THE Prefecture with Harvey and a couple of swallows. Captain Fontaine was the officer in charge. He and Max had a long acquaintance though no-one confused them for friends.

"What did you do to get relegated to the night shift?" Max asked by way of making conversation.

Fontaine glared at him but didn't answer. Harvey was slumped in the corner of the wagon, snoring softly. Max shrugged and pulled his cap down over his eyes. The ride to police headquarters was barely ten minutes but the war had taught him to catch sleep whenever it came around.

The appearance before the night magistrate only took a few minutes; LaFoie had several broken bones as well as a head wound, no water in the lungs so he was dead before he was dumped in the river. The evidence seemed slim to Max but the judge deemed it sufficient to bind Harvey over for trial. Max saw him safely ensconced in a cell and promised to come back later in the day after his lawyer's office opened. Cleroux wasn't the greatest legal mind in Paris but he was cheap and would take cases his more upstanding colleagues wouldn't touch.

Max was a familiar face at the station. Sergeant LePêcheur called him over to the night desk as he was leaving.

"You must be living a clean life," he said. "I hardly ever see you."

"Most of my clients keep bankers' hours." That had certainly been true lately. Business hadn't exactly been brisk and few of his "cases" had involved serious criminals. Not that Max minded. He didn't need the money and it gave him more time to do the things he really liked: dancing with Jacqui at Chez Jake and drinking with Henri and Yesim at Le Coq Bleu. "What are you doing behind the desk?"

"A friend needed me to fill in for a few weeks. Family troubles." He shrugged. "Gereau has been asking after you."

"I thought he retired," said Max.

"He did. He only comes in three or four times a week."

"That doesn't sound retired."

LePêcheur shrugged. "You know Captain Gereau."

Indeed, Max thought. Captain Gereau had little else to fill his days. Never married and most of his close family dead in the war or from the Spanish flu, he had nothing left but his work. Politics had forced him from his job, but nothing would keep him from his occupation.

Max scribbled his telephone exchange and number on a scrap of paper and handed to LePêcheur. "Ask Gereau to call me the next time he drops by."

LePêcheur stared at the paper like it was written in Arabic before folding and slipping it under the blotter. "A telephone? You've come up in the world."

True enough, thought Max, though he doubted the telephone added to his status. The finer class of people looked down on them. Parisians, for all their revolutionary history, were a conservative lot. Still, much had changed in the three years since he had stumbled off the night train from London, freshly demobbed and with no plan for the future more elaborate than a desire to forget everything that had gone before.

Cleroux's office wouldn't open for a couple of hours but Max felt too jittery to head back across town to his bed or to the office he kept above Chez Jake on the far side of Montmartre. Instead, he walked up to Les Halles where the market was already crowded with drivers and porters making deliveries to the dozens of shops and stalls crowded together under the vast glass arches of the marketplace. Several of the larger shops had recently installed refrigerators and he thought he might drop by later to buy a fillet for his supper, to see if the new devices kept the fish fresher than the beds of ice the other shops used.

He took a small table near the back of one of the early-opening brassieres that catered to workers and ordered a mug of chocolate and a basket of pastries. The croissant was surprisingly good; the buttery flakes melted on his tongue, leaving only the faint taste of honey in their wake. Max took three early editions from the rack near the window.

Le Grand Parisien, LaFoie's employer, had a headline two inches high. Journalist Brutally Murdered; American Suspected, though the details in the story below were even sketchier than what had been provided to the night judge. Dark hints of a foreign conspiracy were suggested and by the fourth paragraph, the Protocols of the Elders of Zion had been invoked.

The other papers reported the same meagre facts, though in the first, the headline was only an inch high and the conspiracy was attributed not to Jews but to Soviet infiltrators, another bugaboo of the yellow press. In Le Miroir, the story had been relegated to page two and Harvey had become a key witness rather than a suspect. No conspiracy was mentioned. However, a woman was.

Max had never seen Harvey with a woman but that didn't mean much. People lived several lives at once, lives that seldom intersected. He doubted Harvey had killed LaFoie in a fit of jealous rage. Nonetheless, Max jotted the woman's name – Nicole Bilodeau – into his notebook.

Cleroux's office was on Rue Scribe not far from the Opera Palais Garnier. Max paused to gaze up at the gilded busts of famous French composers gazing down on the passing crowds. Most looked disdainful; others amused. Jacqui had forced Max to take her to a performance of *La forza del destino*. He had fallen asleep in the middle of the third act but woke up in time for everyone to die. He had been overwhelmed by the first opera Havel Barzani had taken him to in 1919, but the novelty had worn off.

Fortunately, Jacqui was catholic in her tastes, if not her religion. She didn't complain about the jazz music at Chez Jake and he didn't ask who it was that took her to the Opera instead of him. Living with Jacqui wasn't what he had been taught to expect growing up in Nova Scotia, but he liked it fine for all that.

THE LAW OFFICE WAS the smallest of three businesses occupying the second floor of a Haussmann era building. It consisted of three rooms, a reception area, a small office shared by a pair of articling clerks and a larger space that Cleroux had to himself. The receptionist, a slim bored-looking young woman with bottle-bright hair and a pronounced overbite, ducked her head into Cleroux's office before waving Max through.

The office was its usual cluttered mess with stacks of books, boxes and files littered on most available surfaces, though the client chair in front of the desk was pristine as was a narrow path that led to it from the door. Cleroux, a middle-aged man with thinning hair, was reclining in a large swivel chair, his back to an expanse of windows that looked out on the street below, his shoeless feet propped on his desk. He was sipping coffee from an espresso cup; a croissant was balanced on his broad waistcoat-covered belly.

He gestured with his cup for Max to take a seat while pointing with one foot to the tray perched precariously on a stack of books at the end of his desk, an invitation to join him in breakfast. Max poured a small cup of dark coffee from the carafe and sat down.

"How can I help you, Monsieur Anderson?" Cleroux asked once they had shared their coffee in amiable silence for several minutes.

"Do you know Erich Harvey?"

Cleroux frowned. "Yes. I have a client who is suing him."

It was Max's turn to frown. "Réjean LaFoie?"

"The same. Did Harvey send you to negotiate a settlement?"

"I'm afraid the suit is settled," said Max. "They pulled LaFoie out of the Seine this morning. Harvey has been arrested on suspicion of his murder."

"Merde!" Cleroux sat up and placed his cup carefully on his desk. His face had tightened and Max thought he might cry.

"My condolences," said Max. "I didn't know you were..."

"It's nothing." Cleroux blew his nose on a large white handkerchief. "LaFoie owed me money. I doubt I can collect it from his estate."

"I was going to ask if you would represent Erich Harvey but if you have a conflict…"

"My conflict died with my client. I would be happy to work on Mr. Harvey's case. You know my terms."

Max took out his cheque book and wrote a retainer. It seemed doubtful he would recover any of it. *Throw your bread upon the waters*, he thought, and had the sudden image of avaricious ducks in a feeding frenzy.

"If it isn't a breach of client privilege, what was LaFoie suing Harvey for?"

Cleroux waved away the thought as one might wave away a buzzing fly. "Alienation of affections."

Max wasn't sure what he had been expecting the lawyer to say but it certainly wasn't that. His expression must have conveyed his confusion to Cleroux for the lawyer went on.

"Mr. LaFoie was engaged to be married." He dug through a pile of files and consulted one briefly. "Mademoiselle Bilodeau."

"Nicole Bilodeau?"

"The same. LaFoie claimed that his engagement was broken off abruptly after his fiancé spent an evening with Mr. Harvey."

Max felt the heat rise to his face. Even after a year with Jacqui and her views on "free love," he found it difficult to accept the idea of casual relations between the sexes. He knew it happened. Jacqui claimed that it was *now* theoretical as far as she was concerned but that was a matter of her choice and not of any obligation to him. "She spent the night with Erich Harvey?"

"The law is nothing if it is not precise. If I meant that I would have said so. Apparently, Mlle Bilodeau is a journalist as well. She and Mr. Harvey spent an evening at one of the bars where such people gather. He told her certain rumours about Mr. LaFoie's activities, which, when she had verified them as true, led her to end their relationship. Mr. LaFoie claimed that this was entirely the fault of

Mr. Harvey. I told him we had little chance of achieving satisfaction in the courts but you know how jilted lovers can be."

"What secrets did Mr. Harvey reveal?"

"I'm afraid Mr. LaFoie was reluctant to disclose them even to me. You will have to ask Mr. Harvey." He slipped a small white card from the folder and slid it across the desk to Max. In neat slanted handwriting, Max read the name of Bilodeau and an address in the nicer part of Le Marais. "Or you could ask Mlle Bilodeau."

Chapter 2 Thursday, September 22nd, 1921

M ax's caseload was slim but it wasn't nonexistent. He spent most of Wednesday at the Hall of Records investigating the relationships of a group of cousins who were in a protracted dispute over an inheritance. By late afternoon he had retreated with sore eyes and an aching head for an early supper at Le Coq Bleu. Yesim, its proprietor, and Henri, his best customer, seemed astonished at the idea of a female journalist and fascinated about the possibility of a 'crime passionnel.' Max left them discussing the history of crime in Paris to return to his empty bed.

He awoke to the sound of urgent rapping at his door and sunlight streaming across his bed from the half-shuttered bedroom window. His clock said it was past two which surprised him until he realized he had neglected to wind it. The rapping came again and Max pulled on a robe over his underclothing and staggered to the door.

A young man in the uniform of the telegraph company was leaning against the jamb. He straightened as Max yanked the door open and offered up a blue-stripped envelope. Max found a couple of francs in a bowl on a shelf and exchanged them for the envelope.

Jacqui's cousin had taken a turn for the worse. Nothing serious but she was delaying her return from Friday to the following Tuesday "to be on the safe side." Dancing at Chez Jake would have to wait for another day.

Max's wrist watch provided a different but no less inaccurate time – 4:12 – so he showered, dressed, and walked across the street to the patisserie that never seemed to close. There he learned that it was actually shortly before ten, neither too late for a decent breakfast nor too early to visit a lady journalist. The rumble in his stomach decided the issue and Max ordered a plate of pastries, fruit, cheese, and a large mug of café américain; it would, he told himself, suffice for both breakfast and lunch. He ate at a table on the sidewalk, enjoying the heat of early autumn and watching the passing flâneurs.

An hour later he was standing in front of a well-kept house on Rue de Jarente not far from Place des Vosges, a spot favoured by duelists in earlier years. Max took a minute to appraise the dwelling before announcing his presence.

The double wooden doors allowing porters access to the courtyard for deliveries were painted a brilliant green, a sharp contrast to the more sedate colours chosen for its neighbours. Like most houses in the district, no windows were at street level and those on the second floor were barred and well curtained from within. A smaller door for residents and visitors stood to one side, its simple stone frame topped with a lintel into which was carved a scowling face. A similar face adorned the heavy metal door knocker. It was not particularly welcoming.

As Max reached for the knocker, the door was suddenly flung open and a woman, her face turned away to call some last-minute instructions to someone within, stepped into the street and into him. She gave a little cry as he wrapped his arms around her to keep them both from spilling onto the paving stones.

They hung like that for a moment, her head tilted back to look up into his face. Her eyes were wide and dark, almost black, in the shade of her cloche cap. Ringlets of black hair dipped below the hat's brim, forming a curlicue line across her smooth brow. Her lips, slightly parted to show even white teeth, were bright red against the paleness of her skin.

Max stepped back, his face suddenly hot, though he kept his hands on her shoulders as she wobbled, heeled shoes making her unsteady on the cobbles of the street. She still had said nothing after the little cry but now smiled at him and then glanced from side to side at his hands until he released her.

She observed him for a moment, one gloved hand resting on her hip. She was dressed in the latest style he had seen on display at the Galleries LaFayette, when Jacqui took him window-shopping – a calf length dress of deep blue, belted loosely at the waist and with a darker open collar that showed the length of her neck. The hat was also blue, with a strip of embroidered flowers along the brim. Max realized she was cataloging his appearance with the same observant eye.

"Mademoiselle Bilodeau?" he asked.

"You have the advantage of me," she replied, her voice a low lilting contralto. "Monsieur...?"

"Anderson. Max Anderson. I'm a friend of Erich Harvey's."

"Poor Erich. Have they released him yet?"

"We're working on it," said Max.

"More than merely a friend, then?"

"I'm a detective. But I'm also a friend." Neither entirely true. The Sûreté did not actually recognize his occupation as much as tolerate it and he was still not entirely sure what his relationship was to Erich Harvey. But it was close enough for now.

"C'est charmant! An American detective in Paris."

Also not true, but Max didn't bother to correct her on his true nationality. Most Parisians didn't see the difference anyway.

"Can we walk together?" Bilodeau asked. "I have an appointment at the American embassy in twenty minutes."

The Embassy was on Rue De Chaillot, well over a kilometre away, not a difficult walk for Max but he wasn't wearing high heels.

However, her shoes didn't seem to trouble the young reporter and she set off at a brisk pace so Max was forced to hurry to catch her.

"What was your relationship to Réjean LaFoie?" he asked.

"As I am sure you already know, he was my fiancé. I broke it off with him several weeks ago. I believe he blamed Erich for my decision – but that is nonsense."

"He had filed a law suit for 'alienation of affections.'"

"If anyone alienated my affections, it was Réjean himself. He was not a nice man."

"You don't seem particularly upset by his death."

"A young woman in Paris soon learns not to be too open about her feelings to men she has only now met. You say you are a detective and a friend of Erich's but how do I know you are who you say you are? You could be anyone."

They had reached Rue Rivoli and turned right to head toward the Embassy. The shop windows were filled with the latest fashions. A scattering of clients still occupied the sidewalk tables of the many cafes and restaurants, sipping coffee and nibbling at the last of their breakfast brioche. Waiters clustered in groups, smoking dark French cigarettes, and gossiping in low voices. The lunchtime rush was more than an hour away and they were in no hurry to clear tables or change the menu boards to advertise the table d'hôte.

Bilodeau paused several times to greet male acquaintances, all of whom rose to kiss her on both cheeks while studiously ignoring Max's presence. They didn't speak again until they reached the Tuileries gardens.

"I have a friend at the embassy, Buchan, who can vouch for me."

Bilodeau stopped and laughed, a low throaty chuckle, then turned and placed her hand on his arm. "I don't doubt you are who you say you are. How do you know Ginger?"

"We've worked together from time to time." Max left out the part where he had once suspected Buchan of murder.

"Fascinating. So then you must know what Ginger does at the Embassy."

Max knew both Buchan's official job and what he really did but he didn't know Bilodeau well enough to mention the latter.

"Whatever's required of him. He's pretty low on the stick."

"As he keeps telling me."

The gardens didn't seem to know the first day of fall had arrived; the trees were still mostly green with the barest hint of yellow and red on a few early turning branches. Max would have suggested they walk through them but didn't want to give the wrong impression. They didn't speak again until they reached La Place de la Concorde.

"How do you know Erich?" Max asked. His real interest was in LaFoie but he suspected she wasn't ready to talk about him.

"We're competitors."

"Erich speaks French but I don't think he writes it that well."

"I wouldn't know. I write in English myself – my mother was English – so we are often trying to sell to the same newspapers. The Paris Herald and Tribune plus the international wire services, of course. Our paths cross from time to time though we are interested in quite different subjects."

"I would think the French press would offer more opportunity..."

"And more competition, too, though that is changing with all the Americans flooding the city. They all think they can write, you know. Erich is finding it more difficult than I."

"Why is that?"

"Because I'm better looking."

Max wasn't about to disagree. He was no expert with women but he wasn't stupid about it either. Besides, she *was* good looking. He had a hard time not sneaking glimpses at her profile as they walked.

"What did Erich tell you about LaFoie that led you to break off the engagement?"

"It is difficult to describe. Everything Erich said I already knew at some level. It was..." she paused to consider. "Have you ever seen those drawings that look like one thing but then your perspective changes and you see they are something else altogether."

"I'm not sure..."

"You know, first it looks like a vase and then you see it is two profiles facing each other. Or a woman in a feathered hat that suddenly becomes the face of an old lady."

Max nodded. Henri had found them printed in a magazine and kept teasing Yesim about them. Try as he might, Yesim could not make his eyes see the second image until Henri pointed them out, tracing the images with his gnarled fingers and laughing at Yesim's sudden realization.

"Erich pointed to a different pattern, a different interpretation of what you already knew. Still, I don't see how..."

"I went from thinking that Réjean was clever and principled, that he associated with the people he did because he was trying to reveal their corruption. But then I saw that he was the corrupt one. Réjean is... was an evil man and I am lucky to be rid of him."

Max was taken aback by the vehemence of the last statement. Bilodeau was not merely untroubled by LaFoie's death, she seemed relieved by it. He wondered if it was more than that. Bilodeau had picked up her pace and Max had to hurry to keep up.

"What kind of people did LaFoie associate with?" he asked.

They had walked another long block before she answered. "What difference does it make now? Réjean is beyond associating with anyone. He is beyond harming anyone."

"It might help Erich's case."

"I know it is your job to help your client but it is hardly mine. Erich had a reason, what do you call it, a motive for wanting Réjean dead. In fact, I think he had several reasons. Sometimes the easiest answer is the correct one."

"You can't really think that Erich Harvey committed murder."

"Why not? Even old men can burn with the fires of passion. But here we are." She consulted a small watch on her left wrist. "And with minutes to spare. Au revoir, Monsieur."

"Can I see you again?" Max said.

Bilodeau gave him a dazzling smile. "That depends."

"On what?" Max felt a twinge of apprehension.

"On whether you like dancing."

Max felt a strange warmth spreading through his body. It wasn't unpleasant but it was unwelcome. "I... I've been known to dance."

"Good. Meet me at Zelli's Royal Box at 9 on Saturday. Do you know where it is?"

"Yes, on rue Pierre Fontaine." He knew it though it wasn't a club he and Jacqui ever went to. Max both felt relieved and guilty at the thought.

MAX WALKED BACK TO the Tuileries and sat on a bench watching young couples stroll by. It did nothing to improve his mood, though he usually found the careful order and simplicity of the gardens calming. After a while, he went down to the river and alternated between staring out at the barges and small fishing boats on the slow-moving water and browsing the book stalls, many of which had been there since before the time of Victor Hugo.

It was all familiar territory now, a far cry from when he had arrived with a few thousand francs in his pockets and few dozen words of French in his head. Now, Paris was his city, his town, the way no place had ever been. He couldn't imagine living anywhere else, couldn't imagine why he would want to.

He had good friends and more money than he could reasonably spend. He had his work and his freedom from it. And he had Jacqui.

So why wasn't he happy?

He let his gaze drift across the river to the bulk of the Hotel des Invalides, the largest hospital in Paris, filled now with the broken bodies and fractured spirits of former soldiers still suffering the wounds of the Great War. A faint echoing throb ran down his leg and Max turned away, his throat choked with inexpressible emotion.

"Must be nice to be able to spend your time daydreaming." The familiar voice of Ginger Buchan brought Max back to the moment. He grasped the red-haired American's hand, relieved there was no need to fathom the rules of the Gallic kiss.

As usual, Buchan was dressed impeccably in the latest styles, a gray pin-striped suit, tailored to make the most of his shoulders and hide his slowly expanding mid-section. He wore a plain white shirt with a high button-on starched collar, but made up for the lack of colour with a wide floral-patterned necktie. A matching handkerchief peeked from his breast pocket.

Buchan had grown a thick ginger mustache in the month since Max last saw him and he felt a faint twinge of jealousy as his own efforts in that regard had never produced much more than a faint wispy discoloration on his upper lip. He consoled himself by noting that Buchan's red hair has begun to thin while his own, like that of his father, was likely to remain thick into middle age.

"I was just talking about you," said Max.

"And like the Devil, I immediately show up."

"Are you free for lunch?" Buchan knew Nicole Bilodeau though it wasn't clear how well. He certainly knew Erich Harvey. At least part of his unofficial job was to keep track of American ex-pats, especially those who had regular contact with "persons of interest" in the eyes of the American government. Erich certainly qualified.

"If you're buying, I'm free." Buchan chuckled at his own joke. "Why don't we try the Café De Pais? The walk will stimulate our appetites and justify our indulgences."

It was a dozen blocks from the river to the restaurant that looked out over the Place d'Opéra. His late breakfast still weighed on him and, despite the exercise, he had little appetite. He ordered a Croque Monsieur and a small beer to be polite. Buchan's politeness was more expansive; he ordered an onion soup followed by a serving of fresh oysters, a small slice of fried beef with mixed vegetables, finished with a crème caramel. He needed a demi-liter of red wine to wash it all down.

"Must be nice to be able to spend your day sleeping at your desk."

Buchan laughed around a mouthful of baguette. "I'm still a growing boy, Max," he said, patting his midriff. "I need to keep my strength up. Besides I assume you wanted some information – this is my payment in kind."

Max sipped his beer. It was colder than he had grown used to, a sop to the growing number of American tourists who were flooding Paris in the wake of prohibition back home. He glanced around; most of the other patrons were Yanks of one sort or another, men in straw hats, women in the latest and most garish Paris fashions, all with loud voices. Max switched to French, less likely to be overheard.

"You are acquainted with Mademoiselle Bilodeau?" he asked.

"Nicole? We've met. Cute thing though not my type."

Max wondered at that; he had seen Buchan with a wide range of women. But he remained silent, picking at his food until Buchan spoke again.

"I was tempted to give it a go when I first saw her. She came to the embassy to interview the Ambassador's wife and I must admit she made quite an impression. Her English is impeccable and those ankles..." Buchan's voice drifted off and he had the appearance of a man contemplating what ankles were attached to. He shook his head, smiling bashfully and continued. "She makes a living writing gossip columns for some of the American and British wire services but she's no flibbertigibbet. I've seen her more thoughtful pieces in some of the smaller French papers. Incisive and insightful. Though I wonder about her politics."

That was what Buchan meant by type. Bilodeau's politics were questionable. Buchan had been appointed to Paris by the Democratic administration of Woodrow Wilson and been promoted by the Republican one of Warren Harding, so it was hard to say exactly what Buchan's own political leanings were, though his membership in the Zionist Organization of America gave some clues.

"Is she a Bolshevik?" Max had had his fill of Bolsheviks the previous summer while investigating the murder of a former American diplomat.

"Hardly that. She claims to be neutral but spends a lot of time writing about the Action Française. She even went down to Italy and interviewed their rising star, that Mussolini fellow. You don't get to see him by being neutral."

Max had dealt with that bunch before, as well as the more radical groups that lurked behind their skirts. He had narrowly avoided a beating once at the hands of the Camelots du Roi, the quasi-military wing of the party who dressed like fops and used their walking sticks to beat unionists, suffragettes, or anyone else whose politics or lifestyle they disliked.

Thinking that someone like Bilodeau – so charming and vivacious – could be involved with those thugs left a vaguely sour taste in his mouth. Though perhaps he shouldn't judge, given that his girlfriend was an anarchist. Jacqui had always been vague about her past, but she had never actually denied taking part in the more violent actions of the anarchist fringe.

"Is she originally from Paris?" he asked. A lot of the Action Française supporters came from farther south.

"Beyond my purview. Her accent is pure Académie Française but that hardly proves anything." Buchan chewed thoughtfully on the last of his steak. "She knows the city better than most but I suppose that's part of her job."

"Have you heard anything about her relationship to Erich Harvey?"

"Harvey. I wondered if you were working for him."

"I'm looking into things."

"Don't look too closely; you might not like what you see."

"You don't think Erich committed murder, do you?"

"It doesn't matter what I think – it's a matter for the Sûreté."

That's true in part, thought Max, though if the Embassy were to intervene, they would likely rely on Buchan's opinion.

"Still..." he said.

Buchan had moved on to the crème caramel and the wine was nearly gone. "Harvey is a drunk and a parasite. You may not like my advice but I suggest you take it anyway. Drop him before he drags you down with him."

Buchan dabbed at his lips with his napkin and dropped the cloth onto his plate. "If you see Mlle. Bilodeau again," he said, pushing himself to his feet, "please give her my regards."

HENRI WAS ALREADY AT Le Coq Bleu when Max arrived shortly after two, sitting at a stool at the bar. His hair was mostly white but still thick and his round pink face unseamed except for laugh lines around his mouth and eyes. His shifts as a porter at Gare du Nord had grown shorter and less frequent now that he had passed his seventieth birthday, though he still worked three or four mornings a week to supplement his pension and "keep fit." He lifted his glass – a small pastis – when Max entered and beckoned him to the empty chair beside him.

Max crossed the room to the far end of the bar where his old friend perched in his usual location, nodding to Yesim on the way by.

Yesim was two decades younger, leaner and several inches taller than his old friend, Henri. His coloring was Mediterranean, his features hawk-like. The stubble on his face, which hadn't been shaved for a day or two was grizzled. Yesim was deep in conversation with a trio of roughly dressed men. He nodded briefly and placed an open bottle of Burgundy and a glass on the zinc-topped bar before turning back to the men.

"New customers?" Max asked.

Henri shook his head. "Old ones, more like. From the days when Yesim was more interested in politics than profits. They showed up here last week and have been here pretty much every day since. Can't say where they've been these last three or four years – prison most likely."

"Anarchists?" Max asked.

Henri looked around the bar as if expecting to spot a police informant or a pair of swallows lurking in the corner. Satisfied, he nodded his agreement. "And not nice ones like your Jacqui."

"If she was here and heard you using the possessive article, you might not think she was so nice."

Henri laughed. "You can't turn a nag into a racehorse. I guess she'll have to take me as I am. In any case, when are the two of you going to make it legal? People are talking."

"Which people? Other than you, that is. I can't see Jacqui wanting to walk down an aisle anytime soon."

"Who was talking about a church wedding?" Henri made a face that indicated what he thought of the Church. "City Hall would do fine. And don't think you know what Jacqui would do unless you've asked her."

Max blushed. He had thought about asking her but was afraid that she might leave for good if he did. Jacqui had very strong views on things even though Max wasn't always sure what they were.

"We missed you at lunch," said Henri. "Working on a new case?"

Max smiled. Maybe it was true what Jacqui said about him being a creature of habit. "You have to be led to new things like a horse on a halter." Then Max thought guiltily about his arrangement to see Nicole Bilodeau – a new girl at a new club. His smile faded.

"Barely," he said. He told Henri about the death of LaFoie and his investigation so far, leaving out the planned date to go dancing. Henri might not follow the teaching of the Church but he had his own code.

The old porter scratched at the stubble on his chin and finished his pastis. He waved his glass in the air for another before saying, "I remember that Harvey. He did some work for you last year. He didn't strike me as the murdering type."

"No," said Max. "Me neither. But if he didn't do it – and even he's not sure that he didn't – then I need to find out who did. And soon."

The wheels of justice turned quickly in France; it would hardly do Harvey any good to be proclaimed innocent if he had already gone to the guillotine.

Chapter 3 Friday, September 23rd, 1921

Perhaps Henri is right, thought Max, as he dragged himself from bed to answer the buzzing of the phone. I have become a servant to a machine. At least this time it's not the middle of the night.

"Max Anderson."

"Gereau. I need to see you." He gave an address in the 4th arrondissement and hung up. The Inspector might be retired but he still gave orders like a flic.

The address proved to be a narrow three-story building tucked away on a side street off Rue Saint Antoine. Gereau's flat on the second floor had clearly been arranged to serve both as accommodation and office. The front room had been cleared of all furniture save a broad oak desk and a couple of chairs. Through a curtained archway, Max glimpsed a long, narrow bed with a small dresser at its foot.

The desk was cluttered with papers and several stacks of books. There was a blotter, a rack of pens and an inkwell but no telephone. Gereau must have called from somewhere close by before returning to greet his guest.

"I have some coffee but I think it's cold," said Gereau, waving Max to one of the chairs beside the desk. Max shrugged and Gereau poured a couple of small mugs from a silver carafe. The thick black coffee wasn't cold but it soon would be. Max took a large gulp, his first of the day, and put the cup on the edge of the desk.

"Your call sounded urgent," he said.

It was Gereau's turn to shrug. "Maybe. Maybe not. Those things make me tense."

Max cocked his head to one side and assumed what he hoped was a sympathetic expression. "Still. You wanted to see me."

"You're looking into the LaFoie murder." A statement not a question. Max waited and Gereau went on. "How sure are you that Harvey didn't do it?"

"How sure are you that he did?"

"Fontaine swears he has the right man." Gereau abruptly stood up and moved from behind the desk. The former police officer had lost weight since Max had first met him but he was still a big man by anyone's standards. He held himself erect but his age had begun to show; the lines around his eyes had deepened and his close-shorn hair and thick mustache had gone grey.

"You used to claim that was a sure sign of the suspect's innocence."

Gereau's fleshy lips twitched beneath the grey bristle of his mustache. "Fontaine needs Harvey to be guilty; that makes him dangerous. How well do you know the man?"

"I've hired him a few times to do research for me. We've shared a few meals."

"And bottles, too, I imagine. Mr. Harvey is a heavy drinker." Gereau had been pacing but now he stopped behind his desk and stared down at the papers scattered there.

"Why did you ask me here?" Max admired Gereau, maybe even liked him a little, but his patience was wearing thin. "What is your interest in this case?"

"That of a colleague." Gereau sat down heavily in the chair behind the desk. Max had heard that the retired inspector had taken on the mantle of consulting detective. He wondered if his connections in the Sûreté made the job easier or harder. "And as a friend."

Gereau took a sip from his mug, made a face, and sat the cup down on the desk. "I miss having constables. Look," he said, after a pause, "Erich Harvey is not exactly what he appears to be."

"Who is? In what particular way is he hiding his true nature?"

"We had a file on him at the Prefecture. It was quite thick. Harvey did things in the war which generated suspicions in certain quarters. Nothing serious enough to have him expelled from the country, though I understand the matter was raised. Since then... who can say? But his association with Nicole Bilodeau and Réjean LaFoie was not a social one, nor, I think you will find, a romantic one. It cost one of them their life. Hard to say what it will cost the others. In any case, I am more interested in the dead man than in who may have killed him."

"What was LaFoie to you?"

"A nuisance while he was alive and a problem now he is dead. I'm working on certain files and..." Gereau's voice trailed off as if he were hesitant or embarrassed to continue.

"Involving anarchists, no doubt." The followers of the black flag were always at the forefront of Gereau's thoughts. He saw anarchist conspiracies wherever he looked. Max always thought it had made him a worse cop. "Is this about Jacqui?"

"Jacqueline Grandet, formerly Jacques Grand, has a history. Surely you don't deny it."

"How do you—"

"I make it my business to know, though for now it can be our little secret."

Max swallowed hard. Of course, Gereau would know of Jacqui's former alias, though apparently, he hadn't informed his former colleagues at the Prefecture. He wondered if he knew her real name, too.

He shook his head. "History started again in 1918. Nothing that happened before then really matters."

"It was all a dream, is that what you're saying? Or a lie? A popular philosophy these days."

Max stood up. For him, it was more than philosophy. His life had ended on the battlefields of France. Only to start up moments later with a shattered leg and a broken spirit. He had recovered from both but saw no link between the life that went before and the one he had now. It might as well have been a dream. It often felt like a lie.

"Jacqui has cut her ties with her former compatriots. She may not accept the strictures of traditional life but she feels no need to destroy it. Her freedom is her own, not something given to her by others." It felt like he was repeating something he had been told, which indeed he was. Still, the words felt true as he held them in his mouth. He glared at the older man until Gereau turned away.

"You may not find her freedom so pleasant," murmured the former police officer, "when it doesn't include you."

ERICH HARVEY SLOUCHED on a narrow bench at the back of a cell that was barely wide enough for him to lie down in. His eyes were bleary and his skin pale and patchy. The only other items in the room were a bucket in one corner, a wash basin in another and an empty wine bottle under the bench. The French were too civilized to let him suffer the pain of alcohol withdrawal on top of everything else.

Max sat on the stool the guard handed him when he let him into Harvey's cell and faced his erstwhile client. Cleroux would have warranted the privacy of one of the visiting rooms but Max wasn't a lawyer; as far as most of the Prefecture was concerned, he wasn't anything.

"What is your relationship with Nicole Bilodeau?" Max asked. Harvey barely looked up, didn't meet Max's eyes.

"A colleague," he murmured.

"Then why was Réjean LaFoie suing you for the alienation of her affections?"

"You've been busy." Harvey stood up and stretched like he was waking from a long sleep. He ran his hands over his face and through his hair. "When am I getting out of here?"

"My lawyer is working on it. As am I. But you could do your part. Bilodeau?"

Harvey reached under the bench for the bottle and held it up to the light. He shook his head sadly and then carefully placed the empty bottle on the floor outside the cell door. Presumably a replacement would appear at some point.

"She and I worked on a couple of stories together. She's..." Harvey paused and sat back down on the bench. "I told her a few things about LaFoie. She decided she didn't like him afterwards. It's as simple as that."

Max had an urge to get up and call for the guard. It was hard to work for a client who wouldn't work for himself. "What did you tell her?"

Harvey looked at Max for several seconds. "If I didn't kill LaFoie, someone else must have. I doubt if he got into a second barfight."

"Seems a reasonable theory."

"Then it was deliberate. Someone decided they wanted LaFoie dead. Framing me may have been part of the plan or it might have been nothing more than a happy coincidence." He gestured vaguely around the cell. "These walls aren't particularly thick."

"Then you'd rather not say." Harvey shrugged and Max continued. "Captain Fontaine has you pegged for the guillotine. Cleroux will do everything he can to delay the inevitable but he's not a miracle worker. I need more from you."

"The size of the blade that slits your throat is irrelevant." Harvey was back to looking into space.

Max stood up. "Fine. I'll do my best. And I'll come to your funeral. Beyond that, I promise you nothing." He leaned against the cell door. "I'm done in here, Sergeant."

"Wait." Harvey joined Max at the door and leaned in until Max could feel his breath, hot and wine-soaked, against his ear. "LaFoie was involved with the Black Fist."

The Black Fist was one of the semi-secret organizations that provided muscle to the various right-wing factions that had sprung up in France since the war. Max had had his own dealings with the Fist and their charismatic leader, Andre Bucard; they were not people to be trifled with.

"Is that what drove Bilodeau away? I thought her own leanings were in that direction."

"That's only half the story." Harvey's voice came quick; the door at the far end of the cell block had clanked open. "I told Nicole that he was playing a double game. His own loyalties were to the Black Flag, not the Black Fist. LaFoie was an anarchist. And quite likely a socialist, too. You can see it in his writing if you look close enough. She never had before I pointed it out."

"She broke off with him over politics." Max and Jacqui, on the rare occasions when they fought, did so over money, or, other, more intimate things.

"Possibly," said Harvey. "But there may have been something else. I don't know – it was something LaFoie said, right before we stepped outside. But I don't remember what it was."

Harvey stepped back as the Sergeant approached. His face had a caved-in look, as if the failing of his memory was a physical blow. He turned away as the cell door opened and shambled back to his bench. Max nodded at the wine bottle on the floor and dug twenty francs out of his pocket.

"Keep them coming, LePêcheur," he said as he pressed the money into the officer's hand.

Chapter 4 Saturday/Sunday, September 24th and 25th, 1921

The Zelli's Royal Box was one of the newer clubs that had sprung up south of Montmartre on Rue Pierre Fontaine to cater to the influx of Americans into Paris. Notably it was designed to appeal to the wives of Americans who wanted the French experience without actually having to deal with the French, or with the working girls who habituated the more lurid bars at the foot of Montmartre.

The main entrance led to a balcony, held up by ornate pillars, where a number of private booths allowed patrons to look down on the action below. There, more than a dozen tables crowded the space around the small dance floor in front of the stage, housed in a mirrored alcove. A quartet was playing the latest dance numbers from Chicago and New York. Along one wall stretched the polished oak bar and beyond that, swinging double doors led to the kitchen.

Bilodeau was sitting alone at a table closest to the band, watching the musicians intently while making little shooing motions with her hand in response to prospective dance partners. They, despite the failures of their predecessors, formed a steady stream, like ants to a mound of sugar.

Glancing at his watch, Max noted it was a few minutes past nine. He sidled up to the bar and ordered a small glass of beer. He sipped it slowly and watched Bilodeau. She barely moved in her seat, though twice she clapped her hands together when the clarinetist, easily the most talented of the four, performed a particularly complex trill.

Max was part-owner of Chez Jake on the far slope of Montmartre where the bands played their own music in a dark and smoky bar only half the size of Zelli's Royal Box. The kitchen was smaller and the food better and Americans only arrived by mistake or at the specific invite of one of the regulars. Max appreciated jazz and he appreciated those who liked it, too, even in the watered-down version being presented here. Maybe, after, he would ask the clarinetist if he would like to come up to Chez Jake some Tuesday night, when they tried out new talent. His answer would tell Max if he was serious about his horn or just in it for the money.

Max finished the beer and ordered a couple of glasses of champagne – there was an empty flute on Bilodeau's table – though he requested it be served in coupes, earning a nod of approbation from the bartender. He wound his way to the table without spilling a drop and slipped into the chair beside her, cutting off a tall blonde who was aiming for the same target.

"I thought you were going to stand me up." She said it without rancour.

"My apologies," said Max. "I'm not used to punctuality in Paris."

"I'm never late for a deadline or a dance," said Bilodeau, taking a sip from her glass. "The good stuff. I'm impressed."

"Money comes and money goes but the taste of bad wine lingers." It was an expression he had heard Yesim use with great success with customers at Le Coq Bleu.

"Sounds like the voice of experience," she said, smiling at him over the rim of the coupe.

Max nodded, though everything he had learned about wine he had learned from the late Havel Barzani, who didn't drink, and Henri LaComte, who drank far too much.

"A man who buys me good champagne is already halfway to, how do you Americans put it, the first station."

Max took a moment to make the connection. "First base. It's a game, like cricket but more comprehensible." A moment later, he blushed. He wondered if she knew what the Americans meant by first base.

"Here's to the sporting life." They clinked glasses, drawing an admonitory stare from the bassist who clearly thought he was better than he was.

They sat in silence for another song but, when the band started on something with a bit more swing to the rhythm, Max held out his hand and Nicole followed him onto the dance floor.

He could feel the eyes of the other men on him and he would have liked to demonstrate why he deserved a dance when they didn't but his wounded leg and his natural reticence limited his mobility. Nicole didn't seem to notice as she followed his every lead. When the number reached its climax, she twirled into his arms as if they had been doing it for years.

Max froze on the floor with her body pressed against him and her face mere inches from his. Her eyes were wide and her lips parted and, after a moment, she said. "Well, either kiss me, or let me go."

Max's face flushed hot and stepped back. Nicole laughed, not unkindly.

"I'm Canadian," said Max, as if that explained everything. "Canadian, not American."

"Truly! I have a cousin in Montreal, perhaps you know him." Then she laughed again and put her hand on his arm to lead him back to their table. Max signaled a waiter and told him to bring them a bottle of Cliquot and fresh coupes.

"And he's rounding first and heading for second," said Nicole in a fair imitation of an American drawl. Max thought she might know the game of baseball better than he did.

"You've been to America," Max said.

"Yes, and Canada, too. It was right before the war. My mother took me on a grand tour for my eighteenth birthday. New York,

Boston, Chicago, Montreal. We sailed into New York but departed from... Halifax, I think it was called."

"In Nova Scotia. That's where I'm from. You probably passed right through my hometown on the train."

"Maybe but I wouldn't know. I was more interested in the people on the train than the countryside we passed through. I've always been that way. People either fascinate or amuse me. When I don't find them repulsive."

"And which category do I fall in?"

"I haven't decided yet, though definitely not the third." She covered his hand in hers and held his gaze without speaking until the waiter returned with the bottle. He stood by the table for a moment as the band finished up a number and then uncorked the champagne with a flourish.

The popping of the cork raised a bigger round of applause than that for the musicians and, as the waiter filled the coupes, several couples held up their glasses until Max and Nicole raised their own to their lips. Max wondered if it was a custom imported from America or something someone had thought up after they got to Paris. It was certainly nothing he had ever seen French crowds do.

After, they danced again, first a fox trot, then a waltz. Max held Nicole closer than was really proper in a respectable club but no-one said anything and even the elderly concierge smiled indulgently. The heat that had filled his face had now found a home in other regions. Nicole's body was supple and her movements matched his own without resistance of any kind. He couldn't help thinking how different it was than dancing with Jacqui who always followed her own rhythms. He felt ashamed that he preferred the compliance of this woman's body to that of his lover.

"That was... nice." Nicole said when they returned to their table. "But that was all. Nice. I don't need any complications right now. Not after Réjean."

"I see," said Max. He shifted in his chair so their legs were no longer touching.

Nicole laughed and put her hand on his arm. He could feel the heat of her touch even through the fabric of his jacket and the shirt beneath. "I'm enjoying the moment, Max, I hope you are, too. But I don't want you to think that what happens tonight – whatever happens tonight – means more than that."

"No, of course, I understand," said Max, though he was fairly sure he didn't. Still, he couldn't help feeling bad. He should be with Jacqui, would be with her if she wasn't still in Marseilles. "Did you come here with LaFoie?"

Bilodeau removed her hand and sat back in her chair. "Now the piper must be paid. Very well, three questions – not counting this one. Réjean had two left feet and appalling taste in music. He liked the accordion. And he was cheap. So, no."

This woman treats everything like a game, thought Max. Three questions – like something out of a folk story. He hesitated before asking, "Was Réjean LaFoie an anarchist?"

"It is easier to tell you what LaFoie didn't believe in, than what he did. Réjean was not a true son of France. He embraced the exotic, the corrupt, the decadent. He would come to listen to Réal del Sartre, the founder of the Camelots, and Andre Bucard and cheer with the others. I was taken in. His accounts of the rallies seemed accurate, even patriotic. Until Harvey pointed out to me how some of his word choices could be taken a different way – as mockery and insult. It was embarrassing. To have my own language explained, explicated, by an American. But once I saw it, I couldn't unsee it. When I listened to what he said when he was drinking – the mockery, the Jew-like imitation of our leader's finest expressions – it was clear to me that he was no patriot."

"Were the Camelots de Roi or maybe the Black Fist aware of LaFoie's politics? Were they angry enough to kill him?"

Bilodeau glared at him. "That's two questions but I'll let it go. The Camelots are misunderstood. They protect our leaders from the assaults of syndicalists, anarchists and immigrant rabble rousers. They do not go out of their way to incite trouble and they certainly don't risk prosecution for murder. LaFoie was a journalist – some thought a good one – and *we* take care of our own. I may have left Réjean behind but I would do whatever it took to bring his killer to justice. No matter who was to blame."

Max nodded. The rivalry between newspapers in Paris was intense but the men and, increasingly, women who worked in them all drank in the same bars and ate at the same cheap bistros.

"You have one more question coming to you."

Max sipped his champagne for courage. "Can I see you again?"

She laughed then and put her hand back on his arm. They danced twice more and finished the bottle and had a pastis to finish the evening. They didn't talk about politics or about past loves but only about music and art and how champagne made everything glow. After, Max walked with her to Rue Pierre Fontaine until she flagged down a taxi and then continued on to his apartment on Rue Lepic, hoping the long walk and the night air would clear his head. But it didn't work.

MAX SAT IN THE SMALL park that separated Saint Germaine-L'Auxerrois from the Louvre and waited for the early morning mass to finish. If Bucard was in town, he would be here or at the restaurant at the Hotel Meurice, a fifteen-minute walk from the church. Normally, he wouldn't disturb someone right after service, though he supposed a man just relieved of his sins might be more likely to tell the truth. In any case, he was feeling a certain urgency about Harvey's fate. His court date had been announced for Thursday and it would be better if Max cleared his name before proceedings began.

Bucard was among the last to emerge, in the company of two younger men in dark suits, one so large it seemed he might burst the seams of his jacket, the other short, wiry and dangerous-looking. Bucard dismissed them with a wave of his hand and came to join Max on his bench; the two young men leaned against a black Voison Town Car and watched them.

"Who was killed this time, Max?" Bucard asked as he settled onto the bench. "It seems the only time you ever come to see me is when someone has died."

"Only if I have reason to think they were involved with the Black Fist."

"I'm nothing but a private citizen," said Bucard. "I have nothing to do with such things."

"Perhaps," said Max. *You're a private citizen the same way the Rothschilds are*, he thought. "But you are always so... well informed."

Bucard nodded in acquiescence and laced his hands over the silver head of his cane. "So who died?"

"Réjean LaFoie."

"The journalist. I had heard he had an unfortunate accident."

"Someone threw him in the Seine."

"Or, perhaps, he fell."

"He was dead before he went in the water."

"There is that," said Bucard. "But you know how it is, old habits die hard. Parisians have been throwing their garbage in the river for generations."

"You didn't like him."

"He was no friend to my friends."

"Was that enough to have him killed?"

"This is the third time you have accused me of having someone killed. It is a bad habit. And as you know bad habits are unhealthy."

"I've always apologized when I was proven wrong."

Bucard smiled. "There is that; you are a very polite young man. A national trait, I understand."

"That and stubbornness," murmured Max. "LaFoie used to cover Action Française rallies."

"Yes. At first, he seemed sympathetic. In the end, he was subtle in his criticisms. The man had a gift for sarcasm and subterfuge."

"That's what Nicole Bilodeau told me."

"Ah, you have met the lovely Mademoiselle Nicole. Charming, isn't she?" Bucard's blue eyes twinkled and a knowing smile played on his lips.

Max had spent half the night tossing in his bed, thinking of her charms. He glanced over at the car. The two young men had been joined by a tall, grey-haired man in a cassock. The three of them were smoking; the priest was doing all of the talking.

"She was certain his murder had nothing to do with politics – or, at least, the politics of the right."

"She is perceptive as well as beautiful. Perhaps the simplest answer is the correct one. I understand that the police have made an arrest. An American. They are such an aggressive people, don't you find? Still living in the wild West – like in the moving pictures."

"I don't think Erich Harvey killed Réjean LaFoie."

"Why tell me? It is a matter for the police and the courts."

"LaFoie was likely an anarchist; Harvey said he had leanings that way. And a socialist, too, if one can be both."

"When one's mind is twisted it is not hard to wind yourself into a knot. I suppose the Camelots might have given him a beating for his insults. I doubt if they would kill him; Leullier is sympathetic but even he can only let us get away with so much."

Leullier was the head of the Prefecture in Paris and notorious for turning a blind eye to the doings of the Camelots or their even more violent brethren in the Black Fist. His treatment of those on the left was not nearly so gentle.

"Why not accept the police story? Harvey hit LaFoie with a bottle. That could be enough to kill a man."

"For someone who knows nothing of these things, you seem to have a lot of the details."

"I read the papers. All of them – so I can get some approximation of the truth."

"Harvey fought with LaFoie on Rue Jacob. That's a long way from the Seine."

"Perhaps he was delirious. As he wandered home, he had a fit and fell into the river. Dead on impact. It could happen."

"And which newspaper suggested that?"

Bucard laughed. "None. But it is plausible."

"I suppose. But without some actual evidence it won't help Harvey much."

"No. To tell you the truth – the city has too many journalists as it is; more all the time it seems. If we can execute one for the murder of another it seems like a reasonable start to me." Bucard stood up. One of the men at the car started forward but Bucard waved him off and gestured for Max to walk with him. Though still an imposing figure, over six feet with broad shoulders, Bucard now used his cane as a tool rather than a prop. "This bell tower was used to signal an ambush that nearly wiped out the Protestants in Paris. Someday it will ring again – when the King, or someone like him, is once more enthroned. Perhaps not in the Louvre but in the heart of Paris. Do you suppose it will matter then if little men like LaFoie and Harvey are here to see it?"

"It will matter to them. It was little men, like them, like me, who fought in the War."

"And by doing so became part of something bigger than themselves. Did you not feel it? The camaraderie – the brotherhood of blood. That was what the War forged and that is what so many are seeking now. To be enwrapped in the flag of the nation, secure that their leader will guide them and see them through."

"I've heard it all before, Bucard. I've even felt it. It's nothing but a dream trying to become a nightmare."

"I sometimes suspect you might be an anarchist, too. Mr. Anderson."

"I'm a guy trying to solve a crime, nothing more. I don't live my life in elegant concepts; I spent four years learning where that led. I'm done with it."

They had reached the edge of the courtyard and Bucard turned and began to walk back toward his car. "Ten years ago," he said, "the Seine overflowed its banks and flooded half the city. Men gathered here beside the Louvre and dug up the cobblestones, uprooted trees, used park benches, whatever it took to stop the waters from destroying the artworks stored here. They did it because they knew that their lives were nothing against the heritage of France. Another flood is coming, Mr. Anderson, but it will take more than cobbles and tree branches to stop it. And when the cleansing waters have washed away the detritus – this, these stones, this bulwark of the people, will remain."

"Ten years ago, my friend Henri carried a stranger on his back to save him from the flood waters. They became the best of friends, despite their many differences. When the flood comes, that is what will endure."

Bucard laughed again, full throated this time. "Why, Mr. Anderson, you're not an anarchist – you're a romantic."

Max had nothing to say to that. He nodded his farewell and turned away from the river.

"Mr. Anderson, say hello to Mademoiselle Nicole when you see her next."

"What makes you think I'll see her again?" Max said over his shoulder without breaking his stride.

"Because I have met her," Bucard called after him. "And I have met you. A collision seems inevitable. I'm sure it would do you good to follow your natural instincts. It would, if nothing else, relieve your tension."

Bucard's laughter, and that of his companions, followed Max along the narrow street until it was lost in the rumble of traffic and the pounding of blood in his ears.

Chapter 5 Monday/Tuesday, September 26th and 27th, 1921

M ax spent the rest of Sunday walking the streets, trying to figure out the best way to pursue the murderer of Réjean LaFoie; other than a few vague suspicions, he had little idea where to begin.

He had dropped by the newspaper where the victim had done most of his work but few of the staff working the weekend shift knew him very well. Those that were acquainted with him were evenly split between those who thought he didn't have an enemy in the world to those who thought the suspects were too many to enumerate. They suggested he come back Monday evening when more of his closer colleagues would be around.

Max wound up at his office in Chez Jake, pushing papers from one side of his desk to the other. The Club was closed Sunday nights but Jake lived on the premises and was always willing to whip up some food in the kitchen for Max and any of the musicians who were hanging around playing for each other.

Monday started out dreary and got steadily worse, wind and rain blowing in from the Atlantic, turning some streets into streams. Max eventually forced himself out for a late lunch at Le Coq Bleu. Henri was not in his usual spot and Yesim was more interested in his new clientele than he was in talking to Max. Eventually Max took a cab to the newspaper and spoke to LaFoie's editor, a lean swarthy man of about fifty, named Braque.

"LaFoie was a good reporter – when he showed up," said Braque, who spoke with a harsh Alsace accent. "He'd sometimes disappear for as much as week, but whenever he came back, he always had a juicy piece in tow."

"What about his relationship with Nicole Bilodeau?"

Braque busied himself with a thick dark cigar before giving an answer. "Business, he claimed. Funny business according to some but I tend to believe the former. LaFoie was quiet about his personal life but I think if he had won over someone like Nicole, he would have been compelled to brag about it."

"But he sued Erich Harvey for alienation of affections?"

"A joke. Réjean was always joking but sometimes he was so subtle about it that no-one knew he was doing it. I learned a long time ago to assume that Réjean was joking until he proved otherwise. It's why he was so good at satire."

"You mean poking fun at the Action Française."

"Them, too. Réjean didn't give a shit about politics. Not really. If he had any of his own, I never knew it. His one political maxim was – if someone was a puffed-up buffoon, it was Réjean's job to prick him." Braque used an expression that implied a more vulgar assault. "Maybe someone decided to prick him back."

Braque didn't seem to have anything else to offer and Max got up to leave. He stopped at the door, remembering a part of Harvey's story that had been nagging at him. "Why would Pierre Delacroix go all the way to the Dome to tell Harvey that LaFoie had been pulled from the Seine?"

Braque answered with a string of explicatives, unlike any Max had heard since he left the trenches. "That bastard: nothing would have made him happier than to spread the word of Réjean's death. If he could cause trouble for someone else at the same time, even better."

"Could he have killed Réjean?"

Braque snorted. "He wouldn't fight in the War; I doubt if he'd do it in the streets of Paris. He's one of those, you know." Braque made a rude gesture calling Delacroix's manhood into question.

"He was with a couple of pirettes when he saw Harvey."

"Protective coloration."

TUESDAY DAWNED CLEAR and Max spent the morning tracking down a few details for his other cases before placing a call to a couple of contacts in Marseilles. The area was a hotbed of anarchist activity – Yesim had had his baptism in the movement while a young man there – and, if anyone knew if Réjean was involved in the Black Flag, it would be those closest to the source. He wasn't happy with what he learned.

Jacqui's train arrived at the Gare Lyon at 1600. It was a few minutes late and Max paced along the marble foyer beneath the high glass roof. Sunlight dappled over the stone and concrete and shone off the four-sided brass clock that dominated the entranceway. The station had been built for the 1900 Exhibition and was cleaner and more modern than the other train stations around Paris, though no less monumental.

Max had hardly left the city since his arrival in November 1918 and he could never enter a rail station without thinking of the trains that had taken him to and from the front lines during the war. His leg throbbed in sympathetic memory – even though, aside from a certain stiffness, the wound that had ended his war had long ceased to trouble him.

At last, the train pulled to a stop with a soft rumble and a final jet of steam that obscured his vision of the platform. Then he saw Jacqui appear out of the cloud of vapour, her tiny figure erect, despite the large bag in one hand and the satchel over the other shoulder. He hurried down the platform to meet her.

She smiled and dropped her bags so he could sweep her up in his arms. She kissed him hard on the mouth and, after a moment, he kissed her back. *Everything will be fine*, he thought, *now that Jacqui has come home.*

Then Bucard's voice came back to him: 'A collision seems inevitable.'

JACQUI'S BAGS WERE barely on the floor of their bedroom before she grabbed him by the hand and led him to their narrow bed. It had seemed plenty big before but now it felt crowded. *As if there was someone else in it with us*, thought Max.

He held her tight and kissed her mouth and face, but when she began to pluck at the buttons of his shirt, he pulled away.

"Didn't you miss me?" Jacqui asked.

"Sure. Of course, I did but... I'm worried about this case. Erich Harvey, you remember him..."

"Not really. Your telegram didn't say much. He's a murder suspect?"

"Yes, of a man named Réjean LaFoie."

"I've heard that name somewhere."

"He was a journalist. You may have seen his name in the paper."

Jacqui's brow furrowed and she shook her head slightly. "I suppose so." She rolled off the bed and went into the tiny space that served as a kitchen. Max could hear her opening and shutting cupboard doors with more force than was necessary. He sighed and got up to join her.

"Is there something bothering you?"

"Should there be?" Jacqui's voice was high and tight.

Max felt a wash of guilt and anger flood through him. He had done nothing wrong, nothing inconsistent with Jacqui's own beliefs. Bilodeau was a suspect, or at least a witness in the Harvey case.

She was the one who insisted on going dancing in exchange for information. He couldn't be blamed for that. "Not that I'm aware of," he said.

"Did you think you could make inquiries about anarchists in Marseilles without me hearing about it?" She had taken two plates from one of the cupboards and filled them with day old bread and cheese and sausage from the icebox. "Do we have any wine?"

"In the cupboard by the table," he said. "I wasn't checking up on you. LaFoie was suspected of being a follower."

"Of course. I knew I had heard that name," Jacqui said, slamming the bottle of wine onto the table hard enough to make the glasses rattle. "But you found out things anyway."

Why doesn't she leave it alone? he thought. *I already said I was sorry, didn't I?* Aloud: "Only that your cousin isn't sick; he's in jail."

"Was in jail. It was a trumped-up charge."

"And he's not even your cousin."

"What is that supposed to mean?" Jacqui filled the glasses to the rim and then took a large swallow. She sat down in front of her plate of food and glared at him.

"You tell me," he snapped. "You must have had a good reason to run off to help him. And to lie to me about it. What is this guy to you anyway?"

"Are you accusing me of being unfaithful to you? You know that doesn't even mean anything to me. Georges was an old comrade. That's all. He got into some trouble and needed some help."

"And there was no-one in Marseilles that could lend a hand. He had to call on you."

"Believe what you want!" Jacqui tore off a piece of cheese with her teeth. "Sit down and eat."

"You can't tell me what to do. We're independent spirits, remember?"

"I thought you loved me."

"I thought so, too."

Jacqui's hand flew to her mouth, as the colour drained from her face. "I see," she said. "Who is she?"

"There is no she." Max looked away. "It's..."

"I think I should go now." Jacqui stood up and went in the bedroom. When she came out, she was carrying her bags.

"Where will you go? Back to your old friends in Belleville?"

"That's it, isn't it? You've never trusted me, never believed me when I said I had left that life, left violence, behind. You were always waiting for me to betray you. Not sexually, but politically. The moment I answer the call of an old friend – a friend! – you assume I am going back to, what you call them, my old ways? My bad habits?"

"Well, aren't you? My informants..."

"They aren't only your informants. Police agents every one. Their job is to sow discord. Wherever they can. All they need is a willing fool to listen to them."

"So you think I'm a fool." He took a step toward her, the emotions welling up from his chest threatening to choke him.

"No. Max, I've never thought that. If I had, I would never have been here. But I think you're acting foolishly and I don't know why. I don't think you do, either." She stepped forward and waited until he moved aside. "When you do, you'll know how to find me."

He was still standing there as the door closed behind her. He didn't move until he could no longer hear her tread upon the stair, until long after he heard the outer door slam.

MAX FOUND HIMSELF IN front of the brilliant green doors on the Rue de Jarente with little memory of the journey there – it was as though he had crossed the city in his sleep. But he was awake now. He tapped the door knocker several times before he noticed the small button imbedded in the wall beside the door. He pressed it and a few moments later the peephole opened and a dark-skinned woman in a maid's cap peered out at him.

"I'm here to see Mademoiselle Bilodeau," he said. "Is she in?"

"Who can I say is calling?" The woman's accent was so thick it took Max a moment to realize what she was asking. He handed her a business card. "Max Anderson."

The small door slammed shut and Max was left to stare at the gargoyle on the doorknocker for several moments before the door opened and the maid ushered Max through and down a long hallway to stairs that led up to the second floor. Nicole Bilodeau was in a sitting room, reading from a small book. She set it on a side table and rose to greet him.

"Max, so nice to see you again."

He kissed her on both cheeks, then stepped back, shifting awkwardly from foot to foot.

"I... I had to see you again."

"Well, I said you could, but I wasn't expecting it to be so soon. Or here." She took him by the arm and led him to a small chaise. She settled in beside him. "You may go, Anna. I'll call you if we need anything."

When they were alone, she asked: "Did you think of another question?"

"No. I..."

"Then why are you here?"

Yes, thought Max, *why am I?* He leaned forward and kissed her. Her hand went to the back of his head, her fingers tangled in his hair, pulling his face tight against hers. He felt his own hand, almost of its own volition, move along her body and across her breast to stroke her face and hair.

After a few moments, she gasped, "Not here. The servants..." She took his hand and led him through a door into a bedroom – her bedroom. She locked the door, turned to him, and began to slowly undress. "What are you waiting for?"

The light in the room was dim; heavy curtains covered the windows, blocking the final light of the day. Still, Max had to resist the urge to turn away as he shed his jacket and shirt, let his trousers fall to the floor. There was an awkward moment when he realized he was still wearing his boots, but Nicole smiled gently and pushed him back on the bed and undid the buckles and pulled them free.

Then she climbed on the bed and straddled him, her body naked except for her silken undergarments. He felt himself grow rigid as she leaned down against him, her breasts pressing against his bare chest through the thin layer of cloth. She kissed his mouth, his neck, his chest, his flat stomach, in the process somehow stripping him of his underpants and removing the last of her own clothing.

Her curves were full and her flesh soft and warm in his hands, so unlike Jacqui's slim muscularity. He pulled Nicole down beside him and caressed her shoulders and then cupped one of her breasts in his hand. They lay like that, kissing and caressing, until she suddenly pulled him across her, her legs parting for him.

He held himself up from her and gazed down at her, her pale skin and dark hair. Her lips were slightly parted and her eyes were wide. Jacqui always closed her eyes. He poised above her for a moment and then rolled to one side.

"I can't," he whispered.

"You most obviously can," she said, smiling and grasping him firmly with one hand.

Max pulled away. "Perhaps, I should say I won't."

"Perhaps that's better," she said, "For both of us. I said I didn't want complications and you clearly come with a basket full."

"I'm sorry."

"Yes. I have to say, you are different at least. I've had men refuse me and men fail me but never one change his mind at the moment of truth. If nothing else, it will make an amusing entry in my diary." She rolled off the bed and gathered up her clothes. "I'll change in the powder room. I'd appreciate it if you were gone when I return."

Max watched her walk, naked, to the door. She paused at the entrance. "I'd also appreciate it if you never came to my house again. Or spoke of this moment to anyone. A woman has her pride."

Max sat on the bed for a few moments after she closed the door, wondering, morosely, if any other man had ever lost two women in a single afternoon. Then he quickly dressed and hurried out before the maid came to show him the way.

IT WAS NEARLY NINE by the time Max returned to Montmartre and the cozy confines of Le Coq Bleu. His journey across the city had been anything but dreamlike, each plodding footstep a turmoil of remorse and confusion. The rain of the previous day had returned and by the time he settled in a stool beside Henri at the end of the zinc bar, he was drenched to the skin.

"Did you take a dip in the Seine?" asked Henri. "I haven't seen someone so wet since the great flood ten years ago."

"Eleven," Max corrected absently. He was familiar with the story of Henri's journey across the flooded city, carrying Yesim, his leg broken and wrapped in a cast, on his back; it had been the beginning of their friendship. "It's been raining for over an hour."

"I wouldn't know," said Henri, gesturing to the three empty brandy glasses on the bar. A fourth was clutched in his hand. "There is this little thing they call a taxi. Or are you saving your money for that ring as I advised?"

Max tried to come up with some offhand remark to change the subject, tried and failed. He looked away from Henri as if something extraordinary could be seen be seen on the darkened street. "No need for a ring. Not for me."

"My God, boy, what have you done?" Henri's raised voice cut through the background babble of the bar. The other patrons looked up from their drinks, perhaps hoping for something more exciting to develop. Yesim stopped wiping the zinc to watch.

"I didn't do..." Max was startled to hear his voice, high and strained, in the sudden silence. He looked down at his hands clutched in front of him until the others went back to their own concerns. Yesim was there with a glass and a bottle of the usual red.

"Whatever you didn't do, you probably need a drink to forget it," said Yesim.

Max nodded and Yesim poured. Henri tapped his own empty glass and said, "I probably need to forget as well."

"You've already forgotten more than I can remember," said Yesim but he poured another shot from the brandy bottle and left both it and the red wine on the bar. "Now, what's not troubling you, Max?"

Max had never been comfortable talking about his personal life with anyone, not even his closest friends but Henri and Yesim had always been his sounding board when it came to his investigations. They were good listeners and knew more about Paris and its complicated politics than he would ever fathom. The words tumbled out before he could stop them – the murder, the question of LaFoie's politics, his call to Marseilles and the fight with Jacqui. He described his night dancing with Nicole, but, in deference to her request, not the events of a few hours before.

When he looked up from his wine glass, Henri was staring at him, his eyes bulging in anger and his face red. Yesim was leaning back against the wall of bottles behind the bar, his arms folded and his expression curiously blank.

"You idiot!" Henri sputtered. "You great blundering Canadian idiot. You went dancing with another woman and then you lied about it. No wonder she left you."

"Don't be stupid yourself, Henri," said Yesim his voice hard. "Jacqui left because Max spied on her, because he doesn't trust her, because he thinks she is an anarchist."

"Well, isn't she?" Max stood up, his arms swinging loosely by his side. "Didn't she run off to join up with them as soon as they called?"

"What if she is? What's wrong with that, hey? You got something against men who think this country is going to hell and want to do something to fix it?"

"Like blowing up police stations and rail cars?" Chairs were being pushed back. Yesim's old new friends.

"Jacqui never went in for that," said Henri. "You know that."

"But she ran off soon enough to help her so-called cousin, her friend, Georges, when he wound up in jail."

"Georges," said Yesim, "has been married for twenty-eight years and has six children. The youngest is a year older than Jacqui. Or didn't your informants tell you that?"

"I didn't know..."

"You're a detective. Maybe you should detect," said Yesim. "And maybe you should do it somewhere else than my bar."

"It's partly my bar too," said Max.

"That's right," said Yesim, raising his voice so the rest could hear. "Money never forgets."

Max glared at Yesim and turned to go. Henri rested his hand on Max's arm but he shoved him away. Henri tumbled to the floor.

"Get the hell out of here, you son of a bitch." Yesim had a small wooden club in his hand.

Max stared down at Henri but no more words came.

MAX WALKED BACK TO his apartment but it took no great skill at detection to know that sleep was a long way off. His hand shook as he inserted the key in the lock but inside, he has frozen, unable to feel the emotions that churned his stomach and knifed pain down his leg. The old blankness threatened to descend and drown him.

He hated violence, hated it more than anything else, yet he seemed to pursue it like an opium smoker pursued the dragon.

Max tore off his wet clothes and toweled his body until his skin burned. Then he dressed again and went out. On other nights – alone or unhappy – he would have made his way to Chez Jake, immersed himself in the music and the drink before stumbling up to his office to sleep on the floor. But Chez Jake meant more questions from people he called his friends. He was in no mood to answer questions. It was time he started asking them.

The rain had slowed to a soft drizzle but Max flagged a taxi and huddled in the back seat as it bumped and lurched through Paris, across the Pont Neuf to deliver him at the corner of Jacob and Rue Bonaparte. A half dozen brasseries and cafes lined both sides of the street. One of them must have someone who had witnessed the fight between Harvey and LaFoie.

The bartender at the unlikely named Le Pré de Sauvage, a place that proudly proclaimed its founding as 1919, looked away when Max asked. Max slipped twenty francs across the bar and asked again. The bill disappeared and the man, his hands long and delicate like a concert pianist, tapped a fingernail on the metal surface. Max dropped another ten and the man nodded.

"You a flic?" he asked, after introducing himself as Luc.

"No." said Max. "I'm a friend of Erich Harvey's."

"He needs a friend. Captain Fontaine is like a dog with a bone. He's settled on your friend and will be reluctant to let go."

"If you know Fontaine so well, you know that dog has no teeth."

Luc laughed and put a bottle on the bar. When Max nodded, he poured him a couple of inches of brandy. "That one's on the house."

"Were you the guy who threw them out on the street?" Luc was tall and thin but the muscles in his forearms looked like steel cables.

"I invited them to take their conversation elsewhere. They were reluctant to go at first but I persuaded them."

Max had no doubt Luc had eloquent methods of persuasion, whether a club like Yesim kept under the bar or one of the many illicit revolvers that still circulated in Paris, three years after the war.

"Did you see what happened next?"

Luc laughed again. Max usually didn't trust men who laughed too much but decided to make an exception for this man. Perhaps, if he couldn't go back to Le Coq Bleu, he could transfer his custom here.

"Take a look at my clientele," he said. "They'd rob me blind if I looked away for a minute."

Max glanced at the dozen or so men slumped around the tables, nursing drinks, and talking in low voices. Most were in need of a shave and few showed signs of prosperity in their shabby clothes or the worn leather of their shoes. But, a lot of people were suffering since the devaluation of the franc and these looked no worse than most.

"What were Harvey and LaFoie arguing about?"

"What do men always argue about? The War, politics, money, and women."

"You forgot religion," said Max.

"I lump that in with politics. This is Paris, not America." Luc laughed again. "Your accent is good but no-one would confuse you for a Frenchman. Let me guess – Canada?"

Max raised one eyebrow – most Parisians didn't make a distinction.

"The fact you can do more than order beer and ask about pirettes sets you apart." Luc rubbed his chin. "It was a woman, I think. I overheard a few of the shouts toward the end. But your friend Harvey kept switching to English. The other one – LaFoie was it? –

seemed to understand. He pulled a knife and I asked them both to leave."

Harvey had told him they fought over politics and religion. Bilodeau might have been at the root of the argument but, according to Harvey, it hadn't been the topic.

"Did anyone go out and watch the fight?"

"Half the bar," said Luc. "But it must not have lasted long. They all drifted back in a minute or two. You might ask those two." Luc gestured to two men in the back corner who had been watching the conversation while doing their best to pretend they weren't. "But be careful how you approach them. If they think you're a police informant, we might be fishing *you* out of the Seine tomorrow."

Max dropped another twenty on the bar and grabbed the half empty bottle before heading for the table in the back. One of the men jerked to his feet but settled back when Max waved the brandy at him. They might be wary but they were thirsty, too.

"I'm a friend of Erich Harvey. The American who got into a fight here the other night." He put the bottle on the table and slid it toward the two men.

"Tall, shabby and old?" said one as he poured healthy servings for him and his friend. He didn't look much more than twenty but the light was dim and appearances were almost always deceiving. The two exchanged glances.

"How do we know you don't work for the Prefecture?"

"I'm told I don't sound French if that helps." Max decided not to offer cash; it was liable to become a bad habit.

"Wouldn't stop those pricks," grumbled the other man. His comrade put his hand on his arm. "We have nothing to hide," he said, "and the gentleman has been generous."

"Wasn't much of fight," said the second. "The little guy had a knife but he didn't look like he knew how to use it. The old man caught it in the flap of his jacket and gave him a little tap on the side of the head. By the time the knife guy was up, the old man had staggered off in search of his next drink. You might try the Le Dur across the street."

"LaFoie got up?"

"Yeah. Everyone else had gone inside but we were..." The younger man nudged him. "...concerned for his well being."

More likely wondering if he would stay down long enough for them to rob him, thought Max. "Did you tell the police that?"

"Sure, we marched right down to the Prefecture and gave our statement," said the younger of the two. The older one laughed like it was the funniest thing he ever heard. His laugh didn't inspire the same degree of warmth in Max.

He took out his notebook and scribbled down what he had been told. When he was done, he showed it to the two men. "Is that about right?"

The older one nodded uncertainly.

"I'm not signing that," said the younger. "If that's what you had in mind."

"No need," said Max. "Just come up to the bar and tell Luc that it's true. He'll witness it. And give you another bottle of brandy."

Max's luck held when he tried the brasserie across the street. The proprietor had been there the night of the fight and remembered Harvey when he came in looking for a drink "to calm his nerves."

"I didn't need trouble so I gave him a small shot and sent him on his way," he said. "LaFoie – he was a regular – came in a few minutes later. He seemed fine, once we wiped the blood off his face. But he was mad – swore he'd make Harvey pay. In fact, he said he would make Harvey look like a fool for what he had done. His words exactly."

"You didn't tell the police?"

"They never asked."

Chapter 6 Wednesday, September 29th, 1921

T he signed statements from the two bartenders were enough to get Fontaine's attention. The captain's sallow face blotched red and his lips pressed so tightly they formed a thin line. Finally, he dropped the two sheets on his desk and snarled at the desk sergeant.

"Bring Harvey up from the cells. Then send a gendarme to verify these statements." Turning back to Max, he said. "If I find you've been lying to me..."

Max shrugged. Fontaine's threats had failed to move Max since the last time he had been arrested for murder. Fontaine went back to his office, presumably to run through his list of suspects now that Harvey couldn't be relied on. Max leaned against the wall and waited for his client to be processed. He wondered what he would do to occupy his time now Harvey was in the clear. He needed something now he no longer had any friends.

"You look like prison agrees with you, Erich," said Max. Harvey's eyes were clearer and there was a spring in his step. His freshly grown beard, more dark-brown than grey, made him look ten years younger.

"Three meals a day and a few good nights' sleep will do that to you." Harvey glanced over his shoulder wistfully. "Believe it or not, this place is quieter than my flat. Cleaner, too."

"I'll walk you home," said Max.

"Maybe we could stop somewhere for lunch," said Harvey. "Breakfast was a few hours ago and I wouldn't want to relapse."

Max suspected that was exactly what the old journalist wanted to do so he was surprised when Harvey ordered nothing more than sparkling water to go with his fish chowder. Max himself took a small beer with his croque-monsieur and roquette salad with balsamic parmesan dressing. Harvey gazed longingly at the beer when it came, then spent the rest of the meal staring into his soup bowl.

"Now that you're in the clear, maybe you can tell me what you and LaFoie were fighting about."

"Nothing."

"It must have been something. He pulled a knife on you."

Harvey glanced at Max. "It was a very small knife. And he wasn't serious about it."

"You thought it serious enough to hit him with a bottle." When Harvey looked away again, Max added, "After all, you might have broken it."

Harvey chuckled and then let it turn into a cough.

"Somebody killed LaFoie – it was no accident – and then they tried to frame you for the job. Surely you want some answers."

"Max, I appreciate what you've done for me but really it is better left well alone. LaFoie was involved with some dangerous people. Obviously more dangerous than he thought."

Max finished his beer and ordered a second. The look in Harvey's eyes was almost painful but Max wasn't going to destroy the man's new-found resolve. The café they had chosen offered a good view of the river. A light mist hung above the water and to the west, banks of clouds had begun to gather. *There would be rain before midnight*, thought Max. He dropped a few dozen francs on the table when the waiter came with the beer. He didn't intend to stay long and didn't want to wait for the bill.

"LaFoie was a friend of yours. Don't you care what happened to him?"

"You're a friend of mine, Max. I don't want the same thing to happen to you."

Max felt a brief clutch of fear below his ribs and straightened in his seat. He had faced worse than a few over-dressed thugs in the war. Still, his mouth had gone dry when he opened it to ask the next question.

"Did..." His voice sounded like that of an old man. He took a sip from the beer, then another as he felt the tightness ease. "Did Bilodeau let it slip to people in the movement?"

"I doubt it," said Harvey. He looked out at the mist on the river, whether to formulate his thoughts or to avoid watching Max drink. "I suspect she deliberately told them. She... How does she come across to you, Max?"

Max blushed and hoped Harvey would not turn and catch the complexity of his feelings. He lifted the beer to his lips and took a slow sip to gather himself. "Full of energy, I suppose. Smart and determined. Well connected and not merely to the supporters of her cause."

"You forgot beautiful," said Harvey.

"Yes."

"Well, she's all that. But more, she is une fidèle disciple of the Black Fist. She would not hesitate to..." Harvey looked back at Max. His skin was waxy and there was a haunted expression in his eyes. The old man's new found sobriety would not last the night.

"To do what?"

Harvey rose so abruptly, his chair nearly toppled. "I should be going. I have deadlines to meet." He staggered as he turned away and caught himself on the back of the chair. His voice when it came was little more than a whisper. "She's dangerous and she's devious. She will do anything to anyone and use any means to advance her agenda. You should stay away from her. I know I will."

Harvey straightened his stooped shoulders and walked with a semblance of dignity through the restaurant and onto the street. Max watched him out of sight and swallowed the last of his beer. He knew he should follow Harvey's advice but knew equally well that he wouldn't.

MAX HAD USED PHILLIPE Latour a few times to aid in his investigations. He was a small man, with a singular ability to trail suspects without being seen. He sent a messenger to the bar where Latour was a regular and arranged to meet him at Pere Lachaise cemetery beside Rossini's cenotaph at four o'clock. They were unlikely to be seen by anyone they knew and it wasn't too far from there to Bilodeau's house.

A steady drizzle had plastered the freshly fallen leaves into a variegated carpet over the red gravel pathways. The unconsecrated grounds housed many of France's most famous citizens as well as those like Rossini and the Englishman, Oscar Wilde, who had made Paris their home. He and Jacqui often walked there on a weekday afternoon when it was largely empty. They visited the graves and monuments of the famous but also speculated over the graves of those unknowns from every religion and every part of the world.

Sometimes, he came by himself when the noise of living became too great. Max wasn't sure he believed in an afterlife but he often felt better after discussing his troubles with the silent stones.

He was checking his watch for the third time when Latour appeared at his side. He was dapper but notoriously tough in a fight. His handsome face was marred by a purple birthmark on his left cheek. Max had not heard his approach across the loose gravel and wondered if the man had supernatural powers.

"I've always liked his music," Latour said by way of greeting. "You?"

"I've only heard it once. I fell asleep."

"Americans," said Latour derisively, though he knew Max was from Canada. "What do you have for me?"

"Tail and report on Nicole Bilodeau. I need to know her movements, where she goes and who she meets. That sort of thing." He didn't mention the connection to LaFoie; it might skew the things Latour thought worth reporting. He handed the detective the card with Bilodeau's address and gave him a quick description.

Latour gave a low whistle of appreciation. "I think I'm going to enjoy this job. How long before I report?"

"I'll hire you for the week and you can report to me at Chez Jake or, if I'm not there, my apartment—I think you have my address."

"Not Le Coq Bleu?"

Max shook his head, not trusting himself to speak of it without emotion, and handed Latour an envelope of cash. He would pay the other half upon receiving the final report. Latour pocketed the money without counting it and took another look at the address.

"Things are moving fast on this one," Max added as Latour turned to go. "If you see anything unusual—and use your own judgement on that—track me down and let me know." Latour raised an eyebrow. "You'll get the full week's pay regardless of when you report. If it gives me what I need."

Latour nodded and strolled away in the direction of the Metro. Max watched him until he disappeared into the misty dusk, fading like a dream until he was gone.

IT WAS WELL AFTER MIDNIGHT when Max was awakened to a pounding on the door of his apartment. He had spent the night at Chez Jake listening to the clarinetist from Zelli's Royal Box jamming with some of the regulars who had made that part of Montmartre home. His head was a bit woozy from smoke and too much pastis. He staggered to the door expecting the gendarmes or possibly some of Jacqui's friends angry at the way he had treated their comrade. Instead, he found Latour, his dark eyes nervously flickering to the street through the small window at the end of the hallway. Max ushered him in and poured them both some anise—the only bottle he hadn't emptied since Jacqui left.

Latour threw it back and held out his glass for another. Max shrugged and poured; he could always buy more in the morning. The small man was clearly shaken.

Latour quaffed much of the second glass and then set it carefully on the small table that half filled the small kitchen. "You might have warned me what I was getting into. I thought this was something simple, like embezzlement or a divorce case."

"You know I don't do those."

"Money talks, people change."

"What happened?"

Latour was disturbed by something he had seen but he was a professional. He straightened in his chair and took a small notebook from his pocket, though he scarcely glanced at is as he gave his report.

"I arrived at Bilodeau's house shortly after five p.m. and tucked myself into a doorway a few metres down the street. Several *anciens combattants* bunk down there at night so I fit right in. A grocer made a delivery on the half-hour and ten minutes later a second delivery arrived, from a milliner by the shape of the box. The assignment didn't make an appearance until ten past six. She exited and went north on Rue de Turenne to a taxi stand. I was able to catch a cab immediately after and we followed her across the city to the Square des Batignolles where the Action Française were holding a rally in a big tent, a slap in the face to the many Communards who were buried there in 1871. I showed my membership card and slipped in behind her—"

"You belong to the Action Française?" Max had always thought Latour was a socialist.

"Sure, and to the Socialists, Communists, and Radicals, too. I've even attended the odd anarchist meeting. It's useful in our line of work to keep your contacts diverse. You should try it."

Max wondered if Latour had met LaFoie in his travels. The men appeared to share a modus operandi. "Continue."

"Bilodeau wasn't on the platform but she was right below it. Bucard—you know him—was standing next to her and she occasionally stretched up and whispered in his ear. Whatever it was, he seemed to find it alternately interesting and amusing judging from the expressions on his face. At one point between speeches de Vesins himself leaned over and shook her hand."

Bernard de Vesins was president of the party and, although he had been defeated in the elections of 1919, retained a strong and vocal following among the anti-Dreyfus right and the disaffected youth of the Camelots de Roi. Bilodeau's contacts within the far right ran deep if she counted both de Vesins and Bucard among her friends.

"She spent the next hour circulating through the room, stopping to chat with this one or that. Most I recognized as players in the movement though a few were new to me. I spotted a couple of police agents—despite the views of the Prefect, many in the prefecture distrust the AF—and she did, too. She spoke to a couple of Camelots and they hustled one of them out of the hall. Then, when Maurras, the chief philosopher of the Action Francais, came in the back, he broke away from his bodyguards and greeted her like a long-lost cousin. They spoke briefly and then she headed out the way he had come in.

"I was sure that would be the end of my night; the back entrance was not for the likes of me. But I decided to try my luck and it paid off. Bilodeau came out of the alley as I was leaving the tent and I had to be pretty quick not to be spotted. In any case, she didn't go far. A couple of blocks farther on is Rue Nollet where one of the little Jewish newspapers, Di Amse Geshikhte or The Real Truth, has their offices. She met two men who had been lurking in a doorway. I recognized one of them, Gustav Reinhardt, a thug for hire from the Alsace.

"The place was dark and locked tighter than a drum but she must have had a key. They went in and came out again ten minutes later. Reinhardt and his friend went back to lurking and she walked a few blocks before hailing a cab in front of the Tuileries gardens. I was close enough to hear her give her own address, so I called it a night."

"So, what are you doing here so early in the morning?"

"About two hours ago, a bomb went off in those offices, shortly after the editor arrived to start the early edition. He was killed but his assistant survived and picked Reinhardt out of a lineup." Latour drained the rest of his glass and went to look out the window. His shoulders were quaking slightly though he didn't make a sound.

"I guess I'm getting too old for this game," Latour said at last. "Reinhardt must have spotted me following Bilodeau. He gave my name to Captain Fontaine as the mastermind. It won't stick but it gives cover to Bilodeau and makes me a target for every Young Patriot or Camelot with a stick in his hand. I'm heading up to Brittainy until this whole thing blows over. I wanted to let you know before I left."

Max went to the safe in his bedroom and got the rest of Latour's promised fee. He added a couple of thousand francs to the pile. "For travelling expenses."

"Thanks, Max. You're a good guy." Latour pocketed the bills and then slipped a grainy photo to Max. "This is Reinhardt," he said, pointing to a man with black hair and sharp Germanic features, "in case you need to find him." Latour took another look out the window as if he expected Fontaine and a pack of swallows to appear at any moment. "If I can give you a bit of advice—stay away from Bilodeau. She will bring you nothing but grief."

After Latour had left, Max tried to go back to sleep. An hour later he was on the street watching the rising sun trying to break through the still heavy clouds. Everyone thought he should stay away from Bilodeau. But she was now his prime suspect in the murder of LaFoie. As if that was her only attraction.

Chapter 7 Thursday, September 30th, 1921

Normally, Max would wander over to Le Coq Bleu to have breakfast with Yesim before the bar opened to the departing night shift from the workshops and small factories that had sprung up on Bessieres since the end of the war. That was out of the question now so he stopped in a small patisserie across the street from his flat for a cheese brioche and a café americain and to catch up with the local papers.

The owner, a very short man with a very big laugh, kept a wide variety on hand, draped over wooden dowels on a rack along one wall. Whatever his own politics, he catered to a diverse crowd. Offering up both left and right periodicals was his way of saying that his café, at least, was neutral ground in the increasingly fractious politics of post-war France.

All of the papers carried reports of the bombing on the first, second or third page. The most liberal papers carried the news, sometimes with photographs, on the front, implying or outright accusing communist agitators of being behind the attack. The Action Français relegated the story to the second page and mostly downplayed the Jewish connection, while bemoaning the failure of the Prefecture to crack down on "notorious foreign thugs who hide in the banlieues," while the socialist and communist papers had put it on the bottom of page three and suggested the explosion had been accidental, that is to say, the result of a failed bomb making attempt by anti-Zionists, thus cleverly slandering two enemies with a single story. Of course, anyone could make a rudimentary explosive device by packing gunpowder in a pipe, but a sophisticated device required real skill. Max wondered how he might track down the person behind the manufacture and made a note to look into it when he had the time.

Still hungry, both physically and intellectually, Max ordered another coffee and added a chocolate croissant, though he knew his stomach would make him regret it, and settled in to see what else was occupying the minds of his adopted countrymen.

The left seemed mostly preoccupied by the now month-old appointment of Auguste Jonnart as an ambassador to the Vatican, a move they claimed would compromise the secular nature of the Republic. They were also furious at the government's intervention in the general strike by northern textile workers on the side of industry and equally outraged at the behavior of American legionnaires who had been welcomed warmly by the President and quickly wore out that welcome by their scandalous behavior. The right, of course, took opposite views on all these matters and also contained lengthy follow-ups on the celebration of the seventh anniversary of the victory at the Marne which had taken place ten days before. The liberal papers gave short shrift to all of these stories and, instead, were filled with speculations on the possible return to public life of wartime leader, George Clemenceau, as well as lengthy reportage of recent French victories on the football field.

Satisfied that he had passed sufficient time that the denizens at Chez Jake would be rousing, he made his way across Montmartre to the bar. Jake himself, looking as elegant as if he were greeting guests for the evening, answered the door, the only sign of his certain hangover, the mumbled greeting, and the weary gesture for Max to find his own way upstairs.

Max didn't have urgent work to do but he always found it soothing to at least go through the motions. There was the case of a missing brother whose presence, or proof of death, was needed to settle an estate. Max had shown his picture around the hospitals and morgues in the city and its outlying banlieues and visited all his known haunts in Paris. He sent telegrams to places he was known to frequent outside the city. Half of the responses had come back negative and the rest would wander in on their own time or not at all. A few leads were left to follow up and he made a list which he promised himself he would begin first thing tomorrow morning, or, at the latest, on Monday.

Equally boring was the matter of investigating the background of a young man who had recently moved to the city and proposed marriage to the daughter of a prominent citizen in the Russian quarter. Max had gotten to know the father during a previous case. While Max didn't handle divorce cases, he was more than willing to prevent a young woman from entering into a bad marriage. He had made the usual inquiries but was resisting traveling to the boy's home town to do on-site investigations.

He checked the mail but there was nothing much there, a couple of bills to pay and two requests for his services—both divorce cases—that he filed in the basket under his desk. It was still too early for lunch and he had no place to go where he'd be welcome. Harvey may have told him to leave it to the police—and he was sure Fontaine would be happy to tap out the same sentiment with his truncheon—but there was one thing Max couldn't stand. Injustice. And one thing he loved: getting under the skin of the incompetent Captain Fontaine.

He put on his jacket and hat and headed back to the offices of Le Grand Parisien to see what else he could find out about the mysterious and complicated Réjean LaFoie.

Braque didn't seem overjoyed about the repeat visit but Max persisted until the editor gave in.

"Ten minutes," he said, waving at a stack of typewritten pages on his desk. "I've got a deadline."

"I'll get to the point. You said LaFoie was 'joking' when he sued Harvey. What was the joke? And did Harvey get the punchline?"

"You'd have to ask him that." Braque leaned over his desk and gestured for Max to do the same. "Réjean kept it to himself—I doubt if more than a handful of people knew—but he had a wife, a woman he had been married to for fifteen years, had two kids with. Any one who did know was sworn to secrecy."

"You said he would brag if—" Braque waved him off.

"Delacroix wasn't the only one to use protective coloration. Réjean would flirt, sure, he was a Frenchman through and through, but to my knowledge, he was never unfaithful to Simonne. He loved her."

"Then why the secrecy?"

"Simonne is Jewish. Given the company he kept... well, like I say, he loved her. And his kids."

A Jewish wife—and therefore Jewish kids. No wonder LaFoie had a hatred for L'Action Française.

"Do you happen to have an address?"

Braque looked doubtful. "What's your interest in this? I heard Harvey was your client and he's out."

Max shrugged. Sometimes his French failed him when he had to explain his feelings, his deepest beliefs. Maybe that was the trouble he was having with Jacqui, his inability to account for the disquietude he so often felt, the sense of despair that had nagged him since the war, as common a companion as the pain now throbbing in his leg.

"A man was murdered. A man the Prefecture would as soon forget." *So familiar*, he thought. It was said the police in Paris had some of the most advanced techniques, the cleverest detectives in the world and yet, for all that, they refused to solve—or prevent—the murders of those they considered marginal to society, or, especially, enemies of the Prefecture.

Braque nodded and wrote a few lines on a scrap of paper. "This is in the 13th arrondissement, just off Tobiac."

"Not the 3rd?" Marais was the traditional Jewish quarter.

"Protective coloration."

THE BUILDING ON MOULIN de Pres was a typical Paris walk-up – six floors high with tiny metal-grilled balconies on the street-side windows, accessed by a pair of arched wooden doors. LaFoie's apartment took up half the second floor. A suspicious concierge took his card and returned several minutes later to usher him to the door of the flat, which was slightly ajar by way of welcome. He rapped lightly on the door. Hearing no response, he pushed though and went down the hall into a small sitting area.

Simonne LaFoie was seated on a deep blue chaise, her face turned toward the window. She was dressed all in black—a long black dress that pooled on the floor at her feet and a black shawl that was pulled up to cover her hair. Seated, it was difficult to judge her height or build but Max had the impression of a tall slim woman, a sense of dignity in the erectness of her posture and the tilt of her head.

The room itself was sparsely furnished and painted creamy white with pale blue trim and intricate wainscoting at floor and ceiling. Other than the chaise, there were three chairs, a simple one beside a small writing desk and two wing-backed ones on either side of a coal burning fireplace. The room was dominated by two floor-to-ceiling shelves, overflowing with books. No paintings or photographs decorated the walls, though a small wedding photo in a silver frame stood atop the writing desk. A thick candle glimmered beside it. Besides the door he was standing in, there was one other exit but the door was firmly closed. Of the children, there was no sign or sound. They were, perhaps, in school or staying with a relative.

"Madame LaFoie," Max said from the entrance of the room, his hat held in his hands before him. She started, though she must have been expecting him.

"You came about... Réjean's death," she said, without turning. Her voice was of medium timbre but quiet, barely audible in the confines of the high-ceilinged room. "Were you a friend of his?"

"No. Not a friend."

"An enemy, then?" her shoulders tensed and Max had a premonition of danger, that his next response might mean more than simply being asked to leave.

"I barely knew your husband. I... was investigating his death for the man who was accused..."

"Of his murder. You say he *was* accused."

"He had an alibi. The police have released him."

She turned then, searching his face for something. Her own face was pale from grief but, judging by the darkness of her brows and eyes, that was not her natural colour. She was younger than he had expected, not much over thirty-five and other than the lines around her mouth and at the corner of her eyes—from laughter more than worry—he would have guessed her ten years younger and not the mother of two children. Her dark eyes were intent and serious but there was something about her gaze, as if she were looking at him through shuttered windows. She remained seated, her body still half-turned toward the window, her hands folded together in her lap.

"You were successful in freeing your client," she said. "What is your interest now?"

How could he explain to this woman—this stranger—when he could barely explain it to himself? He had no paying client, even his work for Harvey had been pro bono, no reason to pursue the death of a man he had barely heard of before a few days ago. If anything, he had several reasons to leave the matter alone, to let the Prefecture deal with it or not as they saw fit. His life was complicated enough without dabbling in the mire of Parisian politics.

"LaFoie's death was..." He paused searching for the words that would unravel the knot in his stomach.

"You are an American, no? Came to win the war, stayed to play the hero?"

"I'm a Canadian, actually. Came to keep my brother safe at home, stayed because... because I needed to fix..." Max felt tears well in his eyes, tears that had not come in the years since he left the battlefields of France, not for doctors, not for comrades or friends, not for Jacqui. "...something broken inside of me."

The pain in Max's leg throbbed and he leaned against the door frame, frozen by grief and anger and something more, something ineffable yet as real as the wood he was leaning against.

"I'm sorry... I should go."

"No." Simonne rose from the chaise and crossed to the small ivory-inlaid table. She placed a small revolver on the table top and then came to Max, taking his hands in hers. Her footfalls were silent and he realized she wasn't wearing shoes. Her gaze was unshuttered now, her eyes deep pools of sadness.

"Réjean was a little like you. He was driven by the things he had seen in the streets growing up in the banlieues, by the violence that seethed beneath the surface of the so-called Belle Epoque, by what he saw later in the war, as a correspondent at the front. I understand why you are here. How can I help?"

"Maybe... a cup of tea?"

"I am afraid we are all coffee drinkers here." She smiled though the pain never left her eyes. "If that will do, sit on the chaise and I will go make it."

Max nodded and sat facing away from the window. He rubbed his hands across his face, and through his hair, trying to stem the flow of tears that, once begun, seemed determined to continue until he was drained dry. He felt ashamed; she was the one who had just lost her husband, the father of her children. Yet, she was trying to comfort him. No wonder LaFoie had loved her. He wondered why he had broken down in front of her, a complete stranger, someone he might never see again. Maybe that was reason enough.

The woman was gone for longer than making coffee would take and he supposed she was giving him time to compose himself. For that he was grateful and, by the time she returned carrying a tray with two steaming cups, as well as sugar and cream, he was sitting straight on the chaise with eyes stinging but dry. She set the tray on the desk and, after fixing the coffee to his request, turned her chair and sat facing him.

"I have no money to pay you to solve Réjean's death," she said at last.

"I wouldn't take it if you did. Money is not an issue to me, justice is." He thought he sounded a bit pompous but she smiled and took a sip of coffee.

"Canada must provide better pensions to its soldiers than Mother France."

Max snorted at that despite himself. "No, not as such. I came in to some money a few years ago and while I make more here and there, if I didn't, I wouldn't starve. Frankly, in your husband's case, I do not believe the Prefecture will make an effort to solve his death. His murder."

Simonne shuddered slightly and slowly closed and opened her eyes. "Then you are sure it was deliberate then. Not an accident or the result of an argument that got out of hand."

"You must have suspected." Max glanced at the pistol still sitting on the desktop. She followed his gaze and slipped it into the single drawer of the table.

"Yes. Réjean had received death threats before but the recent ones were particularly ugly. Particularly specific."

"Did they come here?"

"No. Réjean kept a room in Montmartre. It is what is on his official papers. I hold the *livret* for this apartment."

The Paris police kept extensive records on the movements of its citizens, both French nationals and migrants. They issued certificates of domicile—livrets—and any one whose residence didn't match the official record could be fined or even forced to leave the city.

"But you were worried they might track him here."

"Wouldn't you be? When I heard of Réjean's death—a friend who knew our situation came by—I hoped it was a mistake or, at worst, an accident. But, as you say, I suspected. I sent the children to stay with my mother in Strasbourg until I could decide what to do. And I took precautions."

Max nodded his approval. He still had his Webley .445 revolver, which he usually kept in his desk at Chez Jake, though on occasion it was tucked into a holster under his arm. If Simonne LaFoie felt she needed to keep a revolver handy, perhaps he should start to carry his and hope he didn't get stopped and searched by the swallows.

"Did your husband ever mention a woman named Nicole Bilodeau?"

"I wondered when that name would come up."

"Then you knew about his relationship with her."

She took another sip of her coffee. It had grown cold and she set it carefully back on the tray. The cup barely rattled in the saucer.

"If by relationship, you mean Réjean was sleeping with that *pirette*, you are poorly informed. Réjean had a lot of flaws but infidelity was not one of them. Bilodeau was Réjean's dupe. Oh, I'm sure she tried to charm him and I'm sure he played along, up to a point. But she was nothing but a source to him—the source of a story that Réjean claimed would shake the foundations of the state."

Max knew that Bilodeau had connections to the far right, a dangerous group but not one likely to ever grasp the levers of power.

Yet, some, who publicly decried their tactics, implicitly supported their ideas. Meetings of the Black Fist or, even, the Action Française, were not the only places one could hear the vitriol against Jews and immigrants, the longing for the return of the king, the threats to anyone who did not conform or fit in. Was she also connected to those who called themselves conservative but secretly worked for something else?

"Did your husband tell you the nature of that story?"

"No. Perhaps he thought to protect me. Perhaps it was merely his instincts as a reporter, protecting his 'scoop' even from his family."

Another dead end. Or rather a trail that led him back to the one person he had been warned to avoid. And he wanted to avoid her. Didn't he?

"Then there is nothing more you can tell me about who might wish your husband dead."

"The usual suspects, I suppose. Le Camelots or, perhaps the anarchists. He had written several pieces exposing their activities to the light of day. Like cockroaches, they did not care for the exposure."

Max felt the heat rise on the back of his neck. Those men at Le Coq Bleu. Jacqui. Arcand. Bilodeau. His life was constantly torn between those who would tear down the state and those who would give it supreme power over all.

"Did Réjean ever mention a policeman named Gereau?"

Simonne started at that, her mouth drawn in a tight line. She reached for her cup—forgetting the coffee had gone cold—but her hand was shaking too badly to lift it. She pulled her hand back and clasped it with the other in her lap. After a moment, she drew a long shuddering breath and rose, crossing to the book shelf to the left of the fireplace. She reached behind the books on the third shelf and withdrew a battered notebook.

"This is one of Réjean's notebooks. He left it here by mistake last week; I was holding it for him. I don't know what it contains. Réjean wrote in code but, if you can decipher it, it may tell you what you want to know."

Max took the book; the worn leather of its cover still held the heat of the woman's hand. He flipped it open; more than half of the pages were covered in a flowing script. He had no idea how he would interpret it but at least it was a start.

"But Gereau? Did your husband know him?"

The woman nodded, almost imperceptibly, as if afraid to voice the connection aloud. She turned away to stare out the window into the street.

"Gereau, I think, wanted Réjean to work for him. He was quite insistent but Réjean only worked for himself and his readers. The few times he spoke of the man, it was with suspicion and, I think, a little fear. People like us have reason to fear the police. Now that I know my husband's fate, I will leave this place and join my family. If you are able to bring my husband's killers to justice, you can contact me there at the central post office. Otherwise, I prefer to be left alone."

GEREAU HAD EXPRESSED his interest in LaFoie, ostensibly for his links to the anarchists who had become the older man's obsession. Lafoie had been a clever and determined journalist, had cultivated, if not friends, contacts across the political spectrum. He sought out both those who respected the rule of law and the freedoms expressed in the revolutionary slogan: Liberty, Equality, Fraternity and those who were a law unto themselves, ever willing to subjugate their fellow citizens to their "higher" purposes. Max had assumed that he would find LaFoie's murderer among Nicole Bilodeau's friends but perhaps he should look among Gereau's enemies instead. Gereau had been a policeman for a long time. The list of his enemies could be long.

Gereau had told him that he was investigating certain matters and that LaFoie's death had complicated things. Max had assumed that Gereau was LaFoie's informant—a useful connection both before and after he left the Prefecture. But perhaps it was the other way around, Gereau had hoped to use the reporter as a way to infiltrate anarchist circles. Had LaFoie, despite Simonne's assurances, agreed to do so? No one would ever suspect LaFoie of being a police agent. Until they did.

He had left Gereau's apartment—angry at his implications about Jacqui, implications that he had foolishly pursued—before finding out what Gereau was investigating. It was time to rectify that mistake.

Normally he would have walked from the 13th to Gereau's rooms on Rue de Moussy but his leg, which had been quiescent for months, was now throbbing from hip to ankle so he took the Metro from Italie to Hotel de Ville, planning to walk the last few blocks. However, he spotted Gereau taking a late and solitary lunch—or early supper—in a café at the corner of Moussy and Verrerie. Max slipped into the seat across from him. Gereau didn't immediately look up from the newspaper he was reading but finished the article before folding the paper and laying it to the side of his plate on the red-checked table cloth.

"The chef here is from Gascony," said Gereau by way of greeting. "The duck confit is excellent. Have it with the red cabbage and apple. They serve a nice sauterne but the reds are not worth rejoicing."

"Perhaps later," said Max, though the aromas wafting from the open kitchen were making his mouth water. "I'm still looking into the murder of LaFoie."

"Why am I not surprised?"

"I was told that you and LaFoie had an arrangement." It was hardly true; Simonne had said nothing of the sort, but her reaction to Gereau's name and the provision of the notebook immediately after had told him there must be some connection between the two men. He considered showing the notebook to Gereau. Better to wait and see exactly the nature of that arrangement.

"Who told you that?"

"I'd rather not say."

"Of course, we all need to protect our sources."

"You mentioned that LaFoie's death was, how did you put it, inconvenient?"

"I don't believe I was quite that gauche." Gereau smiled disarmingly and spread his hands wide. "Alright, Max, I'll be honest with you. Perhaps you'll return the favour some day. LaFoie and I did have an 'arrangement.' It was a mixture of common interests and mutual profit. Sometimes money changed hands but generally not. I would provide LaFoie inside information to confirm or direct his inquiries and he would tell me things of interest I could use in my investigations."

"Things must have changed after you left the Prefecture." Gereau wasn't telling him everything but there was nothing unusual about that.

"After forty-five years, you don't suddenly stop being a cop. I... consult. Like our Gascon chef, I have certain specialities."

"The black flag and those who follow it."

"Precisely. Which brings us to your friend Yesim."

"Yesim is a respectable business man."

"Well, he is in business. I'll give you that."

"Commerce and extreme politics aren't exactly roommates." Max didn't like the direction the conversation was going but he wasn't ready to walk out on Gereau a second time. "But go on."

Gereau looked over Max's shoulder at someone on the sidewalk. Max resisted the urge to look around. Perhaps a mademoiselle was passing, or, Gereau, sensitive to Max's desire to protect his friends, was gathering himself to broach the subject circumspectly.

"Yesim is either taking part in violent plots to overthrow the state or is sheltering those who are."

Then again, perhaps it was merely a pretty girl, after all. Max's shoulders tightened and he laid his hands flat on the table to keep from balling them into fists.

"What, no defense of your business partner—yes, we know about that—or his friends?"

"You obviously know that some of Yesim's old friends from Marseilles are in Paris. Yesim makes no bones about his past, or the fact he left it behind, but he is nothing if not loyal. If his former friends came calling, he would hardly throw them out."

"I heard he threw you out."

Max jerked his hand up, then turned it into a gesture to summon the hovering waiter.

"A brandy," he growled. "That had nothing to do with politics."

Gereau frowned and Max thought he was going to argue. Instead, he gestured his acceptance and followed it with a faint smile.

"Friends argue over the stupidest things," said Gereau. "Then if they are truly friends, they get over it."

The waiter returned with the brandy. He also had the bottle of sauterne and Gereau accepted another glass.

"These friends of Yesim. Are you sure they were from Marseilles?"

It was a good question. He had assumed that they were. Yesim hailed from the port city—where his grateful father had named his firstborn after the foreign sailor who had saved him from drowning—and had been active under the black flag there. It seemed logical that these old friends had followed him north but he had no evidence it was the case.

"If not there, then where?"

"We know one, at least, Bernard Dietrich, is from the Alsace."

"A German?"

"He got the name from his great-grandfather who served in the French army before we lost the region to the Germans in 1870."

Retrieving the Alsace, and the rich coal fields they contained, had been a primary objective of the French during the Versailles negotiations, not only for the wealth they would bring but for the crippling effect on the German economy, already struggling from the demands of the French for reparations from the war. Max suspected the world had not heard the last of Alsace-Lorraine.

Gereau continued. "Dietrich is a French citizen and, as far as we know, a patriot—if that term could ever be applied to an anarchist."

"I thought they all believed in international solidarity. Workers of the world and all that."

"You're confusing them with communists. There are anarchists and then there are anarchists—they come in every shade of black." Gereau smiled at his own aphorism. "The anarchists only get along with the communists because they both believe in the withering away of the state. Though the former tends to put more faith in the power of dynamite than the inevitable forces of history."

Max shrugged. He had had plenty of lessons in European politics since he came to France; almost everyone he knew seemed convinced his education had been inadequate. It was true he had been forced to drop out of university by the advent of war but he knew enough to hold his own in most barroom debates. Not that he bothered. Politics bored him, more than that they infuriated them. Dealing with real problems—one at a time—always seemed more useful than big ideas and master plans. Weren't those what had led the world into total war?

"Dietrich is an anarchist and a patriot. What does that look like in real life? I mean, what does he do that makes him so dangerous."

"That's what we would like to know and what Lafoie was trying to find out. It's possible that he was close to an answer, so close that someone decided he needed to be shut up."

"You think this Dietrich killed LaFoie."

"Killed him or had him killed. So far, we've been unable to place Dietrich or his known associates at the scene of the crime."

"Then this is more in the realm of wishful thinking."

Gereau grunted and took another sip of his sauterne. Max thought he caught a hint of redness in the former inspector's cheeks, though he supposed it might merely be the chill in the air.

"You keep using the pronoun 'we,'" Max said. "Who are you working with?"

Gereau laughed. "Sorry, old habits. The police, like royalty, always refer to themselves in the plural. Grants us more authority, I suppose. As I say I am a consultant, like you. Right now, I am, how do they say it in the newspaper business, working on spec, trying to dig up evidence the Prefecture might eventually be willing to pay something for." Gereau looked away and added, almost at a mumble, "A policeman's pension doesn't stretch far these days."

The drop in the value of the franc had made Max richer but was causing real suffering for a lot of French citizens, including his friend Henri who relied on a small pension to supplement his increasingly rare work as a porter. Thinking of Henri caused a lump in his chest. What had Gereau said: true friends get over stupid arguments.

"I'll see what I can find out," he said. At least it would give him an excuse to make amends with Henri, though he was less certain how he would approach Yesim.

Gereau raised an eyebrow at that but nodded. He reached for his wallet but Max waved him off. Gereau looked like he might object but, in the end, he let Max pick up the bill.

Chapter 8 Friday, October 1st 1921

A house in Bobigny, one of the banlieues to the northeast of Paris had served off and on as a safe house for anarchists travelling through the City of Lights. As far as he knew, the Prefecture had failed to find this one and if that was still true, there was a good chance he might find Jacqui there or, at least, someone who could tell him where she was. He wanted to reunite with Henri and Yesim and, to do that, he first had to make peace with her.

The area outside the 20 arrondissements had always housed the working poor and those that fed off of or encouraged their discontents. Those without money—citizens from the French countryside or the many emigrés from the French colonies in Africa and Asia—would crowd into the shabby tenements, often ten or twelve to a flat and eke out an existence in the piecework factories that sprung up from time to time on the outskirts of the city. Many, too, worked behind the scenes in restaurants or hotels, washing dishes, dealing with garbage, or cleaning up after visitors to Paris.

Max never quite felt welcome there—though he had never been treated discourteously—the same way he had always felt uncomfortable in the Negro neighbourhood that existed on the edge of his hometown. His experience in the war had taught him the stupidity of such thoughts but knowing and feeling were often at odds. Perhaps that was why he had waited until morning before visiting. Those who worked during the day would be away and the night shift would likely still be asleep.

These buildings had no concierge to open the front door and, besides, Max knew from previous experience that he would likely receive a warmer welcome—or at least a less hostile one—if he entered from the back alley and provided the password to the inevitable watchman on the fire escape. He only hoped it hadn't changed since his last visit.

The curtains to the third-floor apartment were pulled shut against the morning light as Max walked slowly past the building on the opposite side of the street. A few young men lounged on the corner, assessing their chances, and deciding against taking him on. Max supposed his time in O'Brien's gym had added a swagger to his walk that made the rewards of robbery not worth the risk.

He walked back along the alleyway beneath lines of clothing flapping gently in the fall breeze and past heaps of broken furniture. He paused before climbing the ladder to the fire escape and the stairs to the third-floor landing. He rapped sharply on the door and waited with his arms crossed, the holster containing his Webley pressed tight against his side.

The door opened a crack and a male voice said. "Whatever you're selling, we aren't buying it."

It was the same phrase as his last visit, nearly a year before. "I'm offering a very special price."

"Clear off." The door started to close.

"Let him in." Max had forgotten how soft and sweet Jacqui's voice could be. "I'll vouch for him."

"What makes you think we can trust him?" The door opened wider. The burly man blocking the way had dark hair and a deep scowl.

"He's known about this place for over a year and never told his pal, Captain Gereau."

The scowl deepened but the man moved aside to let Max enter. When he stepped forward, the guard put his hand on Max's shoulder. "If you're so trustworthy, I'm sure you'll leave any weapons at the door. As a sign of good faith."

Max opened his jacket and let him take the Webley. "I'll want this back. It has sentimental value." The man nodded and let him pass. Max bent over and removed the five-shot from beneath his pantleg and handed it to Jacqui. "As a sign of good faith."

"I recall this gun," she said, as she dropped it in her bag. Max smiled, remembering how he had held her, in her guise of Jacques Grand, and Jacques Court at gunpoint in another safe house when he was investigating the death of Havel Barzani. He followed her down the hall, past several closed doors to the front sitting room.

Jacques Court looked up as they entered, his ample frame more than filling the wingback chair in one corner. He did not rise but the second man in the room did, exchanging worried glances with the other two.

"It's all right, Bernard," said Court. "Max is an old friend."

Bernard Dietrich, thought Max. Dietrich looked to be about forty with thinning blond hair and a hard look about his eyes. He wasn't as big as Max but had the air of a man who could handle himself in a fight. He nodded and smiled, showing big white teeth, the front incisor capped with gold, before sitting back on the sagging sofa under the window.

"What brings you here, Max?" asked Court.

"I came to find Jacqui, to apologize for being an idiot."

Court laughed. "You must be serious, to say it in front of witnesses."

"Max is always serious," said Jacqui. "It is both his most annoying and endearing quality."

"I find it hard to believe this *putain* would come all the way out here to say he's sorry," said Dietrich in more than passable English.

"Please, Bernard, there's a lady present..." said Court, gesturing Max to take a seat on the sofa. Max shook his head.

"I don't much care what you believe," said Max in French. "About me or the state of French society."

He had come to see Jacqui, not to engage in a political debate with people he didn't like or trust. Gereau wasn't right to condemn people simply because of their political views but that didn't mean some of them weren't worth condemning for who they were. If Dietrich was one of those anarchists who espoused the propaganda of the deed, committing acts of violence to expose the legalized violence that underlay state power, then Max wanted nothing to do with him or with those, like Court, who gave him cover. But, he wondered, does that include Jacqui?

"I understand you're looking into the murder of Réjean Lafoie," said Court.

Max glanced at Jacqui but she gave an elaborate shrug, as if to say "Court has his own sources." Not surprising since the man kept extensive files on friends, and especially, enemies, that would make the Prefecture jealous.

"I take it you're familiar with him."

"Our paths have crossed from time to time. You know how it is." Court rubbed his thumb across his pudgy fingers. Every thing had a price in Paris, even among those who considered property, and its stand-in, money, to be theft. "The usual arrangement?"

Max nodded, uncertain why he was willing to throw good money after bad for a case that had no client and no likely good outcome. Then he thought of Simonne and her children. *Maybe I have a client after all.*

"If you'll excuse me, I have no interest in hearing you negotiate with this police agent," Dietrich said, this time in French. He heaved to his feet and pulled aside the heavy curtains to glance out the window as if to assure himself that a police cordon wasn't closing in around the house. His expression was contemptuous but if it bothered Court, he gave no indication. Dietrich deliberately bumped Max's shoulder as he passed but Max refused to respond to the provocation. With a derisive snort, Dietrich stomped out of the room as Max finally took the proffered seat.

Jacqui joined him on the sofa though far enough away he couldn't reach out and touch her. Max resisted the urge to move closer. Court smiled indulgently and, after a moment, Jacqui laughed though Max couldn't see what was funny.

"You have to excuse Bernard," said Court. "He's a bit of a purist."

"Though not so pure, he won't eat the food you buy," said Jacqui. Max was surprised at how quickly she and Court had fallen back into their comfortable banter. *A return to her old ways*, Max thought, not unhappily. A sudden pit opened in his stomach as he thought of how close he had come to losing her, how close he still was.

"What do you know about Lafoie?" asked Max.

"That is far too general a question to do either of us much good," said Court. "I could spend an hour and rattle off a bunch of disconnected facts which would not illuminate you or profit me. I have other obligations today."

"Was Lafoie an anarchist?"

Court frowned. "In a sense of the word, I suppose. He didn't trust anything organized—church or state. But that could be said of any *honest* journalist. And he was that if nothing else. If it had stopped there, he might still be alive."

"But it didn't stop there."

"No," said Court. "LaFoie was all too willing to cross the line and try to create the news and not merely report it. Or, rather, create the news and then report it."

"Meaning?"

"To answer your first question, Max," said Jacqui. "LaFoie was playing a dangerous game. He was involved with certain anarchist cells, providing them information to help avoid the Prefecture but also about the movements of those they considered enemies. At the same time, he was informing on other cells to Captain Gereau. At least he was before Gereau was forced out of the Prefecture."

"Gereau was forced out?" He wondered who had the power to force the Captain to retire and why.

"According to our sources," said Court. "It's a pity. Gereau was a determined adversary but he was also predictable. And for a flic, reasonable."

Max turned in his seat to face Jacqui. "When last we... spoke, you had barely heard of LaFoie, but now..."

"I know you. You were never going to let this go, even after you got Harvey released. It's in your nature. I made inquiries, hoping... well, hoping this would happen." She moved her hand toward him and then back. The gesture did not include Court.

"I wish..."

"We all have wishes and dreams," said Court. "Mine is that we can finish this conversation before lunch."

Max turned sharply, a retort springing to his lips, but he bit it back at the look of sympathy on Court's face. *He probably knows Jacqui better than anyone in Paris*, Max thought. *He knows what she's going through, what we're both going through.*

"Then there are anarchists who would be happy to see LaFoie dead, even happy to kill him?"

"Of course," said Court. "I can't... won't give you names but I can suggest places you might go to ask questions. Le Coq Bleu for example."

"I'm not sure I'm welcome there."

"I've heard."

"I could speak to Yesim," said Jacqui. "Say it's all right between us."

"Is it? There was—" Max couldn't force the words out of his mouth. How did he explain his dalliance with Nicole Bilodeau? He couldn't explain it to himself.

"I don't need the details, Max. I won't hold you to a standard I can't apply to myself. If you still want me, if I still want you... then we'll see."

Court cleared his throat. "If you need to be alone, there is a room down the hall." The big man gave no indication that he was about to move.

"I'm a distraction," said Jacqui, rising. "Finish your business. I need some air."

Max watched her depart, wondering when, or if, he would see her again. She had left her handbag on the floor and Max thought briefly of retrieving his gun and forcing Court to talk. But that, he knew, would be the end of them.

"Jacqui is committed to our cause but in her own way," said Court. "But that is the heart of anarchism. Each individual must determine what freedom and justice means to them while attending to the beliefs of those around us."

"Sounds like liberalism to me."

"It is easy to make that mistake but liberals believe in the rights of property, as if things could ever exercise supremacy over people. They believe in the necessity of the state, instead of seeing how it will always favor one group or class over another. Being an anarchist is endless work but it isn't a thankless task."

"And did Jacqui ever..."

"Throw bombs? No. She ran a school to teach the principles of freedom. And for that, men like Gereau would put her in jail."

Max didn't think it was that simple. Not for him, not for Gereau, probably not even for Jacqui. But it would do for now.

"LaFoie wasn't only involved in anarchist groups, was he?" He already knew that the journalist had become a thorn in the side of the Action Française but perhaps Court could provide insight into how deeply he had offended them.

"You've read his articles, so you know he reported on the right as well, often in such detail he must have been invited to their inner circles. If he betrayed their secrets..."

"Or seemed to be mocking their values?" Max remembered what Bilodeau had told him about the tone of LaFoie's writing that Harvey had pointed out to her.

"There are some in the AF, or more specifically, in the more extreme organizations that associate with them, who take offence at everything, suspecting all the press—even their own—of being part of the vast *Jewish* conspiracy that obsesses them."

Did Court know of LaFoie's Jewish family? There was no way of even asking the question without betraying Simonne.

"So both the anarchist left and the anti-Dreyfusard right had reasons to silence LaFoie."

"Undoubtedly, though I'm hardly in a position to advise you on who to talk to on the right, or even, where you might go to safely question them. Now take out your notebook and I'll give you some addresses."

Max retrieved his Webley from the lookout at the door, suddenly remembering that his other gun was still in Jacqui's purse. He remembered the last time one of his weapons went missing and hoped he wouldn't regret the gesture he had made in giving it to her.

For now, he had half a dozen bars and coffee houses to investigate. He would worry about Jacqui and his gun later. As he headed back toward the bus stop that would take him into the city, he took one final look back at the safe house—which he suspected would now be abandoned, despite Jacqui's assurances that he was trustworthy. The heavy brocade of the curtain parted and though he couldn't see who was watching him, he suspected it was Jacques Court. He probably resented having to leave the comfort of his wingback chair and the security of the no longer safe house.

He didn't feel up to facing Yesim and Henri just yet. It would take time for Jacqui to let Yesim know that things were alright between them in any case. Meanwhile, there was another man who might have insight into LaFoie's connections to the extreme right. A man who, like Court, only felt secure in his own house.

Chapter 9, Saturday, October 2nd, 1921

As soon as he had finished a light breakfast of croissant, plum preserves and café americain, Max headed for the flat of Colonel Dominic Ledux in the 13th arrondissement. He had sent him a message the night before and received a prompt reply inviting him to join him at 9 a.m. The blind ex-soldier never left the rooms he had occupied since the war and had lost contact with much of the diplomatic community that had been his life's blood. Still, he had a deep knowledge of the Parisian political scene, especially the more conservative side, and Max valued his opinions.

Ledux was waiting in the parlour where he always received visitors, impeccably dressed in a pale grey suit, white shirt, and red and blue striped tie. Max felt underdressed but supposed Ledux wouldn't mind what he couldn't see and took a seat on an upholstered bench facing the colonel.

"There is coffee in the samovar and some pastries and cigarettes in the silver case on the sideboard. Help yourself if you like." Ledux had a half-finished cigarette in his left hand; two butts were already in the ashtray on the table beside his chair.

"I was up early and had breakfast before coming," said Max.

"Admirable," said Ledux. "And you don't smoke as I now recall."

"I never got the hang of it."

"Wish I never had." Small talk over, Ledux got to the point. "You mentioned you were investigating the murder of Réjean LaFoie. Do you mind telling me who your client is now that Erich Harvey is in the clear?"

Max had anticipated the question. He couldn't betray Simonne LaFoie's secrets. "Themis."

Ledux snorted. "Then the blind shall have to lead the blind."

"What can you tell me about LeFoie?"

"He's dead," said Ledux, smiling softly. "More seriously, his death has stimulated quite a reaction among the fringes of Parisian politics. On the right, groups like the Black Fist are sorry to see him go."

"But I thought..."

"That LeFoie's ridiculing of the Action Française had made him enemies throughout the conservative ranks. Certainly, the AF's leadership and their attack dogs, the Camelots de Roi, had come to hate him as much as they used to laud him when they thought he was on their side. But the feeling wasn't universal. Moderate conservatives like to use the AF for their own ends but they hardly want them to become serious rivals for power.

"Farther to the right, the Black Fist and their ilk are still furious at being pushed aside, even persecuted, by the Bloc National. They blame the machinations of the AF and, while on principle they despise all liberals, they seem to feel vindicated by the constant pricks LeFoie made in the hide of the AF leadership, especially de Vesins. Bucard, I am told, hates the man."

At least I won't have to accuse him of murder again, thought Max. He was surprised that LeFoie might be appreciated by those that followed Bucard and his more extreme views on the future of France, but it did narrow his range of suspects, if only marginally.

"Of course, De Vesins himself would have nothing to do with the murder. He is probably shocked, at least officially. No, if the culprit lies in the ranks of the Action Française, it is likely at third or fourth hand from the leadership."

Ledux stubbed out his cigarette and immediately lit another one. The air in the salon was turning slightly blue and Max resisted the urge to cough.

"Perhaps, I will have a coffee after all. Would you like one?"

Ledux nodded. "Black."

As Max filled two cups, adding several spoons of sugar and a dollop of milk to his own, he asked, "What about Gustav Reinhardt?"

"Ah, I wondered if you had him in your sights. Reinhardt is precisely the type who would take it on himself to 'cleanse the city of Dreyfusard scum.' He's a rising star in the Camelots, you know, ever since his return from Italy."

"What does Italy have to do with it?"

"Reinhardt was sent to Italy to see what Mussolini and his fascists were doing. I'm told it was an eye-opening experience for him. A lesson in the use of terror to cow or even kill the enemies of the party."

"I hear a lot about Mussolini these days – even the mainstream papers seem to take him seriously."

"They see him as a bulwark against the Bolsheviks as if what he has in mind is any less brutal. But he is efficient and has a certain popular appeal especially among ex-soldiers. France has a lot of ex-soldiers, too."

"I take it Reinhardt was a good student."

"Don't sell him short. People who know say he is both tough and cunning with sharp political instincts. He forged strong ties while in Italy and continues to work closely with the fascist operatives here in Paris. Do you recall Jacopo Giamatti?"

Giamatti had been a suspect in a case from the previous year. Max had heard he had returned to Italy. If he was back and associating with men like Reinhardt, he might be a suspect in LaFoie's murder, too.

"Giamatti has come up in the world. I understand you can find him at the Ritz."

AS IT TURNED OUT, GIAMATTI was no longer at the Ritz and Max wasn't willing to pay the size of the bribe the manager wanted to provide his forwarding address. Alain Laurent was still working as a messenger at one of the bigger firms and was more than willing to take time off to look for Giamatti. He had helped Max keep an eye on the Italian the previous year, so knew him by sight. Giamatti was unlikely to remember the bell hop at the small hotel he had been staying at and, in any case, would have no reason to connect him to Max.

"What do I do if I find him?" asked Alain, after he had traded his distinctive company uniform for his rather shabby street clothes. Whatever other benefits running notes about the city provided, a decent wage wasn't one of them. *If Alain works out*, thought Max, *I could pay him better out of the money I save on bribes.*

"Report to me at Chez Jake in two or three days," said Max, writing the address on a scrap of paper. "If I'm not there, you can leave a message with Jake or Smitty." One of the two were always in residence. He handed Alain five twenty-franc notes. "There's five more when you report, twice that if you find Giamatti and can provide an address."

Alain looked at the bills in his hand before folding them and shoving them in his pocket. "You can rely on me, Mr. Anderson."

Max nodded. "I know I can."

On a hunch, Max returned to the Hall of Records and soon discovered a key document which cleared up the relationship of the feuding cousins. Two of them, including the one who had hired him, had a greater claim on the estate than the other three. His client, a young man named Junot, had asked Max to find a conclusion to the squabble regardless of the outcome for his own fortunes. Max would be glad to report that he had ended the argument and provided a significant inheritance to his client as well.

Satisfied with the day's work he stopped for a late lunch of tartiflette, a pastry stuffed with strips of thick bacon, onions and pickled cucumbers in a creamy cheese sauce washed down with a half liter of white wine, before returning to his apartment on Rue Lepic. He found a note stuffed under his door from Jacqui saying she would be at Chez Jake at eight that evening. He could join her or not as he saw fit.

Max was part owner of the night club but he was a silent partner and though he kept an office there to collect his business mail, he never thought of the place as his. Jacqui knew that and offering to meet him there was her way of finding neutral ground – or as least as neutral as the safe house where he had gone to seek her out. The only question was: what should he wear?

In the end, he decided on a tan leather jacket she had always admired and a plain white cotton shirt and dark slacks. At the last minute, he traded his scuffed black shoes for a new pair of two-tone brown Oxfords. He hoped that struck the right balance between normal and special.

He arrived at Chez Jake fifteen minutes early and lingered in a darkened doorway until Jacqui arrived in a dark chauffeur-driven automobile and entered the club – alone. As the long black vehicle pulled away, Max caught a glimpse of the familiar bulk of Jacques Court in the back seat.

Max followed Jacqui into the club as soon as the auto was out of sight and spotted her at the table that Jake kept permanently reserved for his partner. She was wearing a pale blue dress with thin blue stripes cinched at the waist with a rose leather belt that accentuated her slim figure. She had on light grey high-heeled shoes and was wearing a black cloche hat decorated with a long pink feather. He wondered if he should have worn a suit instead but there was no time for that now.

Feeling a faint flutter in his stomach as he crossed the floor, he stopped beside her chair and waited until she looked up at him. Her eyes were glistening as if she were about to cry and he wondered if she had come to say goodbye but when he leaned down to kiss her cheek, she turned her head so his lips met hers. The kiss was brief but it was tender.

The band had been playing a lively swing tune but suddenly switched tempos to a waltz. Max looked toward the stage and spotted Jake, smiling at him, and gesturing toward the dance floor. He took Jacqui by the hand and led her to the small space in front of the stage which was suddenly free of couples. Max's face grew hot but he knew, somehow, he was being tested and he was determined not to fail. He took his girl in his arms and guided her across the dance floor is if they had never parted.

Two waltzes and a foxtrot later—thankfully not as a single couple—Jacqui led Max back to the table where a bottle of Cliquot and two coupes had miraculously appeared. He had not told Jake about the troubles he and Jacqui were having but someone must have, as his partner seemed determined to play matchmaker.

"What should we toast to, Max? Paris? The coming of fall?"

"How about to starting over and doing it right?" said Max raising his glass.

"I don't know what 'doing it right' would entail but I'm willing to drink to it." Jacqui clinked glasses with him and took a sip and then another. "I'd forgotten how good this was. The common ration doesn't usually run to champagne."

"A revolution without champagne? Sounds dull."

"It would be even duller if it had no dancing. Contrary to popular belief, anarchists are not all dull propagandists nor brigands. If you had ever seen Emma Goldman at a dance..." Jacqui smiled. "No one you're likely to meet—but a hero to me."

"Then, to Emma Goldman," said Max, refilling their glasses.

Jacqui nodded toward the dance floor which had now filled for another waltz. "She would approve of a dance club in Paris, owned by a black man where men and women of all races and desires could mingle and enjoy each other as equals. Maybe you're an anarchist and just don't know it, Max."

Max smiled. "I've had a good teacher."

Their banter was interrupted by the arrival of two steaming bowls of seafood bouillabaisse, served by Jake himself. It was accompanied by slices of toasted bread flavored with butter and garlic. He placed two large glasses of a straw-colored wine beside the bowls.

"Hope you have a good appetite tonight," he said. "The kitchen went all out when they heard that Jacqui was back in town." Jake wasn't lying. The bouillabaisse was followed by *alouettes san tetes*, thin slices of beef and prosciutto rolled together with garlic, shallots and paprika and sautéed in white wine with carrots, celery, tomatoes and leeks and served with a bottle of deep red Medoc.

They ate their food slowly, seldom speaking but, by turns, gazing at each other as if to discover the truth of their relationship. When Jake arrived with a dish of chocolate mouse and glasses of pastis, Max once again led Jacqui to the dance floor for a waltz. The band followed with a fast-paced ragtime number that left them both breathless.

"Well, I guess we earned out dessert," said Max, when they were seated again. Jacqui smiled and offered him a spoon of her mousse and they fed each other like that until the bowls were empty. Max raised his small glass in another toast.

"I'll toast but I won't drink," said Jacqui. "The wine has already gone to my head and I have things to do in the morning."

She declined his offer to escort her home. "Court will be waiting for me outside," she said, standing while gesturing him to remain seated. "I've spoken to Yesim. He said he misses his partner. As do I."

She leaned in and kissed him firmly on the mouth. "I'll see you at Le Coq Bleu. Soon. I promise."

Max watched her make her careful way across the club. Smitty escorted her through the front door and returned a minute later and gave Max a thumbs up, a gesture from the trenches that meant everything was okay. Max turned back to his pastis and finished it in a single gulp. He drank Jacqui's more slowly and listened to the music until the second set was finished. He was tempted to stay for the third, which was always more improvisational, but, like Jacqui, he had things to do in the morning.

Jake looked worried that his efforts at sparking romance had failed but Max shook his hand and smiled. "I think tonight was a good start."

"Then it's up to you to finish it," said Jake, grinning. "I can only do so much on my own."

AFTER A MORNING SPENT investigating the disappearance of a client's business partner (he had run away with his mistress but promised to be back in the office the following week), Max, feeling the same trepidation he had felt the night before, headed for Le Coq Bleu in hopes of reconciliation—and lunch. Henri was at his usual spot at the end of the bar, nursing a beer and picking at a plate of cheese and olives. He glanced up and then looked away. Yesim was talking to a young couple seated under the neon parrot but turned when he heard the door open. He nodded at the pair and went behind the bar, a scowl marring his face.

"What are you doing here?" he growled.

"I...I was hoping..." Max glanced from Yesim to Henri, whose shoulders were gently shaking. *Was Henri crying? Had Jacqui misread the mood?* "I guess I was wrong."

Henri turned on his stool, his face split by a grin, a soft chuckle issuing from his mouth. Yesim's scowl transformed into a toothy grin. "You didn't think we'd make it easy on you, did you?"

Before Max could find a reply, Henri leapt from his stool and grabbed Max in a bearhug, before kissing him on both cheeks.

"I'm sorry for being foolish, for our argument, for pushing you, for—"

That's enough," said Yesim. "Though I personally have never done anything foolish, I understand how you must feel. All is forgiven. Now sit down and I'll get you some lunch."

Yesim hurried into the back room, that served as store room and kitchen and reappeared a moment later with a plate of sandwiches and a dish of assorted olives and pickled onions. Henri gestured to the stool beside him and Max took a seat as Yesim put the food in front of him. A glass of pale beer appeared within seconds.

"Eat first, talk later," said Henri, following his own advice by taking a sandwich consisting of a slab of smoked ham between two thick slices of white bread. He took a bite and nodded appreciatively. "Good! You're using that mustard I suggested."

"Henri is using his spare time to advise me on how to run my kitchen," said Yesim, not unkindly.

Max selected a pan bagnat, olive-oil-soaked rustic bread wrapped around chunks of tuna, olives, capers and anchovies. The beer was crisp and provided the perfect counterpoint to the fishy flavours. Yesim satisfied his hunger with a simple baguette stuffed with thin slices of smoked beef and hard cheese. They ate in silence as was their custom, taking their time to savour the rich flavours of their food.

When Yesim had served a second round of beer, he said; "Your old pal, Gereau, dropped by last week with a couple of 'bodyguards' to question some of my clients, not to mention me. Now that he can't call on the swallows to protect his back, he seems to have recruited some ex-soldiers down on their luck to do the job. He had the nerve to try and order lunch but I told him to try Gagnon's down the street. They had a recent outbreak of food poisoning."

"I had heard he had finally been forced to retire," said Max, not mentioning he had heard it first from Gereau himself and later from Jacques Court.

"Maybe," said Henri, "but he still has friends in the Prefecture who lend him an office and access to police files. He may be an ex-Captain but he still has some sway."

"And he still thinks anarchists are the antichrist," added Yesim.

"Maybe it's just a spelling mistake," said Henri.

Max didn't like it that Gereau would continue to act like a police captain at the same time he was begging for Max's help to provide him with information. Max thought of the coded book LeFoie's widow had given him. He was sure if he could decipher it, he would be a lot closer to discovering who had killed the journalist and what, if anything, his relationship to Gereau had to do with it.

"I'll speak to him," said Max. "and, if that doesn't work, I'll find out who pushed him out of his office."

"I heard you could start with Fontaine," said Henri.

Not my favorite flic, thought Max. *The things we do to help our friends.*

"Did you see the Action Français last night?" asked Henri.

Max shrugged. He was familiar with the organ of the party with the same name but was not a regular reader. Henri was more catholic in his tastes, reading half the twenty papers published in the city every day and sampling the rest from time to tome.

"Bucard had a long article about a supposed unholy alliance between the parties of the left to overthrow the will of the people. The usual nonsense you would expect from the former head of the Black Fist, full of obscure religious references and veiled hints about the return of the king. I guess it caught my attention simply because it was there. Bucard's star has been sinking and, his recent attacks on de Vesins had made him persona non grata in most hard right circles – yet there he was. On the front page, no less."

"I'll have to track down a copy," said Max. "I don't suppose you still have yours?"

Henri and Yesim exchanged looks. "I'm afraid," said Yesim, "that I used it to wrap garbage."

Chapter 10 Sunday, October 3rd to Monday, October 4th, 1921

Pierre Delacroix was a stringer who filed stories with whoever would buy them. He wrote a semi-regular gossip column for Le Petit Parisien. He was a frequent contributor to the sports pages of Le Journal and, less often, Ce Soir, though his work might turn up on almost any subject from politics to the latest theatre production in any paper that wasn't an official party organ. Though he reported on politics, he seemed to have none of his own, unless *joie de vivre* was considered an ideology.

Max spent Sunday at the Velodrome and the Colombes sports stadium but had no luck finding the reporter at either, though he found the high-speed bicycle racing strangely entrancing and enjoyed being reintroduced to the sport of football, which he played in university—though then he had known it as soccer. He arrived home late that evening and fell into his unmade bed, too tired to even eat.

He woke the next day early, awakened by the grumbling of his stomach rather than the buzz of his alarm clock. He breakfasted at his favorite café on Clichy before beginning the rounds of visits to the various news offices scattered around the central arrondissements. Either Delacroix hadn't been around for a week or Max had "just missed him." As his frustration grew, he began to wonder if it was even worth it to track down the elusive reporter but finally caught a break at the offices of Le Figaro. Delacroix had delivered a short article on the impending signing of a treaty to finally end the war with the former Ottoman Empire. As he departed, he had announced that he was off to Le Rotonde to meet with "a ravishing blonde."

The restaurant was nearly empty when Max arrived shortly after four p.m., the lunch crowd having drifted away. Most of the serving staff were gathered to one side of the restaurant smoking and keeping an eye on the three or four tables with paying customers. Only one had a blonde sitting at it and Max supposed he might be considered ravishing if you were interested in muscular young men. The man sitting opposite apparently was. His gaze seldom left the young man's face as they talked in low tones, leaning across the table so their conversation remained private.

Delacroix himself was certainly handsome, with even features, large dark eyes, and a thin mustache over a strong mouth. He appeared to be in his thirties though Max knew from his inquiries that he was approaching fifty. Max wondered if his dark hair was dyed. If so, it had been done professionally. Delacroix was dressed impeccably; he was clearly a man who cared about his appearance.

Max watched the couple for several minutes before approaching the table. "Pierre Delacroix?" he asked in a low voice.

Delacroix looked up, a startled expression on his face which he was quick to control. His eyes ran over Max's face, taking in the few small scars he had accumulated in the course of investigations before running his gaze down Max's body in a way that made him feel uncomfortable.

"Who wants to know?" The reporter's voice was resonant, like that of an actor or a politician, and again Max wondered how much of this man was real and how much a cultivated appearance.

"My name is Max Anderson. I'm looking into the death of Réjean LaFoie."

"I'll see you later at the Zig-Zag, Ernst," Delacroix said to the blonde youth who promptly stood, gave a small bow to both

Delacroix and Max, turned on his heel and quickly departed. The reporter gestured for Max to sit. "Ernst is with the unofficial German embassy. He has been a useful source of information."

"I'm sure."

"I've heard of you, Anderson. You're one of these new private detectives, like in the magazines. Your French is very good for an American."

"Canadian," Max corrected automatically.

"Canada! I spent an enjoyable few months in Montreal before the war." Delacroix waved to a nearby waiter and ordered a bottle of Chablis and two glasses without asking Max if he wanted to join him.

"What can I do for you, Mr. Anderson?" asked Delacroix, after the waiter had delivered the Chablis along with a basket of bread and a dish of assorted olives.

"Why did you seek out Erich Harvey and tell him Lefoie was dead?"

"Because they were friends. I thought he would want to know."

"Friends? What made you think that?"

"They shared a girlfriend. You can't get friendlier than that." Delacroix smirked. The word he had used for girlfriend was slightly vulgar.

"Did you know LeFoie was suing Harvey for the 'alienation of affections' of said girlfriend?" Max used the polite word.

"Between LeFoie's crowing and Harvey's whining, everyone in Paris must have known about it."

Delacroix called the waiter over and asked for the menu. The waiter raised an eyebrow but went to fetch the carte. When he returned, he laid one in front of both men. Max pushed his aside. He hadn't found time for lunch but he had no desire to dine with Delacroix. The scent of dishonesty was stronger than the smell of the aftershave he doused himself with.

"You don't like my type, do you, Mr. Anderson?

"What type is that?"

"Oh, the type who lives outside the constraints of arbitrary morality."

"I'm not bothered by that," said Max. "I've known too many good people who live by their own rules." Barzani, Henri, Jacqui. "I thought you meant people who go out of their way to hurt others, to cause trouble, just because they can."

Delacroix studied the menu for several minutes. When he looked up, he contrived to look surprised. "Are you still here, Mr. Anderson?"

Max stood and leaned over the table so Delacroix had to look up to see his face. "I don't believe people do things without a reason, without a motive. Yours may have been innocent enough or it may not have been. But eventually, I'll find out what it is and if it leads me to think you were somehow involved in LeFoie's death, I'll be back."

"I assure you, Mr. Anderson, that my motive was simple enough. Erich Harvey is a drunk. Worse than that he is a dishonest drunk, pretending to be a journalist when he is nothing but a spy for American interests. I heard about LeFoie from a friend who covers the crime beat. I knew about his little contretemps and when I happened to see him... Well, when fate gives you a chance to prick a balloon, you take it."

"And that's it?"

"One other thing. If you think I feel threatened by you, you should search out a different way of thinking. I've spent my life being threatened by tougher men then you. I learned long ago that the pen is truly mightier than the sword. If you don't want your private affairs spread across the city, I suggest you keep your nose out of my business."

Max had been threatened with beating and even shooting, he had been thrown in jail and thrown out of bars, but this was a new one. He laughed.

"Do your worst. I've got no secrets."

"Everyone has secrets. I assure you; I can find yours."

"Listen to him, Max," said Erich Harvey from ten feet away. "This muckraking bastard could find shit in fresh laundered trousers but he couldn't find morality in the dictionary."

"Your French has improved, Erich," said Delacroix. "Too bad the same could not be said of your fashion sense. Or your bathing habits."

Harvey was his usual dishevelled self but he was freshly shaved and seemed surer on his feet than the last time Max had seen him. He wondered if his stint in jail had really persuaded him to cut down on the booze. He took several steps into the space between the tables and raised his fists in the semblance of a boxer's stance. What he lacked in form, he made up for in his eagerness to fight. Delacroix didn't move from his seat.

"Stand up, you snivelling coward!"

"Or, what? You'll bash me in the head like you did LeFoie?" Delacroix's eyes flicked past Max and settled on the waiter, who scurried toward the kitchen, undoubtedly to fetch Libion, the irascible owner of the restaurant.

Max stepped around the table and put his arm across Harvey's shoulders. "Come on, Erich. Let's go to the Dôme and grab a bite. It has a nicer clientele."

"I've already eaten." Harvey gave a final glare at Delacroix but let Max lead him away. "But I'll join you for a... coffee. I've got something to report."

Le Dôme was only a few steps away and its clientele hardly differed from that of the Rotonde, mostly artists and writers, though, with more Americans and Brits. Max ordered skate with black butter and a half liter of chilled sauterne. Harvey relented and ordered a cheese-topped onion soup but stuck with coffee. Max admired Harvey's new found sobriety, though he didn't envy it. Like all converts to Parisian life, he couldn't imagine life without wine.

"You had something you wanted to tell me?" he asked, as they finished the last of their meal. Harvey looked down into his nearly empty coffee cup, then gestured the waiter for a refill. Max waited in silence until the waiter had departed.

"Nicole... Mademoiselle Bilodeau asked me to tell you she would like to see you." Harvey blushed. "What you do is your own business, but—"

Max held up his hand to cut him off. They had been chatting in English since they took their seats but Max now switched to French. "Whatever she wants me for, it's not what you're obviously thinking. When did she make this request?"

"Sunday, no, Saturday morning." Harvey shook his head. "The days all seem the same now."

Harvey might be stronger without the drink but he seemed no happier. "That was two days ago. You know where to find me."

"It didn't seem that urgent and I had other things to do." Max wondered if Delacroix was right, that Harvey was a spy for American interests. If he was, Max hoped they were getting more for their money than he was.

"Did she say where I should meet her?"

"At her home. I guess you know where that is."

Heat filled Max's face and he looked away. He still had visions of Nicole's naked body and the anger in her face when he rejected her. He wasn't sure he wanted to enter her den again but he supposed he had to risk it. He owed it to LaFoie's widow, if nothing else.

"Yes, I know." Max cleared his throat. "Do you have anything else for me?"

Harvey ran his hand through his uncombed hair and took a quick look around and Max followed his gaze.

The Dôme was beginning to fill, half the tables were full and the bar was lined with young men and a few women who preferred to do their drinking standing up. Max thought he saw Ernst, Delacroix's friend, watching them but he turned away quickly so Max couldn't be sure. No matter, he wasn't close enough to hear.

Harvey turned back to Max and leaned across the table. "I hear things. Here and there. Most of it is bull but there have to be a few grains of truth in the pile."

Max nodded but said nothing, waiting to see if Harvey could actually tell the difference.

"There are a bunch of Italians in town, all of a sudden."

"Giamatti?"

"Yeah, but this time he's brought some friends. They make Jacopo seem like the reasonable one."

Max always thought Jacopo Giamatti seemed reasonable, which is what made him so dangerous. Anybody could be a thug but the thugs who could cover themselves in a veneer of reason and civility were the ones you had to watch. He hoped Alain would be careful in his search for the gangster.

"Paris has always shivered at the thought of Italian gangsters ever since one of them stole the Mona Lisa."

"In Italy, Vincenzo Perugia is hailed as a national hero and a patriot. In any case, Giamatti may well be Cosa Nostra but he's much more than that. He has close ties to Mussolini."

"He told me that himself. No one seems to think it will amount to much."

"People in the know don't think that. Giamatti has been meeting with higher-ups in the AF, the Camelots, and they say he is recruiting hard men who belonged to the Black Fist before it blew up in Bucard's face."

"What's this got to do with LeFoie's murder?"

"Maybe nothing, but Giamatti showed up in town two days before it happened. LeFoie was no friend to the far right."

The timing of Giamatti's arrival was news, though Max was uncertain how it might be tied to LeFoie. Still, it and the message from Bilodeau met the criteria of their unwritten deal. He slid seventy-five francs across the table. When Harvey looked disappointed, Max said: "I'll pay for your lunch, too."

"I should have eaten more." Harvey swept the bills off the table and stuffed them in his pocket.

"I'm sure Ginger Buchan will give you an advance."

"You shouldn't believe everything you hear in bars, Max; they're full of liars."

True enough, thought Max, as he watched Harvey stride out of the Dôme into the glimmering lights of Paris.

MAX TOOK THE METRO across the river to Saint-Paul station and walked the final blocks in the gathering gloom. The green double doors were closed but the visitor's gate was ajar and Max pushed his way through. The front door was also open and Max suddenly shuddered. His Webley revolver was in its holster back at Chez Jake; Jacqui still had his five-shot pistol. He snapped open his clasp knife and gripped it in his right hand and slipped the brass knuckles he always carried onto his left. As he stepped through the door, the silence of the house was ripped by a sudden scream and the pound of running feet. A door slammed at the rear of the house but the screaming didn't stop.

Max climbed the stairs that led to Nicole's bedroom. He was met half way up by the dark-skinned maid, her screams now reduced to sobs. She clutched at him as he searched his memory for her name.

"Tell me what happened... Anna."

It took several moments before she could recover enough to say: "They killed her; they killed my mistress." She pointed up the stairs with a shaking hand.

"Who? Who did this?"

"Two men," she whispered. "One big, one small."

Max's stomach lurched. That description could fit a lot of people but it could just as easily fit Jacqui and Jacques Court. The latter claimed not to be a man of action but anyone could kill if the motive was strong enough. But what motive could he have that would stir his considerable bulk from its comfortable chair? Loyalty to a comrade seemed too thin a soup.

The door to Bilodeau's bedroom was open. Drawers had been ripped from chests and the dresser had been flung open and some of the clothes thrown in a heap. The bed clothes had been pulled off and dumped on the floor. It took Max a moment to see the body, half hidden in the scattered garments. Nicole was lying on her front, arms stretched out in front of her, legs akimbo. He put his weapons away and moved closer.

Bilodeau was dressed casually, clearly settled in for the night and not expecting visitors. She had been strangled. A colorful scarf was wound loosely around her neck but Max could tell by the marks on her flesh that it was not the murder weapon. Whoever had done this had used their hands, thick fingers leaving widely spaced bruises in the pale skin.

Max pulled the scarf free so he could more closely examine the wound. He froze when he recognized it; he had bought the hand-painted silk at an artist's studio, a gift to Jacqui for her birthday. Tears pricked at his eyes and he shook his head to clear it of the dark thoughts that ran through it. He heard footsteps outside the door and, without thinking, stuffed the scarf in his jacket pocket.

It was Anna, standing framed in the doorway. Her sobs had stopped but she was trembling, supporting herself by clutching at the door frame on either side. "Should I send for the police?"

"I work... with the police," said Max, buying time with a half-truth so he could examine the scene. "You don't need to see this. Go down stairs and gather yourself; the police will have questions."

She nodded blankly and turned away. Max waited until he heard her slow tread on the stairs before resuming his investigation. Not every place in the room had been searched; the killers had been interrupted in their work by the maid and had fled rather than risk capture if passing swallows had heard the woman's screams.

He pulled out the remaining drawers but found nothing unusual, small items of clothing and pieces of jewelry. The more expensive items he had seen her wear were gone, either stolen or locked in a safe in another room; there was no evidence of one here. In the back of the wardrobe, Max's fingers found a hidden door that popped open when he pressed it inward. Inside was a leather-bound book. He flipped through it but could make no sense of what he saw though there was something familiar about the hand. He tucked it into an inner pocket of his coat.

He was about to abandon his search and fetch the police when he caught a glint of metal under the small mahogany desk that set beneath the window. It was a gun. Had they threatened Bilodeau with it, demanding who knows what from her? Had she struggled and knocked it away? Had she been murdered in a fit of anger? None of it made sense. He took a handkerchief from his pocket and reached for the gun. Before he even got a clear look at it, he could tell by the weight whose gun it was.

It was his. The one Jacqui had taken. He knew he should leave it where he found it, the scarf, too. The book had been hidden, though he supposed it was the object of the search, but the gun and the scarf were clearly evidence—evidence that pointed directly at Jacqui.

Although, he thought, *only I know where these must have come from.* He dropped the gun into his pocket to nestle with the scarf.

The maid was sitting on a stool at the foot of the stairs, staring blankly at the opposite wall. Max laid his hand on her shoulder but she didn't respond, lost to shock and horror. Max had seen the same look all too often on the faces of men new to the trenches. Back on the street, he flagged down a pair of swallows on bicycles and reported the murder. One of them took station inside the front door while the other constable sped off in search of a more senior officer.

To Max's surprise, he returned a few minutes later with Sergeant Lepêcheur who approached Max with notebook open and a scowl on his face.

"Freed from desk duty, Hubert?"

"I go where I'm told, Monsieur Anderson," said Lepêcheur. "But what brings you here?"

Max made it a habit to be as honest as he could when talking to the police, especially if it served his purpose. "I'm still looking into the death of Réjean LeFoie. Unofficially, of course. Erich Harvey said Nicole Bilodeau—this is her house—wanted to see me. He didn't say why but she knew LeFoie, so I thought it worth coming."

"I've met Mademoiselle Bilodeau. Are you sure LeFoie was your only reason for coming?"

Max felt his face flush. Lepêcheur couldn't know of his liaison with the dead reporter, could he? "Nicole was an attractive woman, though less so now that she's been strangled."

"You've seen the body?"

"I arrived even as the murderers made their escape. Two men, one large and one small according to the maid, whose screams alerted me to the crime. She's waiting inside for you to question her."

"Large and small, you say. Not particularly useful don't you think? Size is a relative thing." Lepêcheur waved the constable aside so he could pass. "Wait here, I will have further questions."

"Of course. Her name is Anna. She may need a doctor."

"She was injured?"

"On the inside," said Max.

Lepêcheur nodded. "I'll handle her with care." To the constable: "Fetch Doctor Jacobs; he's two doors down on the right."

Max was impressed. The sergeant might be new to the neighbourhood but he had done his homework. He probably knew every street and alley of the Marais and half its residents.

The police officer returned a few minutes later, shaking his head. "It looks like a robbery gone wrong. The maid confirms it was two men, one large, the other quite small, though she couldn't be more specific. She didn't see their faces, they were masked, the kind we all wore last year to protect against the flu. They pushed past her when she opened the door to take her mistress her evening tea. We found the remains of the cup smashed on the landing. She also confirmed that you arrived moments later. She said you had a knife."

Max removed the clasp knife from his pocket, careful not to let it clink against the gun. "It's a useful tool; I've carried one since I was a boy."

Lepêcheur examined the knife, pulling out the blade and running his finger across the edge. It's very sharp for something you use as a tool."

"My father taught me to keep my tools in order." He held out his hand for the knife which the sergeant reluctantly returned.

"Did you notice anything missing? The maid said you had been in Mademoiselle's bedroom before."

"I don't deny it but she can also tell you I didn't stay long. We had private matters to discuss that she didn't want the servants to overhear."

"There were other servants."

"So she said; I only ever saw the maid." He didn't raise the matter of the jewelry. He was sure robbery was not the reason for the attack.

Lepêcheur made a note in his book and then asked: "What was Bilodeau's relationship to LeFoie? What could she know about his death?"

Max explained about their former engagement and their later estrangement. The sergeant scowled again at the mention of politics. He undoubtedly heard all he wanted to from his superiors at the Prefecture. It was one of the things he liked about the man; Lepêcheur was a policeman first and foremost, everything else was a distraction. He left out his own flirtation with the dead woman. It was irrelevant as well as embarrassing.

When he had finished, Lepêcheur snapped his notebook closed and put it in the breast pocket of his uniform. "I may have other questions but you can go for now. Don't leave the city."

Max nodded. He hadn't left the city since he had arrived nearly two years before. He would not leave it now, not until his own questions were answered.

Chapter 11 Tuesday, October 5th, 1921

M ax woke with a sour taste in his mouth. He had stopped at Le Coq Bleu for a drink and to tell Yesim and Henri of the latest shocking developments, though he left out mention of the scarf and gun. Henri shook his head in sorrow at "such a terrible waste." Yesim was less kind, implying without saying it that she had only got what she deserved for associating with thugs and corrupting the morals of youth, presumably meaning Max.

One drink turned to several and only the memories of their recent breach prevented it from becoming acrimonious. Henri had walked him home but only after Max had extracted a pledge from Yesim to inquire after Jacqui's current whereabouts. "I'll try," he had said, a touch sadly, "though most of my former comrades don't talk to me anymore."

He searched his cupboards but they were empty save for a couple of stale hunks of bread, a piece of hard cheese gone mouldy and a half empty bottle of pastis, the smell of which made his stomach churn. He needed to get his life in order but that would have to wait for another day. First, he would find breakfast; then he would find Jacqui. He had to know why her scarf and his gun were found at the scene of Bilodeau's murder.

He walked down Ave. de Clignancourt to a new bistro that offered a full "American" breakfast and a range of newspapers in both French and English for their patrons' perusal. He was interested to see what a Parisian thought Americans ate for breakfast. If it was any good, he would recommend it to Buchan, who was always complaining about the French habit of surviving the morning on pastries and coffee.

The menu was a pleasant surprise and he ordered two eggs over easy served with sourdough toast and four rashers of thick bacon and a small pot of strawberry jam for any toast that lasted past the initial onslaught. He substituted café americain for a café au lait to soothe his stomach. While waiting for his food, Max selected copies of Le Petit Parisien, L'Humanitie and the Paris edition of the Chicago Tribune, mostly to see if Erich Harvey had a by-line.

It was always amusing to see what editors thought should be the blaring headline below the masthead and as usual, the three papers had all chosen to highlight quite different stories. However, all of them had a brief story on page one of a bomb blast that had occurred in the early hours of the morning, just before the papers had gone to press. The details were sketchy but it again involved a small newspaper office. No-one had been killed but only because the editor had been delayed for an hour at home. The paper was run by a faction of the moderate right, which was the main difference to the one Latour had witnessed. Oddly, none of the papers carried news of Bilodeau's murder. Perhaps Lepêcheur was keeping it quiet for his own reasons.

The office was only a few Metro stops away so Max hurried through breakfast, leaving with the last piece of toast still clutched in his hand. The wreckage of the newspaper office was still smouldering but only two firemen were still on scene dumping water on any spot that looked like it might erupt in flame. The upper floors of the building were still intact; the residents of the apartments above were milling on the sidewalk or drinking coffee at a shop down the street.

Several constables were poking through the ruins under the watchful eye of Captain Fontaine. Max was surprised to see the latter. He usually dealt only with murder cases, and no one had died here, at least according to the papers. Of course, they might not have had the whole story.

Fontaine was unlikely to welcome his appearance so Max stood on the sidewalk across the narrow street and observed from a distance. When Fontaine left, he would question any swallows who remained on scene. They might let slip details that would link this attack to the previous one and therefore to Bilodeau's and, perhaps, LeFoie's murder.

A few minutes after he took up his position, he saw Gereau approaching at a brisk pace from the direction of the Metro stop. He called to Fontaine as he approached and the Captain turned with a sour expression on his weasel-like face. The two engaged in a brief but apparently heated conversation, their voices low—Captains did not shout at each other in front of their men—but their faces florid and angry. They stepped closer and closer together, forcing Fontaine to look up into the bigger man's eyes. Surprisingly, Fontaine did not give an inch and Gereau finally threw up his hands in disgust and crossed the street to stand beside Max.

"Fontaine couldn't find his nose with a handkerchief," Gereau muttered by way of greeting.

"I'd be surprised if he could find his handkerchief."

Gereau snorted. "What are you doing here? Don't you have lost dogs to find?"

"I leave such complicated cases to the Prefecture. I'm more interested in simple things, like murder."

Gereau shook his head. "Nothing good will come of poking your nose into a hornet's nest. LeFoie's death has been put down to misadventure. He had a spell after his brawl with Harvey and fell in the Seine."

Max raised his eyebrows at that; it was the first he had heard of that theory. "There has been another murder."

"Bilodeau. I didn't know you were aware of that."

"I discovered the body, moments after the killers had escaped."

Gereau glanced at him, his face neutral but a certain tension in his shoulders and neck that Max had not seen before. "I was not... apprised of that detail."

That must be hard on him, thought Max. Gereau has always been at the centre of things. His contacts at the Prefecture had informed him of the death but not the details. They say you are often forgotten before the smell of your cigar fades from your office. Max resisted the urge to put his hand on Gereau's shoulder; he doubted if the older man would appreciate the gesture. Gereau was proud—stubborn some would say—and would consider it condescension rather than condolence.

"You have a theory about this bombing?" Max asked although he already knew what the retired Captain would say.

"I've been a witness to countless anarchist attacks," Gereau said. "Since before you were even born. This has all the hallmarks of their approach."

"Haven't most French anarchists denounced illegalisme?"

"They don't speak with one voice; they *are* anarchists. Besides a zebra without his stripes may look like a horse but he is still a zebra."

"But what motive—"

"The same motive as always. To destabilize the state and bring terror into the hearts of ordinary citizens."

"Seems like a strange motive to blow up a conservative newspaper, let alone a Jewish one."

"You have other ideas?"

"Bilodeau was seen at the Jewish paper hours before it was destroyed. And she had connections with both LeFoie and the more aggressive wing of the Action Française. I think there is a connection between their deaths and these bombings. What if—"

Gereau cut him off with a rude gesture. "You would be of more use helping me track down the real culprits. Bernard Dietrich and those who aid and shelter him."

Max had seen Dietrich in the company of Jacques Court. Jacqui had been there, too. Was it chance or choice that brought them together?

Captaine Fontaine appeared to have finished his investigation, although a few constables were still picking through the wreckage. The rest of the street was slowly coming back to life. Concierges were busy sweeping the steps of apartment blocks and gossiping with their neighbours. A cart filled with crates of fruits and vegetables was unloading produce under the watchful eye of a shop keeper, who kept glancing at the still smoldering office down the block. Paris, as usual, was too busy to pause for anything as mundane as a bomb.

Fontaine made his way across the sidewalk to Gereau. He glanced at Max. "Birds of a feather now, are you?"

"What do you intend to do about this?" Gereau made no effort to keep the sneer from his voice. "Sweep it under the rug?"

Fontaine looked over his shoulder at the scattering of bricks and glass on the sidewalk. "That would take a lot of sweeping. I understand you're for hire now?" He had taken Gereau's insults for years, now it seems he was ready to take his revenge.

"Careful, Marcel, I may have left my office but I still have my files."

Fontaine flushed. "What about you, Anderson? Have you joined the hunt for the ever-elusive anarchist mastermind who will, any minute now, bring down the Republic?"

Max didn't want to embarrass Gereau; they were friends of a sort and the former officer had been helpful to Max in the past. Still, he knew Gereau was on the wrong track, at least about the bombings. If anarchists were involved, it wasn't in the way he thought. "I couldn't say. Have you any further word on the murders of LeFoie and Bilodeau?"

"The way you ask, it sounds like you think they were linked."

"Well, they were, at one time, engaged."

"Sure, but nothing more than a coincidence. LeFoie was hurt worse than it appeared from Harvey's attack—we may yet have him before a judge—and fell in the Seine, dead before he hit the water. As for Bilodeau, a robbery gone wrong. The maid says some jewels were missing. We are following several leads. I assure you; an arrest will be forthcoming."

The usual Fontaine approach: do nothing until the pressure mounts, then find a convenient scapegoat. If justice was to be served, it would be up to Max.

MAX RETURNED HOME TO find Alain Laurent sitting outside his door. The young man leapt to his feet as he approached and stood at something approaching attention. Max was surprised he didn't salute.

"What do you have for me, Alain?"

Alain paused to gather his thoughts. He had filled out in the year that Max had known him, the boy growing into a man. The cuffs of his worn trousers did not quite reach his ankles and the hand-me-down shirt was tight across the shoulders, though still too long in the sleeves. Though he was a hard worker, Max knew he was living day-to-day. Alain's father had been killed in the last months of the Great War and his mother had returned to Lyon with his younger siblings. He had chosen to remain in Paris, barely fourteen but with a stubborn streak of independence and a love for the excitement of the city of lights. Max realized that Alain reminded him of his younger brother, Ben.

I seem to be acquiring people who depend on me, he thought. *Alain and, I suppose, Henri.* He thought then of Jacqui, who was determined to depend on no one but herself. He sighed.

"Sorry," said Alain. "I'm just trying to get things straight in my head."

Alain could read, but his writing skills were limited, something Max would have to deal with if he did decide to take on Alain as a full-time assistant. "The sigh wasn't for you. I also have a lot on my mind."

Alain smiled and began his report. "I checked all of Mr. Giamatti's former hangouts. The hotel I used to work at, the Ritz and a couple of restaurants I remember him asking about when I was a bellhop. He wasn't at any of them, or at least, not while I was lurking in the shadows."

Max suppressed a chuckle. Henri had loaned Alain some of the detective novels he loved. Clearly the boy had been reading them.

"Then, I thought, Mr. Giamatti's from Italy; maybe he might get his mail at the Italian embassy on de Verennes, or need some service or other from the consul. I knew I couldn't hang around an embassy without drawing attention to myself, so I borrowed a shine kit from a friend at the messenger service and set up across the street. I split the money I made with my friend but it was on your time, so—"

Max shook his head. "That kind of initiative deserves reward."

"Thanks! I set up on Sunday around supper and was there most of Monday as well. I decided to give it one more try this morning and got lucky for once. I spotted him go in the embassy at about nine and by the time he came out half an hour later, I had packed up my kit and tailed him to a restaurant near the Jardin des Tuileries, at the Hotel Meurice. Luckily the weather was fine so he walked the whole way."

"The Meurice?" Max had been in that restaurant himself. The memories weren't particularly pleasant.

"That's right. About ten minutes later a big car pulled up and a heavy-set gentleman of about fifty got out and went inside. He had two bodyguards with him, one built like a gorilla, the other, short but with a way of moving that gave me the chills. The small one went inside with him and the other stood in the doorway and turned other people away. He started staring at me so I took off. I went to Chez Jake like you said and left a message. I thought I should come here, too, to see if I could catch you before my shift."

"Good work, Alain," said Max, taking out his wallet and paying the promised reward.

"Another thing, Mr. Anderson. I recognized the gentleman from the car. I've seen his picture in the AF newspaper. It was Andre Bucard, who used to lead the Black Fist."

Bucard. *Well, I know how to find Bucard. Now I know how to find Giamatti, too.*

Chapter 12, Wednesday to Friday, October 6th to 8th, 1921

Bucard was in none of his usual haunts when Max went looking for him on Wednesday morning. The priest at Saint Germaine-L'Auxerrois confirmed that he was still one of his parishioners but he hadn't seen him since Sunday mass. The restaurant at the Meurice was closed for "a family emergency" but would open again on Thursday evening.

Yesim still had no word on Jacqui's whereabouts but promised to keep looking. Max contacted Alain and offered him a full-time job as his assistant at a salary that had the young man grinning broadly as he set off on his first assignment, to track down anarchist safe-houses in the city proper and in the banlieues, known as the red belt.

Frustrated, Max headed for his office above Chez Jake to check on his mail. Ginger Buchan was waiting for him, his feet propped up on his desk and a croque monsieur on a plate in his lap.

"Smitty remembered me from previous visits," said Buchan, "and agreed to let me wait up here. The fewer people who know I'm here, the better."

Max glared at Buchan's stylish shoes—spats they were called, until he shifted them to the floor, careful not to kick over the glass of beer perched on one corner of Max's crowded desk. The sandwich looked good; Jake had come up with a recipe that combined the traditional thick ham and cheese with a hint of creole spice and grilled onions. Max called down to the kitchen for one of his own plus a jug of beer and a second glass.

He cleared a space on his desk for the food before turning to his visitor. "What brings you all the way from the American embassy on this chilly October morning?"

"My doctor says I should exercise more," said Buchan. "A good walk before lunch to visit an old friend seemed like a good way to start."

Max had met the attaché to the United States embassy during the negotiations of the Treaty of Versailles nearly three years before. He didn't know what Buchan's job was then and he didn't know it now but they had gotten along well enough that he supposed the term "friend" would apply. He was, Max realized, one of the few people close to his own age that he had formed a bond with since arriving in Paris.

They exchanged pleasantries for a few minutes until the food arrived. Max refilled Buchan's glass before pouring beer for himself. He shut the door and sat behind his desk. Buchan had finished his own meal and he gestured at Max to start on his.

"You eat, I'll talk. I hope you don't mind if I do it in English; I'm not sure my French is up to the complexity."

Max had eaten little for breakfast so he was agreeable to listening to Buchan in either language and took a large bite of the sandwich, savouring the smoky flavour of ham mixed with the creamy nuttiness of the gruyere cheese. The spice took a moment to kick in but, when it did, it offered a pleasant counterpoint to the other flavors.

"Something serious is in the works, Max. Something bad."

Buchan's usual obsession was with the red menace, just as thoroughly as Gereau was preoccupied with anarchists, so Max was surprised when he said: "There are rumours of a right-wing coup in the works. There are those among the extreme faction of the Action Française, and their paramilitary allies on the far right, who are furious at being left out of the Bloc National alliance that swept the elections two years ago. Even their leader failed to win his seat as a result. Increasingly, they feel their views are being ignored, their members ostracized.

"It's hard to fathom their motives. The conservatives are in decisive control of the government and the left is in disarray. The AF still clings to the idea of the return of the monarchy which bemuses most of the citizenry and simply confuses people like me. Anyway, they seem to think that, despite their small numbers, they can stage some sort of popular uprising and force their way into government without the benefit of an electoral victory."

Max paused, the second part of his sandwich halfway to his mouth. "Wasn't the war about saving the world for democracy?"

"That's what those in charge said. How do you feel about those in charge?"

"I..." *How do I feel?* The trenches were a slaughterhouse and the generals and politicians didn't seem to care. All the old values seemed like shiny lies in the wake of so much destruction. But what was there to take their place?

Buchan nodded as if he had read Max's unspoken thoughts. "Exactly. People feel lost; many feel betrayed. America looks inward while Paris parties and Berlin experiments with moral chaos. Many, especially former soldiers, want answers, simple solutions to what look like intractable problems. There are men more than happy to provide such answers. The Bolsheviks have the edge right now but you've seen the Camelots marching in the streets; that's nothing compared to what is happening in Germany and Italy. I don't see how we can avoid another war, if not soon, certainly in our lifetimes."

Max recoiled at Buchan's words and a wave of nausea forced him to push the rest of his lunch away. A phantom pain twinged in his leg and he sat motionless, unable to speak. Buchan waited patiently while Max recovered himself.

"I can't stop a war, Ginger," he said at last.

"I'm not sure anyone can, though I imagine some will try. I'm more interested in stopping what is going on in Paris right now."

Max nodded. He wasn't sure what he could do to achieve even that modest goal. Solving a pair of murders almost seemed simple, but if those murders were somehow linked to this rumoured plot, maybe it would help.

"Do you know who's involved in this? Has Andre Bucard's name come up?"

"No, and I've asked around, but that doesn't mean he's not involved: the absence of evidence is not evidence of absence. Even with the dissolution of The Black Fist, he still has a lot of influence, and he's not the only member of his family with their fingers in this pie. It seems doubtful that he doesn't know about it even if he is not directly involved. Maybe you could talk to him. It would be awkward for me to do so."

Buchan was always careful about whom he would or would not see. Still, he had extensive contacts throughout Paris, not to mention farther afield.

"I could do that, though surely you have someone better placed, more trusted by Bucard."

"I do. But not one I trust as much as you. Besides there is something else. One of my informants says that someone high up in the prefecture, though not the Prefect himself, may be involved, either directly or by providing cover, information, support, that sort of thing. I can't be seen poking around in the internal affairs of the French government, but you have contacts..."

"I have a few. Gereau is retired but may still have useful suggestions."

"Gereau retired? Funny, I hadn't heard that."

"I don't think he's very happy about it; he may be keeping it quiet. I'll talk to him and see what he says."

"That's great." Buchan stood up and brushed a few crumbs off his pale blue vest and straightened the navy cravat around his neck. He slipped his dove grey jacket off the back of the chair and put it on. He glanced around before running his fingers carefully through his thinning red hair. "You really need to get a mirror, Max. How is a guy to know he's put together without one?"

"I'll take it under advisement." Max stood and offered his hand. Buchan grasped it warmly, then extracted a card from his vest pocket. "This is my new address in the 5th. Better to contact me there than at the embassy."

MAX SPENT THE REST of the morning going through his mail. A factory owner named Bourgeois had contacted him on the recommendation of a former client about missing goods from his shipping warehouse. He had already changed the locks and increased security around the building but the disappearances hadn't stopped. It sounded like an interesting problem so Max sent a note agreeing to take the case and outlining his terms.

Four of the letters were requests to follow wayward spouses, something Max had no interest in doing. He used to send polite letters explaining his position and recommending detectives who did that kind of work but had grown tired of doing other people's research and now dumped the letters in the waste basket under his desk.

Finally, two families were seeking information about soldiers who had not returned from the war. Nearly three years after the peace, such letters continued to trickle in. No pictures were included but general descriptions and distinctive features were listed. Max felt it was his duty to help them, though usually the men could not be found or if found, were past returning home, so he sent replies agreeing to search, quoting a token fee so they understood that their request had value. The rest of the mail were bills, either personal expenses or those of Chez Jake. He wrote cheques on his own account for the former and prepared ones for the latter for Jake to countersign.

He spent the rest of the afternoon reading the half dozen newspapers he had delivered every day, more to practice his French skills than because he thought they would reveal anything useful for his investigations.

A short article in Le Libertaire, an anarchist paper, caught his eye. It reported on the disappearance of several Italian anarchists after a series of bombings at Rome newspapers had been blamed on them. The writer, identified simply as L. Pierre, claimed they had been kidnapped or killed, though Max supposed they could have simply gone into hiding. Pierre implied that it was a plot of right-wing extremists carried out in cooperation with the Rome police. The parallels to what was now happening in Paris were disturbing.

By the time Max looked up from his reading, the sun had long set and he could hear musicians warming up in the bar below. Max stacked his mail and the copy of the paper for further examination and carried the plates and glasses down to the kitchen before retiring to his usual table near the stage to take in the music—a trio of guitar, piano, and drums—and eventually eat a late supper. He enjoyed the music and made a point of telling the musicians before leaving after the second set for the short walk home. The evening air was crisp and the lights of the city inviting and Max thought of walking further but he felt a sudden lassitude as he approached his apartment and decided that sleep was a better idea.

When he woke the next morning, his bedroom was flooded with sunlight. He threw open the window that looked down on Rue Lepic to cool the apartment while he heated some day-old croissants and opened a fresh pot of jam. As the coffee perked, he leaned out the window and listened to the chatter and laughter as the local cafes opened their shutters and invited passers-by to partake of their fare.

A young man stood on the corner, selling newspapers, calling out the headlines to anyone within earshot. Max's head jerked up at the announcement of yet another bombing, this one in a bus stop across from the offices of Le Figaro, Paris's leading conservative newspaper. Two pedestrians had been injured, one seriously. Max hurried down the stairs and purchased several editions to peruse over his breakfast.

The prefecture had issued a warning, asking people to avoid unnecessary travel and to report any suspicious packages or activities. A list of possible targets, including all newspapers and magazines, printing presses and political party offices were listed. A cordon had been thrown around the National Assembly with police checking papers and searching bags. No arrests had yet been made but Captain Fontaine had been assigned to head up a special task force.

"The whole city will be blown up before he figures it out," muttered Max.

None of the targets were near the restaurant where he hoped to find Bucard and Giamatti so he sent a messenger to confirm a reservation for two for 8 p.m. He would take Henri, more to treat him to a dinner out than to help with his mission.

In the meantime, he could work on his other new cases. The Invalides hospital was a good place to start to look for the missing soldiers. Even after three years, a few badly injured or disfigured soldiers were still in beds there, though most had been released to return to their villages, to other hospitals or to fend for themselves on the streets of Paris. Max made it a habit to carry a few francs in his pocket to drop into outstretched hands or old military caps laid on the paving stones. He couldn't help them all but he couldn't ignore them either, the way many of his fellow Parisians had taken to doing.

He shoved the families' letters in his jacket pocket, both to show the hospital staff that he was on "official" business and to answer any police questions as to why he was out and about. Even if the missing soldiers were no longer in the Invalides, there might be something in the files as to their current whereabouts.

Pierre Garnier had, according to the records, never been admitted to the hospital and no one remembered him from the description in the letter. They did provide a list of the few institutions in Paris that still housed men who were too damaged or disturbed to be released, which he might send Alain to visit on Friday. No record existed for Andre Lambert either, but when Max mentioned that the man had the tattoo of an anchor on his left bicep, an orderly standing near the office piped up, "He might mean Andre the Sailor. He's confined in Ward 6."

The administrator shrugged but agreed that Max could take a look. "But don't expect too much," he said. "Residents of Ward 6 are unlucky to be alive."

The orderly led the way down a long hallway lined with marble arches and memorial plaques and statues of France's fallen heroes and then up a stairway to a narrower darker hall lined with barred doors. They stopped halfway down at a door with "VI" on a plaque and the orderly fumbled with a ring of keys until he found the right one.

"I'll come in with you. The men here can get...excitable when confronted with a stranger." He pulled the door open on squeaky hinges. The quiet babble of voices fell silent as they entered, then started up again, louder and more frantic. Eight beds lined the two sides of the ward, thin half-curtains separating them to give the pretence of privacy. Only six were occupied; five men stretched out under patched sheets, a sixth sitting on the end of the bed staring up at the ceiling and mumbling the same words over and over: "Viande avariée." Rotten meat.

The air was stale. The smell of disinfectant masked but did not hide the odors of human waste that permeated the room. Beneath it all was the all too familiar smell of festering wounds and approaching death. Max suppressed a gag and fought back the urge to turn and go.

"How can they be left like this?" Max glared at the orderly who blushed and dropped his eyes.

"It's not what it looks like," he said in a low voice. "Most of what you see they do themselves, fresh injuries where old ones have healed. We tried binding them but they still find a way. We bathe them twice a week and there is a toilet through that door." He gestured to a narrow grey portal at the end of the ward. "But we can't make them use it. These are men looking for death but they don't know where to find Him."

Max made himself look at each of the men as he passed their beds. Each of them was missing one or more limbs; those who still possessed eyes were staring blankly at something no one else could see. The babble resolved into separate voices. This one was praying; that one cursing. Another was calling out for his mother; a fourth cried a woman's name between shuddering sobs, though his mouth was so badly torn, Max could not tell if it was Annette or Antoinette. Only one was silent, lying flat on his back with a sheet covering most of his face.

"This is Andre. He's quieter than the rest, though when he speaks you can make some sense of it."

"How do you know his first name and not his last?"

"Not every soldier arrived with papers in hand; some barely had the tatters of a uniform to show they were soldiers at all. He must have told someone; it was before my time."

Max looked at the orderly, really looked at him for the first time, seeing the man behind the white jacket. He was young, probably too young to have served in the war, his broad intelligent face bare except for a wispy trace of mustache. He was a few inches shorter than Max but broad, the muscles of his arms and chest straining the cloth of his uniform.

"What's your name?" he asked.

"Hugo Pomeroy."

Pomeroy reached down and gently touched Andre's remaining leg. The man lurched upright, the sheet falling away to reveal a mass of scars on the right side of his body. His arm on that side was truncated below the elbow and his left hand was missing its two smallest fingers. The left side of his face and head was unmarked but his right ear was gone as was his right eye, leaving only an empty socket. The nose was a crumpled mass but the mouth and chin were untouched and the lips now curved into a beautiful smile.

"Hugo," he said.

"That's right, Andre. Hugo. This is Max."

Andre looked at Max with his single blue eye. "Max." He touched his breast and said: "Andre"

"Hello, Andre. I'm pleased to meet you. How are you?"

Andre looked around at his fellow inmates and shrugged. "Better than them."

Max laughed at the unexpected response. Andre's grin got bigger. His brow furrowed before he spoke again, slowly, enunciating every word. "I'd leave this place but I don't remember where to go."

Max wasn't sure that any of the others would ever leave this place; they hadn't shifted their gaze or changed their rhythmic muttering, but Andre seemed alert, despite his horrific injuries. "Do you know your last name, Andre?"

Andre shook his head, his smile fading.

"Is it—" Max cut Hugo off with a gesture before he could ask his question.

"Is it Garnier?"

Andre shook his head. Hugo looked at him curiously but said nothing.

"Is it Bucard?" Max wondered why he had thought of the rightist leader.

"No. No."

"Is it Laurent?"

Andre's brow furrowed and he pursed his lips before shaking his head. "No, not that."

"How about Lambert?

Andre's head jerked up, his eye wide and staring straight at Max.

"That's right. I'm Andre Lambert. Andre Lambert. Andre Lambert." The man was almost bouncing on the bed, his voice filled with wonder and delight at the sound of his own name. "I'm Andre Lambert from Mont... Montrésor. I'm from Montrésor."

It was Max's turn to grin. The family had written from Montrésor, a village in the Loire valley. This was their missing son. "Your family is looking for you."

"They sent you to find me?" Andre sobbed. "They will not want this."

"They said in their letter that that they wanted to have you home again, no matter what your situation or condition."

"Truly. They will accept this..."

"All they will see is their son." Max turned to Hugo. "Can he be moved to a better accommodation while I make arrangements for his return home?"

"Of course," said Hugo, a catch in his voice. "I'll escort you back and ask the administrator where we can put him. He'll be waiting for you when you return."

"How did you do that?" asked Hugo as they walked back to the office.

"You weren't in the war, were you?"

"I was too young. My brothers both served. One didn't come back; the other was here for almost a year. It's how I came to work here after seeing the care the doctors and the Sisters give to the wounded, to my brother. Still..."

"Sometimes you see men in the trenches after a bad battle. They couldn't remember where they were, where they come from, even what their name was. Often all it took was some clue, some hint and it would suddenly come back. He couldn't remember his name but I thought he might recognize it. I got lucky; it worked."

"The doctor will be amazed—and relieved. Most of the men in these wards only leave in a box. Ward 6 is not the worst of it."

Max offered to pay for a private room but the doctor in charge was so pleased to hear of Andre's improvement and prospects that he refused to take Max's money.

"He'll get the best of care," said Hugo as he walked Max to the front entrance. "I'll see to it myself."

"Thank you. Hugo, do you like jazz?"

"I might. If I knew what it was." Hugo smiled.

"That's the right attitude." Max took out a business card and scribbled a note on it. "Show this at the door, It will guarantee you a seat at Chez Jake any time you care to come by. Bring a friend if you like." Jake would seat him at Max's reserved table and make sure he was well taken care of. With any luck, Max would be there himself. It was time he broadened his circle of acquaintances.

BUCARD HADN'T BEEN at the Meurice on Thursday night. Max woke to the news of another bombing, though it wasn't clear if it was connected to the previous ones. A small blast ripped apart a tobacconist shop in the 4th arrondissement, causing serious damage to the shop and the apartment directly above but injuring no one. There wasn't a newspaper office within five blocks and when Max dropped by the Prefecture to see if Gereau was about—he hadn't been at his apartment—Lepêcheur told him the tobacconist, who was deep in debt, had been arrested on suspicion of planting the bomb himself. "It happens," he said. "They say that half the 'anarchist' bombings before the war were actually insurance fraud."

He sent Alain to check for Pierre Garnier at the half dozen hospices on his list and went to the Bourgeois's factory, which produced speakers and other radio parts, to interview the owner and his foreman. The latter would not meet Max's eyes when questioned but Max knew some people were like that. His answers seemed straight-forward enough and Max didn't think he was involved. He would look into his background anyway. Instincts were valuable but facts were what proved the case. He obtained a list of other employees, including the security guards, as well as any local competitors to the business.

Satisfied with the day's work, Max dropped by Le Coq Bleu to see if Yesim had any news of Jacqui before resuming his search for the elusive Bucard. Henri was alone behind the bar, wiping the zinc top with a dirty rag and keeping an eye on the two tables of guests in case they wanted something. He looked up as Max entered and waved him over, leaning across the bar to speak in a low voice.

"Captain Fontaine was here with a squad of swallows. They took Yesim and several of our customers. Jacqui was waiting to see you and they took her, too."

Gereau had won his argument with Fontaine, or his superior, and the round up of anarchists had begun.

Chapter 13 Friday-Saturday, October 9-10th, 1921

Bucard forgotten, Max had gone to the Prefecture on Île de la Cité but had been turned away at the door. Police vans and wagons were coming and going, disgorging prisoners in groups of three or four. Officers carrying rifles—a rarity in Paris—surrounded the entrances and lined the nearby streets, alert for any sign of trouble.

He found Lepêcheur commanding one such group on the Pont au Change. He offered him a cigarette which the sergeant gladly took. Max didn't smoke himself but he kept a pack in his jacket for such occasions. Lepêcheur didn't know many of the details of the arrests, other than several of the most sought-after radicals had escaped the net. Jacqui would likely be held at the women's prison on Saint Lazare in the 10th arrondissement. Yesim was probably still in the holding cells in the Prefecture itself unless he had already been transferred to La Santé in the 14th. He promised to find out for sure and send word to Max as soon as he could.

Fortunately, Blaise Cleroux was still in his law office when Max stopped by a few minutes before five p.m. "Most of the 'suspects' will be released tomorrow or, at the latest Monday, if the Prefecture remains true to form—though the bombings put a different light on things. There has been nothing like it since before the War. Still, Fontaine will have cast a wide net hoping to catch a whale; he'll be in a bad mood if all he gets are minnows."

"Whales aren't technically fish," said Max. Cleroux gave him a sour look. Lawyers hate to have their eloquence blunted by a technicality. "What can he do? If they don't run to form."

"Nothing really. It isn't against the law in France to hold contrary views. If it was the streets would be empty and the jails would be full. Probably, some don't have their papers in order or have failed to report a recent move to the Prefecture. Hardly hanging offences. He might keep those he thinks he can make a case against but the judges get annoyed if the wheels of justice don't spin in a timely fashion. Bring them to court or let them go is the way they like things to run."

And once in court, a speedy conviction was the desired result with transportation to the penal colonies, imprisonment in one of the overcrowded penitentiaries or execution the most likely outcomes. Acquittal rates were low and at the very least, Jacqui and Yesim could have their passes revoked and be sent back to Marseilles to live. Max had never been to the southern port but he doubted it could hold a candle to Paris.

Max doubted if Yesim was in any danger. He hardly left Le Coq Bleu except to shop for the kitchen or go drinking with Henri. A group of old friends, anarchists from Marseilles, had hung around the bar the previous year but, Yesim said, "they were lousy customers who scared away the good ones." Max hadn't seen any of those ones in months. Max hoped Yesim's attitude towards the latest arrivals from Marseilles was the same and he had already moved them along, though it would be troublesome if he hadn't.

Jacqui was another question. Even without the incriminating evidence Max had removed from Nicole Bilodeau's bedroom, Jacqui had several strikes against her, not least her long-time partnership with Jacques Court, whose role in the anarchist movement was secretive but significant. As far as he knew, the Prefecture didn't yet know that Jacqueline Grandet and Jacques Grand were the same person but they had spies everywhere and it might come out or

Gereau might tell them. Still, she was arrested in the company of other anarchists and Max doubted she had a reliable alibi for any of the bombings, except the first one, though even that was no sure thing.

"I know a helpful judge who should be able to get you a pass to see both Yesim and Jacqui sometime tomorrow." Cleroux said, after the silence had dragged on for several minutes. "I can drop them by Chez Jake tonight at about ten. You can buy me dinner for my troubles."

TRUE TO HIS WORD, CLEROUX arrived at ten with the requisite paperwork, by which time Max had heard from Lepêcheur. Jacqui was at Saint Lazare while Yesim was still packed with twenty others in the holding cell at the Prefecture. Max shared a meal of braised leg of lamb served with garlic potatoes and green beans almandine with Cleroux but left him to enjoy desert alone after the first set. He had a feeling he would need all his energy for the ordeal ahead.

Early the next morning, he made his way to the Prefecture and, after a brief delay while the desk sergeant tried to find flaws in the documents Max presented, a constable led the way to the holding cells in the basement. Max could have found his way without a guide—he'd been a guest there a couple of times himself over the years and had frequently visited clients as well.

The four cells were all full. Designed to hold two or three prisoners at a time, they each held five or six men. Anarchism apparently covered all classes as the occupants were dressed in everything from shabby workman's garb to business suits and most styles in between. Still, it was remarkably orderly for a group that claimed that personal liberty was the highest aspiration of human society. He recalled Yesim's lectures on the self-organizing principles of anarchist society and it seemed it was at work here.

The benches had been arranged so that the prisoners could sleep in shifts and relative comfort rather than slouched against a wall. The buckets that served as toilets had been shifted from the corner to a spot near the cell door. Max wondered at that until the smell brought him—and the accompanying constable—up short. The constable blew a whistle and two civilian employees appeared to remove the buckets and bring fresh ones. The anarchists had figured out a way to make the guards suffer as much as them, prompting better service than afforded most prisoners.

"Yesim Coriveau," called out the constable. "You have a visitor."

A lump stirred on one of the make-shift beds and unfolded itself into Max's friend and business partner. The other occupants of the cell drifted to the rear of the small room to give them some privacy to talk. Max glanced at the constable who moved to the end of the hall where he could watch the interchange but not listen.

"Are you here to break me out of here?" asked Yesim. "Or to gloat?"

"Mostly to gloat," said Max, smiling. "And to make sure they are treating you right. Are you getting enough to eat?"

"I've managed to choke down a few bites. They won't be giving this place any Michelin stars." The tire company had begun publishing travel guides in 1904, as a way to promote tourism by automobile, and rewarded exceptional restaurants from one to three stars. Chez Jake had recently received one of the coveted stars; Le Coq Bleu would never be in the running.

"You'll be back eating your own cooking before you know it," said Max. "You'll go before a magistrate on Monday morning. Cleroux will be there to represent you and pay bail if necessary."

"I'd rather rot than give these thieves my money." Yesim could never decide who he hated more, the police or customers who left without paying their bill.

"Think of it as a favour to me. And the customers at Le Coq Bleu. Henri is tending the bar and serving sandwiches while I'm bussing the tables." In truth, he had decided to limit the hours of the bar to the supper hour, opening at six and closing by ten. He had asked Alain to come in to help out Henri and the young man had proven a cheerful worker.

"I better get out on Monday or I'll have no custom left. Have you seen Jacqui yet? Can you get her out on Monday, too."

"I'm going to see her at Saint Lazare as soon as I leave here. Cleroux says the women won't be seen until Wednesday, something about them being considered more of a risk to society than men. Anarchism apparently removes them from the category of 'the gentler sex.'"

Yesim nodded knowingly as if this wasn't unexpected news. Were anarchist women more dangerous than men? If so, could Jacqui have been involved in Bilodeau's murder? A hard knot started to form in his stomach.

Yesim reached through the bars to grip Max's forearm. "It's going to be alright, Max. All of it. These bombings weren't done by these men or the women either. Illegalism has been universally denounced, at least in France. People will find their freedom another way. And Max, don't be too hard on yourself, or on Jacqui. I've seen the way you look at each other when you think the other isn't looking. It's time you started looking in her eyes."

It was unexpected advice from Yesim, who was better known for his crusty sarcasm and his scowls. Max felt a sudden wave of warmth for the older man. He put his hand over Yesim's and squeezed it gently. "Maybe I'll do that. Thanks." The two men looked into each other's faces for a moment and then looked away. "If there is anything else you need?"

"Some beer would be nice—but make sure there is enough for everyone; everyone suffers together, everyone shares." Yesim stepped away for the bars and seemed to grow taller. *He still believes*, thought Max, *despite everything he still believes in liberty, equality, and fraternity.*

"I'll see what I can do." In Canada, it would have been out of the question but in France, justice was harsh but it was also civilized. Men would be punished severely if guilty but treated decently until it was proven so.

As he turned to go, he spotted a familiar face in one of the other cells. Pierre Roget was leaning against one wall but came over when Max beckoned him.

"You're an anarchist now, Roget?" Roget had, over the last few years, gone from a bodyguard to a notorious criminal and a member of the Action Française to being an assistant to a socialist deputé. He supposed anarchy was a logical next choice, given Roget's love of a fight.

"I'm here, aren't I?" His answer was neither an affirmation or a denial. Roget drifted over to the bars; the other men shifted back to give them space to talk.

"My lawyer will be in court for Yesim on Monday morning. I suppose he could handle two cases as well as one." Roget was by no means a friend but they had a shared history and the man had proved helpful in the past. *It would cost little to put him in my debt.*

Roget shook his head. "I'll be alright." His expression seemed to say he had already arranged a way out. *Not an anarchist, then*, thought Max, *but a police agent.*

"If he hadn't retired, I'd say this operation had all the hallmarks of our friend, Gereau." Roget glanced down at the mention of the former captain's name. It wasn't much but he knew Roget well enough to know he had hit the target. Gereau's agent, not the police.

"Captain Fontaine is getting desperate." Roget's mouth twisted in a sneer; his contempt for the man almost matched Max's own. "When he couldn't think what else to do, he resorted to the tried and true. But he doesn't have the brains to pull it off. The big fish, Jacques Court, Émile Armand, and Bernard Dietrich, all escaped his noose."

Max supposed that was good news of a sort; if Jacqui wasn't considered a big fish, she might get off lightly. It was time he found out exactly what her situation was. He bid good-bye to Roget and for a hundred francs arranged for beer to be delivered to Yesim and his cellmates before heading for the women's prison on Saint Lazare.

THE AIR WAS CHILLY but the sun was shining and the walk was a pleasant length. He crossed the Seine on Pont au Change stopping on the other side to admire the Tour Saint-Jacques with its leering gargoyle rainspouts and statues of the saint overlooking the river. He continued along the slow rise of Boulevard de Sebastopol with its tree-lined sidewalks, many statues of men famous or forgotten, and many small parks. He thought of stopping in one of the glass-covered shopping plazas to buy a small gift to make Jacqui's imprisonment more comfortable but thought better of it, daunted at finding something she could share with her comrades.

Saint Lazare prison was an intimidating pile of stone, parts of it dating beck to the Middle Ages when it had served as a leper colony and later as a prison for aristocrats during the Revolution. It had been converted for the exclusive imprisonment of women in the mid-18th century and, he had discovered, held such notables as Mata Hari, the German spy who had been executed by firing squad in 1917. Max trusted a similar fate did not await Jacqui.

The guard at the front desk examined Max's papers before leading him to an austere office where a stout woman with steel grey hair drawn back in a bun introduced herself as Sylvie de la Roche, the assistant matron of the institution. She indicated a chair in front of her desk.

"What is your business with this prisoner?" She had no real right to ask him that; the papers were quite clear that he was to be granted access. However, it was clear she would be answered. He slipped off his dark wool coat and fedora and took a seat.

But what was his business with Jacqui? They were far more than friends but he doubted that occasional roommate and bed partners was not the answer de la Roche wanted.

"She is my fiancée." He hadn't known what he was going to say until he said it, yet the words felt exactly right. Despite everything, including Jacqui's adamant rejection of the institution of marriage, he wanted her to be his wife.

De la Roche raised one eyebrow at that. "I thought anarchists didn't marry. Free love or some such nonsense. How can you be engaged?"

"I'm a very persuasive man," said Max.

That earned him another raised eyebrow and a closer look as well. Max had worn his best suit for the visits—to impress the guards if not the prisoners—a blue pinstripe with wide lapels and a single button, the matching pants with newly fashionable cuffs. The jacket fit perfectly at shoulder and waist, showing off his triangular torso.

"I can see you might be." The woman looked down at a form on her desk and jotted a few notes. "Please empty your pockets."

Max had left his brass knuckles and clasp knife at home in anticipation of a search so the contents consisted of a billfold, a handful of change and a couple of wrapped mints. De la Roche examined them cursorily and returned them.

"You can leave your overcoat and hat in the wardrobe outside my door, A matron will escort you to Mademoiselle Grandet's cell."

A uniformed woman led him through the dank halls and up several worn stone staircases to a line of iron doors, each of which had several openings to observe the prisoner or deliver trays of food. She unlocked the first on the left and ushered him in.

"You have fifteen minutes. I'll be right outside."

The room was larger than he had expected, with a single bed along one wall and a dresser with several drawers and a chair and a mirror along the other. A small door in the back likely led to a commode, a distinct improvement over the bucket Yesim had to share with his cellmates. He had seen worse rooms for rent in the area around Rue Lepic.

Max stood inside the entrance until the door closed behind him. Jacqui had risen from the bed where she had been sitting reading a book. She took a step toward him, then hesitated, her face calm but her eyes searching his face, an unspoken question resting on the curve of her lips.

Then they were in each other's arms, Jacqui's face pressed into his chest, her arms wrapped around him. He held her tight with one arm while his other hand stroked her hair. Jacqui gave a little sob and Max's throat constricted and his eyes stung.

"I love you," he said.

"Even if I'm a jail bird, a criminal in the eyes of the state." Jacqui's voice was barely audible.

"The state has been wrong before."

They stood like that for several minutes before Max stepped away. "We only have a few more minutes and there are things that I have to tell you... and ask you."

"Alright." She returned to the bed and sat on one end. Max pulled the chair close so they could converse without being overheard.

"I've arranged for Cleroux to defend you, and Yesim, too. He'll be at your hearing Wednesday and will arrange bail if he can."

"Yesim might get bail; he owns property, which is the only thing that matters. I'm homeless, rootless, and a known agitator, even if my agitating days are long behind me. They'll make me go to trial even if the evidence is thin."

Max was afraid she was right. He was certain there was nothing to connect her to the bombings; he now doubted anarchists had anything to do with them at all. He was not so certain that she wasn't connected to other crimes but, he suddenly realized, that didn't matter. Not in any real way. This was the woman he loved and he would stand by her no matter what.

"You remember the gun I left with you?"

"The one I appropriated from you, don't you mean? I don't have it any more."

"What happened to it?"

"I put it in the arms locker at the safehouse. When I went to retrieve it, someone had taken it. No one seemed to know who. The quartermaster was quite embarrassed. I didn't tell you because I kept hoping it would reappear. It didn't. I'll buy you a new one."

Max wasn't sure where a homeless, rootless ex-agitator would get the money, though Jacqui always seemed to be able to pay for her share of meals when they went out, no matter how much Max objected.

"It's alright. I found it. At a murder scene."

"Oh." Jacqui got off the bed and went to the dresser to pour a glass of water from a ceramic jug. She took several sips before returning to the bed, the glass still clutched in her hand. "Someone was killed with your gun."

"No. The gun wasn't used, except maybe as a threat. The victim was strangled."

Jacqui took several more sips of water, her other hand rising unconsciously to her throat.

"I found your scarf, the one I gave you for your birthday beside the body. But, no, it wasn't the murder weapon. There were finger marks around the neck. Whoever it was had large hands, bigger than mine."

"I see. I haven't worn that scarf, since... since we had that fight. I suppose it could have been taken at the same time as the gun."

Max nodded. It was possible that the gun and the scarf were stolen and planted at the scene, perhaps to incriminate Jacqui or to send a message to someone. But who? Was it a message to him? If so, what did it mean?

"Two people were seen leaving the crime scene, one large and the other quite a bit smaller. They were dressed in dark clothing and wore hats. No other details were given." That he knew of. Perhaps Lepêcheur had gotten more from the maid than he had.

"A small person. Like me, you mean."

Max shrugged. "I could never imagine..."

"But you did imagine it, didn't you?"

Max knew he was standing on a precipice. What he said now would determine his future. If he said the right thing, it would be alright and if not, it would be over with Jacqui. If only he knew what the right thing was.

"I..." His throat constricted. He reached for the glass of water, his fingers brushing hers as she let him take it. He took a long swallow and set the glass on the floor. "I imagined it."

Jacqui looked away, her eyes glistening. "You better go."

"Wait, hear me out. Please," said Max. Jacqui looked back and nodded.

"I thought of everything I knew of you, recalled every word you had spoken, saw your face in my mind with all your moods flickering over it. Then I knew it was nothing but my fear, nothing real. You could no more kill someone or be party to it than you could sprout wings and fly. You told me, you swore to me that you had never participated in violent acts, that in the end you had renounced violence altogether. How could I say I loved you if I did not believe your solemn word? What kind of love would that be that didn't recognize a vow?"

"People break their vows all the time, Max."

"Yes, they do. But not us. Not to each other."

Jacqui smiled and reached across the gap between them and stroked his face. The space disappeared and their lips met.

"That will be enough of that," said the matron from the open door. "Your time is up."

AFTER THE INTENSITY of his visits to Yesim and Jacqui, Max felt the need to burn off energy. It had been a couple of weeks since his last visit to Kid O'Brien's gym. Twenty minutes on the bags and a half hour in the ring was exactly what he needed.

O'Brien didn't spar with him anymore since Max had knocked him out, using the unsportsmanlike moves the Kid had taught him. Still, there were always those willing to box, palookas for a couple of francs or young men trying to prove themselves. The recent influx of Americans had produced a raft of willing dance partners and Max was soon shuffling around with a heavy-set blond from Arkansas. After shadow boxing for a few minutes, O'Brien came over to referee, sending them both to the corner with the usual admonitions against low blows and sucker punches. A couple of other Americans volunteered to be corner men while Jo-Jo, who mopped the floors and kept the equipment in order, worked the bell.

"Three two-minute rounds. Go to you corner when the bell rings. Winner by knock-out or my judgement." O'Brien tapped their gloves together and sent them to their corners. Max barely had time to get his mouth guard in before Jo-Jo rang the bell to start the match.

The American, who had introduced himself as Frank, came charging across the ring, intent on pinning Max to the ropes where his heavier build would prove the advantage. Max danced aside, moving to the left to hide his weaker leg, tagging Frank with a couple of light right jabs as he passed. Frank turned, fast for a big man, and tried again. Again, Max danced aside, giving Frank, who had raised his guard, a hard left to his ribs as he passed.

Max knew he could do this all day, racking up points with O'Brien while Frank grew increasingly frustrated, but he had come to work off steam not dance the afternoon away. The next time, Frank charged, Max feinted left and then stepped forward inside Frank's flailing fists, and landed a hard right-left-right combination to his belly, before lifting a hard uppercut to his jaw as Frank tried to clinch.

The bigger man staggered back, stunned but not seriously hurt and surprised Max by charging forward again, almost leaving his feet in his eagerness to press Max to the ropes. Max stumbled from the weight of the man crashing into him, but then accepted his fate, leaning back against the ropes to let his opponent wear himself out with wild punches, most of which Max dodged or absorbed on his gloves or arms. The one or two that snuck through stung but only served to get his blood up. Every time Frank paused in his flurry of punches, Max snapped out a jab, on the theory that he would eventually tire of being hit in the face.

He didn't have a chance to prove his hypothesis before the bell rang to end the first round. O'Brien had to pull Frank away and shove him to his corner, warning him that if he didn't break clean at the end of the next round, he'd be penalized the round, no matter what he had accomplished in the previous minutes.

Max sloshed out his mouth with tepid water, while his corner man inspected his face for cuts. Finding none, he patted him on the back and pushed him to his feet just as the bell rang for the second round. Max's eye caught a familiar face working out on the heavy bag. He was sure it was Gustav Reinhardt, though it was hard to be certain based on the photograph La Tour had given him. Max's uncertainty almost cost him the fight, as Frank caught him with a roundhouse right on the side of his head that sent Max staggering.

He spent half the round moving out of the American's reach, while recovering from the blow. When he was ready, he stood in the centre of the ring, swaying slightly and his guard slightly lowered. Frank took the bait and rushed in to finish the job. Max met him with a combination of punches to his ribs and head that the other man, now breathing heavily from chasing Max, could barely counter. On the eighth or ninth punch, his knees buckled and he toppled to the canvas, awake but with the fight knocked out of him.

O'Brien directed Max to a neutral corner and then did a slow ten-count, giving Frank every opportunity to get up and resume the bout. Frank declined and, as soon as O'Brien turned away in disgust, Max helped Frank to his feet and back to his stool. "Never assume your opponent isn't trying to trick you. Be brave but beware."

"Good advice," said Frank, a wry smile crossing his lips. "I think I'll take a few more lessons before I step in the ring again."

Once he was sure that Frank had suffered no lasting damage and that his corner man was seeing to his well-being, Max slipped from the ring in time to see Reinhardt finish his workout and enter the locker room. Max performed a quick stand-up wash while the other man showered and was dressed and waiting outside when the Camelot thug exited the gym.

Reinhardt obviously wasn't worried about being followed but Max kept half a block back in case the man's suspicions should be aroused. Max felt warm after his match and was glad this quarry chose to walk in the crisp afternoon air. It was more pleasant than the Metro and easier to maintain a pursuit. As they approached the Trocadero gardens, not far from the American embassy, Reinhardt stepped into a small café. Max drifted past, daring a glance inside as he did. He was sitting at a table deep in conversation with Erich Harvey and Ginger Buchan.

Chapter 14 Saturday evening to Monday, October 10th to 12th, 1921

Max returned home, somewhat perplexed by what he had seen at the café but determined to get to the bottom of it. But not today. He needed some time to think, to consider what he had learned and what he still needed to uncover. Before he could do that, he needed something to eat.

Saturday was always a busy night at Chez Jake and tonight was no exception. The bar and dining room were full and, judging from the line-up outside, the overflow rooms Jake had recently added were full, too.

A couple of tow-headed Americans expressed their displeasure when Max walked past them and went through the main doors, but Smitty explained to them in a few choice gestures that who got in and when was none of their business. The fact that Smitty was a large black man didn't make them any happier but Mac noticed they didn't leave either. Chez Jake wasn't as popular as the larger places in Montparnasse but it had the caché of Montmartre where artists and musicians had been gathering since the Belle Epoch. It was one of the places you went to when you "did" *le vrai Paris* as opposed to the tourist sites of the Eiffel Tower or the Louvre.

Max's usual table, somewhat sheltered from the main room but close to the stage, was kept free until the second set started unless Max had told Jake he wouldn't be in that night. Max had barely settled in his chair from which he could see both the stage and main entrance before Jake himself glided over and took a seat.

"The special tonight is Pigeons Muscovites, which, despite the name, is lamb and vegetables wrapped in white cabbage with a madeira sauce," said Jake. "I've got a nice bottle of Saint-Émilion from Bordeaux to wash it down with. If that sounds a little heavy, we have a sole almandine with lemon potatoes and roasted green beans. Plenty of choices for a white wine but the chef recommends something light and fruity."

Max had spent a lot of time in the Russian quarter the previous year and had acquired a taste for the food so he ordered the pigeons and a half bottle of the Bordeaux. He might have something else later if the band was good, but for now he needed to keep a clear head.

Max had finished the soup, a light fishy broth with chunks of perch, potatoes and turnips. As the main course arrived. the band, a six-piece mixed-race band from Chicago headed by a cornet-playing black man everyone referred to as King, began to play. The music was up-tempo with plenty of solos by King as well as the clarinet and piano players. Max enjoyed the music but found it really didn't suit his mood and he left after the first set, taking the long way home along Avenue de Saint-Ouen before turning onto Clichy to reach his small apartment on Rue Lepic. As he climbed the short hill to his door, a soft drizzle began to fall.

It had been a long day and he was tired but sleep wouldn't come. He crawled out of bed shortly after two and slipped on a silk robe that Jacqui had given him for his birthday. He poured himself a small brandy and sat at the table, watching the neon lights from Pigalle flicker against the wet cobblestones.

What have I really accomplished in the last three weeks since the call from Erich Harvey? Other than nearly destroy my relationship with Jacqui and my two best friends, what can I put in the ledger to my credit?

He had cleared Harvey of the charge of murder. There was no question in his mind that the man was innocent of that at least, despite police threats to reopen the case if the true killer wasn't found. Though with the recent spate of bombings, they might have more on their mind than the death of a journalist. Still, he wondered what Harvey was hiding, because there was no doubt he was hiding something. And what was his relationship with Buchan and, more interestingly, with Gustav Reinhardt?

Max found a pencil and a piece of paper and began to make a list of people he would need to find and question and what questions he would need to ask them when he did. He started with Eric Harvey then added Buchan and Reinhardt.

He had come to suspect Nicole Bilodeau was somehow involved in LeFoie's death but her murder had turned that theory on its head. Was it a revenge killing for LeFoie and, if so, why and by whom? The obvious suspect was Simmone LeFoie but she had left Paris and, besides, Max couldn't imagine she would countenance such a thing. He had found his gun and Jacqui's scarf at the crime scene along with a mysterious journal that Bilodeau had hidden in a secret drawer in her wardrobe. He retrieved them and put them on the table along with the notebook LeFoie's widow had given him. That notebook was somehow linked to Gereau but Max hadn't yet found the courage to ask the former police captain what that link was. Perhaps he should seek out Pierre Roget to see if he was still working for the former Captain and could shed light on what Gereau was working on.

The first bombing had somehow involved Bilodeau and the Camelot soldier, Gustav Reinhardt, although he only had Philippe Latour's word for that. He had never thought of Latour as a coward but the man seemed completely unnerved by the bombing, or did he have some other reason for leaving town, if, in fact, he had left town? Two bombings followed the first, three if you counted the tobacconist shop though he was inclined to follow LePêcheur's lead and deem it unconnected to the rest. In any case they had all followed the murder of Bilodeau.

Two people had been seen leaving the scene of the murder—one large and one small, though their exact dimensions were unclear. He was no closer to determining who they might be than he had been on the night of the killing. Was Bucard involved or Giamatti? The latter was average height and build but the former would qualify as large. Bucard didn't like to get his own hands dirty but his two most recent bodyguards fit the profile. For that matter, Giamatti had arrived with colleagues, dangerous ones by all accounts. In any case, he hadn't been able to find either of them. They remained wild cards as did the flamboyant Delacroix whom Max was sure knew more than he was telling. It would be worthwhile to see him again.

Max didn't think anarchists were involved in any of it but he admitted he might be biased. If any were, the mysterious Bernard Deitrich, described by Gereau as both a terrorist and patriot, was the most likely suspect, given his penchant for violence. Even if he weren't directly involved, he almost certainly knew something and Max needed to talk to him—probably threaten him—to find out what it was.

LeFoie himself was the heart of the mystery but neither he nor his widow were available to answer questions, though Max supposed he could track down the latter if need arose. The editor where the journalist did most of his work had shed some useful light on the man, who had far more integrity and idealism than his public persona suggested. It would be worth talking to Braque again and perhaps some of LeFoie's closest colleagues.

He could hardly start banging on doors in the middle of the night but maybe he didn't have to wait until morning to begin his investigation. The two victims were sitting right in front of him in the form of the journals that both had chosen to keep secret. They were written in code and, so far, his efforts at deciphering them had met with failure. LeFoie and Bilodeau had once been close, obviously not engaged but willing to pose as such until Erich Harvey said something to split them up.

Or had he? Maybe what Harvey had said endangered the secrets both were hiding. Suppose they had been working together not as lovers but as fellow journalists, investigating a common story by coming at it from different angles. Bilodeau's ties were to the Action Française and its less legitimate allies while LeFoie had, it was rumoured, infiltrated certain anarchist cells. She came at the story from the right and he from the left. What would he find where they met in the middle?

Max opened the two books and sat them side by side. The first page of Lefoie's journal started with a sequence of number pairs, in several lines and divided by commas. 1-4, 2-6, 3-7, 4-2 and so on. Beneath the line of numbers were line after line of words, seemingly chosen at random. Max had tried using the numbers to form sentences. The fourth word of the first line, the sixth word of the third and so on. It had simply produced gibberish.

Bilodeau's notebook was similar, though the numbers appeared at the bottom of the page. Again, using a simple line-word selection produced nothing sensible. But if the two journalists were working together maybe their journals were working together too. Max used LeFoie's numbers to select words from Bilodeau's book and vice versa. It still didn't make sense, but it almost seemed like it should.

In a sudden flash of intuition, Max tried reading Bilodeau's numbers from the end of the string, thus selecting words from the other journal going up the page. Once he had the two lists of words, it was obvious that they were meant to be read interspersed with each other—the first word from Bilodeau's list—ladies first—and the second from LeFoie.

The first page produced: If you are reading this, we are both dead or in prison. We only hope you are a patriot who will do what is needed to save France.

THE MOMENT HE HAD DECIPHERED the first pages, sleep fell on him like a hawk on a pigeon. He barely had time to hide the books in two separate places in his small apartment before falling into bed. He slept until nearly ten. His usual café across from his home was closed for a family celebration of some sort so Max strolled up Lepic toward Le Coq Bleu, stopping at one of the other small bistros that dotted the neighborhood for a croque monsieur and a large café americain.

Henri, who was staying in the rooms above the bar while Yesim languished in jail, was just opening the bar in the hopes of attracting newly cleansed church-goers on their way home. "I like to give them something to confess for next Sunday," he said when Max questioned the propriety of serving liquor on a Sunday. "Besides, in Paris, Sunday is no excuse for abstinence."

The weather had turned warm again so Max helped Henri put out a few tables for passing flaneurs and made sure the bar was replenished from the cellar storeroom. A few stale sandwiches remained in the tray on the bar. Max threw them out despite Henri's protests and walked a couple of blocks to pick up new ones at their favorite patisserie, which in exchange for telling patrons the source of the food, gave them a small discount.

Max enjoyed spending time in the bar with Henri who always had a new joke to tell or some salacious gossip to spread about local politicians and other members of the ruling elite. While they waited for customers to arrive, Max outlined what he had learned so far about the murders and their possible connection to the string of bombings that had the Prefecture in a turmoil.

"This woman," Henri's tone of voice suggested he had not yet forgiven Bilodeau for corrupting Max, "was in cahoots with the murdered man. It sounds nefarious to me."

"I don't think so. I think they were on the verge of uncovering a serious plot. I'll need to decipher more of the journals to know what's involved but I finally feel I'm making some progress."

"I hope you're right. Maybe then we can get back to normal with Yesim growling behind the bar and you and Jacqui pretending you're not made for each other."

"There is still a lot of work to do," said Max. "Both Bilodeau and LeFoie died before the second bombing so the journals aren't going to tell the whole story. That's going to take a lot more legwork."

"Then you better eat one of those sandwiches to keep up your strength." Henri gestured to the empty tables both inside and outside Le Coq Bleu. "It's not as if anyone else is going to eat them."

Henri's prophecy proved false; fifteen minutes later the bar was filled with a group of American Catholics returning from mass at Sacre Coeur. Their French was so bad that Max had to switch to English to take their orders. Their boisterous laughter and loud conversation attracted several other tables and lunch stretched well into the afternoon.

Max went for some more bread while Henri prepared a cauldron of soup in the little kitchen and cut up meat and cheese to serve the supper crowd. Henri's pessimism had been transformed into wild optimism by the Americans' generous tips and Max was sure he'd be taking charcuterie home for his supper. It was his turn to be wrong; the supper crowd, mostly French this time, showed up in sufficient numbers that they were left with little more than a snack for their own meal when they closed the doors at nine o'clock.

He and Henri finished off the soup and other bits while toasting their successful day with half a liter of decent Beaujolais from Yesim's private stock.

"If this keeps up," said Henri. "I'll have to quit my job at the station and work here full time."

Max nodded. *That isn't a bad idea*, he thought.

xxx

Max rose early the next day to begin work on deciphering the contents of the journals. Constructing the sentences was tedious work and, even after he had a dozen laid out in front of him, it made little sense to him. No one was referred to by name but instead by nicknames such as Ironhead, Dunce, Weasel, and Sailor Boy. While some dates were in standard form others were also referred to obliquely such as "my brother's birthday" or "The day you stumbled."

Despite the obscurity of the text, it was clear to Max that they were sincere in their concern about a growing plot that could, if successful, endanger the state and, even, plunge France back into war. It had something to do with the reparation payments that Germany had only recently begun to make to France and England but beyond that, the nature of the plot remained hidden. Whatever it was, it had obviously cost both of the journalists their lives.

The break had been in reaction to what Harvey had told Bilodeau though not in the way it had first appeared. The revelation of LeFoie's political masquerades had warned them that eyes were beginning to be turned toward them. They feigned their broken engagement to provide cover for her infiltration into the AF, adding a further layer of camouflage with LeFoie's ludicrous lawsuit against Harvey. Their machinations had obviously failed them since both had wound up dead, presumably by the same hand.

It all seemed logical to him and was borne out by the veiled hints in the journals but, beyond that, he had no hard evidence proving the link between the two deaths or to the series of bombings. Still, the past few years had taught Max to trust his instincts. They had saved him more than once on the battlefield and had led him to solve several murders where the Prefecture had failed or, in at least one case, deliberately looked away.

By noon, Max had a headache. Progress on deciphering the journals had slowed to a crawl and other lines of inquiry were demanding his attention. After a light lunch of carrot soup and a fougasse dotted with sun-dried tomatoes, Max took a walk through the Montmartre cemetery to visit the grave of Havel Barsani, the friend whose murder had started his career as a detective. He stood over the simply marked grave in silence; out of respect for his friend's faith, he brought nothing to memorialize him but his thoughts.

Thinking of Barzani always reminded Max why he did what he did—to become a better man and to seek justice in an unjust world. After each visit, he determined to act more in accordance with his values and to avoid the mistakes of the past. When his resolve wavered, he always remembered what Havel had said to him more than once. "You are a good man, Max, but you are still only a man."

It had taken several phone calls and a reconnaissance by Alain but Max knew that Harvey had switched his usual lunch spot, though whether for culinary reasons or financial ones, it was unclear. He descended into the nearest Metro station and emerged a quarter of an hour later at Ecole Militaire, not far from the Eiffel Tower. He spotted Harvey through the window of La Fontaine de Mars, a popular café near a small fountain of the same name. He was alone, his head down over a modest lunch. Max slid silently into the chair opposite and Harvey's head jerked up in surprise.

"You scared me."

"Do you have reason to be frightened, Erich?"

"Usually." Harvey glanced around as if for emphasis.

Max picked up the menu, though he wasn't particularly hungry. Still, he had found people were more open when they shared a meal so he waved a waiter over and ordered duck confit served with mashed potatoes and braised green onions. Harvey recommended he take a glass of white burgundy and Max nodded his agreement.

"Can I get you anything, Erich?"

Harvey glanced longingly at the wine list but shook his head sadly. "Doctor's orders. No alcohol until supper and then no more than a half liter. I usually find it easier to skip it altogether."

Harvey's skin was sallow and the whites of his eyes had a faint yellowish tinge. There was a slight tremor to his hand when he lifted a forkful of cutlet to his mouth. Max had known Harvey for several years, had even employed him from time to time and used him as an informant on numerous occasions. They weren't exactly friends but he wished him no ill will.

"If there's anything I can do to help..."

Harvey shrugged. "I appreciate that, Max, I really do but..." He shrugged again. "This isn't your usual haunt. I assume you want something."

"Sure. Usual rates?"

Harvey smiled softly as if happy to be back on familiar ground.

"How sure are you that Bilodeau was a genuine member of the Action Française?"

"That's... an interesting question. I know she went to the rallies and knew many of the leadership, at the very least, on a first name basis. There were rumours of more private encounters. I can't attest to that—we only met in bars. If you had asked me a few weeks ago, I would have said, yes, absolutely. Now I'm not so sure."

"Why the change of heart?

"I went to her funeral. Other than a few colleagues, her maid, and a few members of her family, no one came. Usually, there'd be an honour guard of Camelots, other members of the AF in black crepe sashes or armbands. They make a big show whenever someone important to the movement dies—especially if they had been killed by enemies of the cause. I started to think she wasn't as close to them as she appeared. I started to think that maybe she hadn't been killed by enemies of the cause."

"You think someone on the far right was responsible for her death."

"No, I have reason to believe they weren't involved, at least not the AF or the Camelots."

"Because Gustav Reinhardt told you?"

Harvey leaned back in the moleskin-covered banquette and let his gaze slowly drift up to the green and pink wallpaper to the brass light fixtures high on the wall. The tremble in his hands was more pronounced and he rested his palms on the table to steady them.

"Perhaps I should find a new doctor," he said, smiling faintly. "A pastis might be in order."

Max signalled the waiter. Harvey was a grown man; he could make his own decisions. When the drink arrived, Harvey downed it in a single gulp and nodded for another.

"Mr. Reinhardt is more than he seems at first glance," Harvey said. The waiter returned and put the glass on the pink and white tablecloth. Harvey eyed it speculatively but didn't reach for it.

"More than a thug who sets bombs in Jewish newspaper offices?"

"Much more than that, I'm afraid."

Max's food arrived but what appetite he had had was now gone. He pushed it to one side and leaned across the table. "I'm afraid I don't understand. Gereau told me he was a rising star among the Camelots with connections to like-minded operatives in Italy, maybe Germany, too."

"Gereau has gone into retirement for a reason. He no longer has a grasp on the way things work. The British started it, during the Boer War, but everyone else soon caught on, some faster than others. Spies and counter-spies. Double agents. Reinhardt was recruited by the French, before the war. He's from the Alsace, speaks German as well as he does French. Italian, too, I hear. He proved useful, providing information on German troop movements.

"He moved to Paris in the summer of '15 but the French couldn't find much use for him here. Besides the Americans paid better."

"He's a spy for the Americans?"

"He spies for them, and does other things as suits his interests, but I don't think you could say his employment is exclusive. He's useful though not necessarily reliable. I believe that Buchan thinks much the same about me."

Max didn't doubt it. After all, Harvey was willing to tell me Buchan's business for the price of a drink or a few francs. "If Reinhardt doesn't think that the far right is responsible, who is?"

"I think he knows but isn't ready to show his cards, yet. Maybe he's waiting for a better offer than Buchan is willing to make."

Harvey was eying Max's untouched lunch. Max pushed the plate across the table and the journalist, hunched over it as if he hadn't already eaten. *Making up for the calories he used to get in liquid form,* thought Max.

"Who do you think was involved?"

"Bucard would be my first guess," said Erich, around a mouthful of duck. "He's eager to push himself back into the center of the action. Bombs aren't his usual style, but desperate times, as they say. If not him, then some wild card, operating for less dogmatic reasons. Anarchists used to be known for their bomb throwing but the targets seem off, almost deliberately so."

Max didn't relish confronting Andre Bucard with yet another accusation of murder. The man already considered it a bad habit and Max wondered when he might decide it was a habit that needed breaking. Still, Bucard had been seen associating with Giamatti and Giamatti was linked to Mussolini and his "Blackshirts," a version of the Camelots not averse to the use of arson against their enemies. Fire was nothing but a slow-motion explosion.

If it wasn't Bucard and Giamatti behind it all, Max had no idea how to proceed. How did you find a wild card, someone whose motives were as obscure as his actions? Dietrich seemed like a likely place to start: an anarchist who was also a patriot.

Chapter 15 Tuesday, October 13th, 1921

Max slept late the next day. Between his shifts helping Henri at Le Coq Blue and the frustrations of chasing all over Paris in pursuit of justice for Bilodeau and LeFoie, he had begun to feel stretched thin. He hadn't felt that way since the dark days of 1917 when it appeared the war would never end, or, if it did, would end in favour of the Germans. Still, his bed on Rue Lepic was far more comfortable than his bunk in the trenches and the morning sounds of traffic and happy voices were a vast improvement on the rattle of machine guns and the whine of descending shells.

When he arrived at Chez Jake to collect the receipts from the weekend and sign any cheques Jake needed to get the week started, he was surprised to find Phillippe LaTour waiting for him. He was slouched at a table just inside the door, a carafe of coffee and a plate of yesterday's pastries in front of him. He looked up from under the brim of a battered Homburg and invited Max to join him.

"Small town life doesn't suit me," he said by way of explanation of his return. "I thought I'd check in with you to see if you had any further work for me. I feel I still owe you from the last job."

Max glanced around before answering. No one else was in sight, other than Jake himself, who was talking animatedly on the recently installed telephone. Max slid into the chair opposite the diminutive operative and poured a dollop of coffee into the extra cup. "As a matter of fact, I could use your help tracking down a man called Bernard Dietrich. Do you know him?"

"I know of him. An anarchist from Alsace, right?"

"That's the one. I need to talk to him."

"About Bilodeau's murder?"

"You heard about that?"

LaTour shrugged. "Vannes may be a small town but we still get the Paris newspapers. Crime is our mutual business, is it not? Do you think her death is related to that of LaFoie?"

It was Max's turn to shrug. He did think they were related but wasn't about to reveal it to the smaller man, at least not until he knew what the two journalists had been working on together. "If so, I can't find the common element."

"But you want to question Dietrich about her death, right?"

"Not about the murder directly, though I think there may be a connection. I'm interested in a series of bombings that followed the one you witnessed."

"Almost witnessed," Latour corrected him. "Any idea where I might find him?"

"If I knew that..." Max laughed. After a moment Latour joined him. "I've checked the usual anarchist hangouts, some bars on the other side of Montmartre and a few safehouses I know about in the red belt. The last round of police raids has sent him to ground. You mentioned your wide range of connections, left and right; you might have better luck than me."

Latour nodded and Max gave him a description of the man and the names of those associates Max was certain about. Max went up to his office and returned with five hundred francs as an advance against expenses.

"Business must be good," said Latour as he slipped the cash into the inside pocket of his three-piece suit.

"Consider it danger pay," said Max. "Dietrich is slippery. I'll need to be taken to him or have him brought here. Hire muscle if you need it; I'll cover the cost."

Latour shook Max's hand to close the deal, grabbed another brioche from the plate and headed out the door to pursue his assignment.

MAX WAS GOING THROUGH the mail in his office, his feet on his desk and a fresh café americain in his hand, when Alain Laurent stuck his head through the doorway.

"I found the hotel where Mr. Giamatti is staying," he said to Max's inquiring glance. "He's at the Hotel Majestic in the 16th."

The Majestic was a large luxurious hotel near L'Arc de Triomphe. It had been built on the site of a palace constructed for the exiled queen of Spain and it was rumoured that the Queen's bathroom fixtures, including a marble tub had been retained and installed in the presidential suite. It had served briefly as a military hospital during the first year of the war before reopening in 1916 as one of the premier hotels on the Champs Elysée. Giamatti clearly had a sizeable expense account. Max wondered where the money came from.

"Any chance of catching him, now?"

"He was ordering lunch as I left—that was thirty minutes ago. He might still be at table if you hurry."

An hour or more at lunch wasn't uncommon in Paris, especially if Americans weren't involved, so Max dropped the unopened mail on the desk and slipped his five-shot Kolb into his jacket.

Alain's eyes widened at the sight of the gun and he gulped audibly. "Do you need me to come with you?"

Alain had been too young to fight in the war and, though guns were not uncommon on the streets of Paris, it was not something one saw everyday. Max made a mental note to give Alain some training with weapons. He might need it someday if he was going to continue working as a detective's assistant.

"I might need you to track down Giamatti again; he's a slippery fish so it's better if he doesn't see you with me."

Alain looked relieved. "Is there anything else I can do?"

"As a matter of fact, there is. I've accepted a couple more missing soldier cases – or I will once you post these notes for me. Then, check the hospitals and invalid hospitals for these two men." Max handed Alain the original letters and the two to mail. "Use the letter of introduction I gave you the last time, if there are any questions."

He handed the youth five ten-franc notes for his expenses. "Report when you have some results or you need additional cash."

A BRISK WALK AND A short Metro ride brought Max to The Majestic. While it couldn't match the Meurice or the Ritz for either location or cachet, its suites and private dining rooms were considered some of the finest in Paris and it was particularly popular with Spanish and Italian aristocrats as well, it was rumoured, the elite of the Parisian artistic scene.

The main dining room was half full and Max spotted Giamatti holding forth to two other men, both of average build, and a woman at a table against the far wall. They appeared to have reached the dessert and pastis portion of lunch and Max only felt a little guilty at interrupting them.

"Mr. Giamatti, you're a hard man to find."

Giamatti turned slowly and flashed a brief toothy smile, a glint of gold catching the light before his mouth closed. "My *friends* have no difficulty finding me."

"I'm sorry. I don't mean to interrupt your lunch—"

"Yet, here you are." Giamatti switched to what Max assumed must be Italian, strangely familiar yet frustratingly unintelligible. One of men, an older man with a dark beard flecked with grey answered briefly, before rising. The other two followed suit. Giamatti stood and kissed the two men on both cheeks before bending over to rest his lips on the woman's outstretched hand. Giamatti's male guests ignored Max but the woman gazed at him appraisingly with grey eyes.

"You must be Mr. Max Anderson, the Canadian trouble-maker. Jacapo has mentioned you." The woman's voice was low with the hint of an accent that Max couldn't place.

"I try not to make too much trouble. Mademoiselle?"

"Yet, here you are?" The woman gave a tinkling laugh. "It is Madame Novak. In case we ever meet again."

She hurried to join the other two men, her long strides quickly closing the gap they had opened. Giamatti had resumed his seat and gestured Max to take a chair in front of an unused setting. A waiter appeared immediately and Max ordered a coffee and a pastis, though he knew he would regret the alcohol on an empty stomach.

Giamatti hadn't changed much since Max had last seen him, over a year before: a few more flecks of grey in his dark curly hair and perhaps a few more lines cutting through his olive skin. The come-and-go smile was the same, other than the addition of the gold tooth.

Giamatti filled the minutes until the waiter brought the drinks with idle chatter about the weather and the increasing number of Americans in the city. "Americans are all right," he concluded. "Half my relatives are Americans now."

When the waiter retreated to his station, Giamatti's face took on a darker expression. "I don't like being interrupted while doing business with my friends."

"I can apologize again if you like. I've been wanting to talk to you for a while and, when I heard you were here—"

"Heard from whom? Have you been following me?"

"I remember the last time I tried to follow you; I was spotted in a minute. Do you think my skills have improved so much?"

Giamatti laughed. "I don't know, have you been practicing?"

Max smiled and shrugged. "I've been cultivating my contacts. You'd be surprised what a few American dollars will do even in a fancy place like this."

"Yeah, I heard that life has gotten a bit thin since the last devaluation. Well, you're here now. What was it you wanted to talk to me about?"

"There have been a series of bombings—"

"I don't know nothing about that." Giamatti put both hands flat on the table as if he would abruptly rise but then he leaned back in his chair and waved for Max to continue.

"Your name came up a couple of times. In a good way."

"Yeah?"

"As somebody who was well connected but also 'above the fray.' Some one who might have a few insights as to what's going on in certain circles."

"Circles like the Action Française and their friends."

"Especially their friends."

"If you mean Andre Bucard, forget about it. Bucard is a spent force."

"That's what people say about old lions. Until they feel their fangs around their neck."

Giamatti gave an elaborate shrug. "Maybe you know better than me. I'm only a visitor."

"A frequent visitor."

Another elaborate shrug. Giamatti waved to the waiter and ordered two more pastis without asking if Max was thirsty. Max pressed on, ignoring the Italian's frown at the waiter's presence.

"If not him, what about Gustav Reinhardt?"

Giamatti said something in Italian but it was close enough to the French expression for Max to get the drift.

"I'm not sure Reinhardt's parentage is particularly relevant."

Giamatti laughed and toasted Max and then swallowed the liquor in a single gulp. Max sipped his to be polite. "What else do you know about him?"

"He's a slippery fellow. Came down to Rome to see how we operate."

"You mean how Mussolini operates. Is he really the coming thing?"

Giamatti paused before answering, taking the time to scan the restaurant, pausing every few seconds to gaze at something or someone in the room behind Max. He resisted the urge to turn. Instead, he studied Giamatti. The man exuded certainty and strength but he had often seen the same thing in the war; men who came across as fierce but were the first to break when things went bad. He looked too old to have seen action himself but who could say? Towards the end, the French, who bore the brunt of the fighting for more than three years, were sending old men and boys to the front line. Maybe the same had been true of the Italians; it would explain the scars on Giamatti's face. For the first time he noticed that the small finger on the man's left hand was partially amputated.

As if reading his thoughts, Giamatti said: "A lot of men came back from the war, wounded in body and, more importantly, in soul. Many found they were not welcome back home. Sure, they had a parade or two in their honour but, after, no one liked the grim reminder of wounds, of broken spirits. They grew angry that nothing had changed, that the rich were still rich while the people struggled.

"Il Duce offers them hope. More, he offers them healing by helping them find their proper place in society, creating something greater than themselves, the way a bundle of sticks, bound together, are stronger than any one rod. They are the fasces; Il Duce is that which binds them together."

"I've heard similar things from other people." Max wondered, as he always did when men spoke forcefully about politics, where this was going.

"Of course, you have. This idea has power; it draws people in. Eventually every one will see, but mark my words, Italians will see it first. They will embrace it first." In his enthusiasm for "the coming thing," Giamatti had forgotten about Max's original question.

"And Reinhardt was impressed."

Giamatti blinked, almost as if he were waking up. "Yes, yes, he was. And he was impressive, too. We thought he would be... useful... in the larger struggle. But since coming back to Paris..." Giamatti concluded with another shrug.

"Too slippery?"

"Yeah, like three-day old fish. Slippery and a little off."

"I thought Mussolini was a nationalist. Italy for Italians and all that."

"That first, of course. But he has larger ambitions. Rome will rise again."

Max wasn't sure if Giamatti meant the Church or the Empire. Probably both but it wasn't any of Max's business what happened outside Paris. At least, not yet.

"Reinhardt was linked to the first bombing. Along with a woman called Nicole Bilodeau."

Giamatti flashed another gold-tinged smile. "I met her at a couple of Action Française rallies. Journalist, right? She gave me something nice to look at when the speeches went on too long."

"She was murdered nearly three weeks ago."

Giamatti looked genuinely shocked. He made the sign of the cross and dropped his eyes, while mouthing a brief prayer. As he always did, Max found the spontaneous display of faith both moving and slightly embarrassing, as if he was witnessing some secret that he wasn't meant to see.

"Who did it?"

"That's what I'm trying to find out. Another journalist was killed earlier. Réjean LeFoie. Ever hear of him?

Giamatti shook his head. "All this talk of dead journalists is a little creepy. Il Duce is a newspaperman, you know."

Max didn't but it made sense. If you could communicate well in writing, it wasn't unlikely you were a good public speaker, too. Max had heard his share of demagogues since leaving Canada. They both impressed and worried him. Crowds could be whipped into a frenzy by a powerful speaker, a frenzy that all too often ended in a riot.

Giamatti had little to offer after that. He volunteered the names of a couple of his contacts who might be able to shed some light on Reinhardt and the bombings. Max doubted much would come of those leads; Giamatti likely thought of him as a police informant and wouldn't risk key contacts simply because Max asked him. He would check them out, of course, even a small man might hold a big secret.

MAX RETURNED TO CHEZ Jake to see if either Alain or Latour had reported back. They hadn't but there were several letters of interest. The mayor of Givors had responded to his inquiry about the suitor of the Russian mademoiselle. Although he was circumspect in his language, it was clear he had a very low opinion of the young man, who had run up significant debts before disappearing from the town in the middle of the night. The report should be sufficient to break off the engagement without the likelihood of a lawsuit. Max copied the salient details in his journal and sent the letter to Valery Petrovitch Denisov, the girl's father.

Another letter solved the matter of the missing brother; he had died in a racing car accident when a vehicle driven by one of the Renault racing team lost control and drove into a crowd of spectators. The brother was the only fatality though two others had been injured. The driver walked away unscathed. The death had occurred nearly eight months before but a mix-up in reporting had resulted in the certificate being misfiled. Max wondered how many other missing men and women had suffered the same bureaucratic mistake.

Having wrapped up two of his pending cases, Max made his way to Le Coq Bleu, taking a circuitous route that took him past Pigalle and along Rue Blanche before heading back uphill to Gabrielle. Several small clubs had opened up in the last month or two, featuring black jazz musicians from America and he wanted to see if, first, there were some good players he could send on to Jake and, second, if the places were any competition to his own club. The answer to the first was decidedly yes and he gave cards to a trumpet player named Briggs and to Bechet, a clarinetist. They were passing through Paris and hadn't yet heard of Chez Jake on the other side of Montmartre but promised to check it out.

The answer to the second question was: not yet. The clubs were small and somewhat shabby with the atmosphere of transience filling the space. They would close but more would follow; jazz was quickly becoming the hot thing in Paris.

Max was relieved to see that Alain was at Le Coq Bleu helping Henri. Business was slow and Henri was sitting at the bar with Alain beside him, teaching him by drilling him on the finer points of written grammar. A young woman whom Max didn't recognize was behind the bar, chatting amiably with a couple of older male patrons.

Max raised his eyebrow at Henri. "That's Alain's cousin, Josette," he said. "She's new to town and needed a job and Alain vouched for her so..."

Max wondered how Yesim would feel about all his new employees when, and if, he was released from jail. He had already decided that he would ask Yesim to take Henri on a permanent basis. He was well-known and well-liked by the regulars and was still strong enough to shift cases of wine and casks of beer. A young woman might be good for business, provided Yesim made sure some of the rougher types who sometimes frequented the bar were kept at bay. Alain, in the meantime, was proving useful as an assistant and the detective business showed no signs of slowing down.

It will all work out, he thought. *Unless someone throws a bomb through the window.*

Chapter 16 Wednesday-Thursday, October 14-15, 1921

The weather had changed sharply overnight, shifting from the sunny warmth of late summer to the dreary drizzle and cool air of early fall. It would be his fourth winter in Paris and, while it was never as chilly or snowy as back home in Nova Scotia, the cold was damp and seeped into the scars on his leg and arm. Perhaps this winter he would travel south to Italy to see this Mussolini up close or to take in the bullfights in Spain. He had avoided them during his first trip there, still too haunted by the blood of the war, but he felt stronger now and curious about the men who deliberately put themselves at risk in the sand-covered ring.

The images of bright sunshine and spectacle stayed with him over the course of the day and helped ward off the gloom of the low-hanging clouds. He checked in with Cleroux to see if he had made any progress on getting Yesim and Jacqui released but the lawyer had little to report other than someone with pull with the Prefecture was doing all he could to keep them behind bars. Max wondered if that someone was named Gereau.

He dropped by the cells only to discover Yesim had been moved to "more permanent" accommodations at a facility in the 16th arrondissement, as far from the centre of the city as you could be without crossing into the banlieues or, in the case of the 16th, the Bois de Boulogne. It was too late in the day to make the trip and still have time to see Jacqui, who was still being held in Saint-Lazare, but he promised himself he would go see his friend first thing the next morning.

Jacqui greeted him with quiet dignity, not much else being possible under the watchful eye of the matron. She was happy to hear his plans to have Henri work full time at the bar. "He's getting too old to carry trunks at the railway station."

"Don't let him hear you say that."

"Now about this pretty young barmaid you've hired..."

"That Henri hired. She's pretty enough I guess but not my type."

"Oh, and what is your type?"

"You. You're my type. And there's no one else like you."

Jacqui smiled and touched his cheek with her fingertips. "Then we are a matching set."

They kissed then, though ever so briefly before the matron separated them and showed Max the way out.

A FIFTH BOMB HAD GONE off early the next morning and Max spent an hour scouring the newspapers for details. A flat of a journalist who wrote for L'Humanité, the paper controlled by the French Communist Party, had a grenade tossed through the window. The reporter escaped with minor injuries and refused to talk to the police. Although a journalist was involved, neither Max, nor the police, according to the various reports, could see a connection to the previous bombings.

The rest of the day was largely taken up with his planned visit to Yesim, who eagerly ratified Max's decision about Henri but expressed some doubts about having a young woman behind the bar. Previous experiments with women staff had not been propitious; the first had absconded with the petty cash, the second had married one his regulars, who was never seen in the bar again. Still, he agreed to give it a try.

When he got back to his flat, a note was shoved under the door, telling him to meet Latour at the Brasserie Lipp on St. Germaine. The Metro delivered him to the restaurant in under thirty minutes and he spotted Latour at a table by the window, eating the house specialty, pig's feet stuffed with foie gras and drinking a beer.

Max slipped into the chair opposite and signalled for a beer and a menu. He quickly ordered the soup of the day, chunks of spiced trout and onions in a fish broth, and some paté with dark bread.

"You have news about Dietrich?" he asked after the waiter delivered the food. "Where has he run off to?"

"No place at all," said Latour. "He's staying here in the Latin Quarter, passing, if you can believe it, for an American. Even has the papers to prove it."

Money would buy you anything in Paris if you knew where to shop. Max had no doubt Dietrich knew all the right places. He had heard the man speak English and although it was only a single sentence, he could well believe the man had the ability to mimic some sort of American accent. Unlike Canadians, American speech was as variable as the British and, as long as he wasn't too specific about his origins, he could certainly fool the French—and maybe the Americans, too.

"Do you have an address?"

"I do," said Latour, passing over a sheet of paper with an address for a flat on Racine. "He hasn't been there since yesterday—I've got a boy watching the place—but he's bound to return soon. All his belongings are there. But I heard he's been frequenting Le Dôme for the last couple of nights. You might find him there in an hour or two."

Max finished his food and had another beer to keep Latour company. He had thought it might be a chance to get to know him better if they were going to work together on a regular basis. However, the man had a talent for talking a great deal without really saying anything and Max left the table no more acquainted with Latour than when he sat down.

He spent an hour or two drifting around the area that surrounded the Montparnasse cemetery—one of the three graveyards Napoleon had permitted to remain in Paris before moving the rest of the dead to the outskirts or into the boneyards that filled the Catacombs at one corner of the burial ground. Tourists would pay a couple of sou to go underground and view the macabre arrangements. Max had seen too many bones in the trenches of France to have any interest.

Rumour had it that this was to be the new cultural heart of Paris, with many of the artists who had made Montmartre their home, now moving their studios and domiciles across the river. Max had never paid much attention to the painting or sculpture of Paris but lately had begun to visit some of the small galleries that remained near his apartment. *Perhaps I'm growing up*, he thought. Americans, too, seemed to favour this district and more of them arrived in Paris every day. After four years of hearing mostly French, he was now catching snatches of English wherever he went.

At about nine, he headed for Le Dôme in hopes of cornering Dietrich and finding out what he knew about the bombings and the murder of the two journalists. He was beginning to despair of ever solving it. Whoever he talked to claimed no knowledge of the events and suggested someone who might. They then said exactly the same thing. Still, someone had to know. Paris was a major city, yet the key players, right, left, or otherwise seemed to know each other. Persistence would pay off if nothing else did.

The restaurant was packed, almost every table inside and out surrounded by a boisterous crowd, with more spilling onto the sidewalk. Max pushed his way through the mob, using soft words and sharp elbows to make his way to the bar, where he grabbed the lone vacant stool. From here, he could see most of the darkly paneled room with closely spaced tables covered in white linen to one side and a series of leather backed booths on the others.

He scanned the crowd looking for the man he had only met once and that briefly but his eyes kept coming back to the singer. She was a strikingly beautiful young woman with bright scarlet lips and jet-black hair. The dress she was almost wearing consisted of little more than sequins and lace and every man she touched as she passed jerked as if jolted by electricity. She was singing, not beautifully but with gusto, and when Max listened to the words, he felt the heat rush to his face. Yet, the sweetness of the delivery somehow made the bawdiness of the lyrics more amusing than shocking.

"Who is that?" he asked the man next to him.

"That's Kiki."

A single name but it was enough for her apparently. Max now remembered that Jake had pointed her out at the club, dressed more demurely but still striking. She had been there about two weeks before with an American, a recent arrival to Paris with deep-set eyes and a previously broken nose. The same man was sitting at a table with several others watching her every move—a mixture of adoration and cynical evaluation on his face.

Kiki finished her impromptu performance and returned to her seat, while the rest of the bar got down to the serious job of drinking. In some of the booths, Max saw the sudden dip and lift he had come to associate with cocaine users. He glanced nervously around, still seeking Dietrich, but also aware that police agents were undoubtedly watching in case things got out of hand, as they often did in the new bars and restaurants of the district.

He spotted Delacroix at a table nearby, staring at Kiki and her companions, though whether it was the girl or the men who surrounded her that was drawing the man's gaze, Max couldn't tell. He was still trying to decide when he spotted Dietrich moving toward the exit. Max moved quickly to intercept him, taking him by the elbow and leading him to a momentarily vacant booth.

"I need to talk to you," he said in his best American drawl.

Dietrich laughed and answered in like manner. "Buy me an expensive drink and I'll consider it."

Max ordered them both a snifter of the house's best Armagnac. Dietrich nodded in approval as he sniffed the heady bouquet.

"You have good taste for an American."

"Canadian and you have a good American accent for a Frenchman."

"You pay the fat man for information. Do I get the same deal?"

"If you like. I'm surprised you'd take money from a '*putain*' and a 'police informant.'"

Dietrich laughed. "Words spoken in anger are never forgotten. Times are tough and a man has to earn a living whatever way he can. Maybe I'm saving to go to America for real."

"They don't have a lot of time for anarchists in America."

"Sacco and Vanzetti were framed. I trust the courts will eventually figure that out. America may hate anarchists but I suspect they hate immigrants more. If I go, I'll make sure my papers show I'm an American born and bred."

Max knew of several people who claimed to be able to make authentic looking forgeries, though he wouldn't want to test their honesty at a border crossing.

"The deal I have with Court is fifty francs for every valuable piece of information and I determine its value." Max had switched to French. After four years of avoiding English, the words had felt strange in his mouth.

"Sure."

"Do you have any idea who's behind the bombings of newspaper offices?"

"Not anarchists—or at least not French ones. The Germans, the British, the Italians threw bombs at each other for four solid years and it changed nothing. The state didn't wither away; the banks didn't shutter their doors. We are seeking a different path to freedom now."

"Peaceful revolution?" Max had heard similar things from Jacqui but he found it hard to know what she meant.

"Certainly. Look at Kiki over there. She's an anarchist even if she never waved the black flag in her life. Does what she wants with whoever she wants. Defies the strictures of society and makes a living doing it. Freedom is the inevitable state of mankind. I can lend you some tracts—"

Max held up his hand. He hadn't come for lectures on the inevitability of anything. "If not anarchists, then who?"

"Look around. There are plenty of suspects. I'd suspect the Prefecture itself if it now wasn't full of bumbling idiots. What better way to discredit the left than to plant a few bombs and blame it on the anarchists? Two birds with a single bolt. As to who is really behind it—it's Andre Bucard. He's gathered together the remnants of his organization and is using them to attack socialists and Jews. All the old targets are in his sights."

"I suppose you can prove this."

"As a matter of fact, I can. I have letters, photographs, names, and addresses. They all point to Bucard and some of his allies."

"Like who?"

"I'm not spilling that for fifty francs. What I have is big and will bring down a lot of dirt on the right. An avalanche of it. I'll give you the whole thing—for fifty thousand."

"That's a lot of money."

"I know you've got it. Besides what's it worth to you to stop the bombings and solve the murders of LeFoie and Bilodeau."

Max's heart hammered in his chest. "Then it's all linked?"

"I've got the goods on all of it. Meet me here on Friday at 1700. Bring me the cash and I'll bring you the evidence and then—shit!" Dietrich leapt out of the booth and began pushing his way toward the kitchen. Seconds later, the shrill call of police whistles broke through the clatter of music and conversation.

"Halt in the name of the Sureté! You are all under arrest!"

Patrons bolted for the doors, only to run into the arms of waiting swallows, their black capes billowing in the breeze. More enterprising or experienced drinkers leapt out of windows or tried to bolt through the kitchen into the back alley. Some escaped, most didn't.

Meanwhile Kiki and her table mates continued to laugh and drink as if nothing were happening. Others followed suit, staying at their tables until police officers led them away. Bowing to the inevitable state of confinement, Max followed them to the police wagon. Hopefully, Cleroux could get him out of the cells in time for breakfast.

The steady clop of horse's hooves on stone was oddly soothing and Max tried to relax and collect his thoughts but Delacroix, seated beside him on the bench of the wagon, insisted on conversation.

"That was a handsome man you were talking to, Max."

"Just a friend passing through."

Delacroix waved at the interior of the wagon. Nearly a score were crowded on the benches or the floor. Most were slumped over and silent but a few of the younger women were weeping. One young man started yelling in bad French about his rights but a quick cudgel blow put paid to that. "One who can smell the police before they even enter the room."

Dietrich had apparently avoided capture; the man was a whiz at slipping out of traps. Max wondered if he would keep his appointment in two days. Max wasn't sure he could rely on him to show or to have what he claimed. Still, it was the only real break he had had in the case and, while fifty thousand francs was still a lot of money, it didn't come close to emptying his bank account.

"I've been thinking a lot about Réjean LeFoie," said Delacroix, after a few moments.

"Really. I didn't think you were that close."

"Nobody was ever close to LeFoie. He liked it that way."

Max thought of the dead man's wife and children. They would surely disagree. LeFoie was like two men; the man the public and colleagues knew and the secret one, kept from all but those closest to him. He wondered why Braque was the singular exception. He would have to talk to the editor again.

"Why is that?"

"It preserved his independence and protected his integrity."

"Integrity?"

"I know, not the word people usually used with Réjean but I always thought he was the most honest of us all. Journalists are like everyone else, you know, from scallywags and scoundrels," Delacroix gestured to himself with his thumb, "to pillars of virtue determined to reveal everything bare in the glare of truth. If I am at one end of the spectrum, LeFoie was at the other. He was no saint but he was dedicated to his art, as much or more than any of the poseurs who share this car with us. There was no one he would not reveal to the world, from the lowliest cutpurse to the President of France himself, if he thought he was in the wrong.

"You can look where you like for his murderer and that of Mademoiselle Bilodeau, too, but, mark my words, it will be someone whose secrets he had uncovered and was about to expose. I pointed the finger at Harvey out of pettiness and spite, because, sadly, that is who I am, but it will be someone less likely, someone above reproach that committed these crimes against us all."

Having said his piece, Delacroix leaned back against the side of the wagon and appeared to fall asleep.

"It is a relief," he said, "to know who you are, even more to reveal it to a stranger. I don't know why I chose you for my confessor, but it was easy. Perhaps though, you could keep it to yourself, the way a priest is sworn to do."

Delacroix was drunk and maybe something more but his words were strangely powerful and moving. Relaxed, his face revealed his age and the depth of his loneliness that he guarded the way LeFoie had guarded his family and his values.

"I have a friend at the Prefecture," Max said. "If he's on duty, I could put in a good word for you. No need to spend the night in jail with these—"

"Oh, my dear boy, don't waste your favours on me. I have no place else to go. I may as well spend the night with my tribe."

The wagon lurched to a halt, the snorting of the horses announcing their arrival. The back doors swung wide and a pair of constables ushered the crowd onto the sidewalk. The night had grown cold and puffs of breath clouded the air and blurred the lights of the streetlamps. It might as easily have been 1821 as the present day and Max shook his head to clear the illusion.

A familiar voice called to him before the officers could usher him through the doors of the Prefecture to the waiting cells. LePêcheur was indeed on duty and was sorting the crowd into two groups. One, consisting mostly of women and well-dressed men was kept on the sidewalk, while the clearly inebriated and those known to be troublemakers, including Delacroix, were herded through the tall gaping doors of the Prefecture and into the now empty holding cells below. LePêcheur beckoned Max to join the former group.

"Still working the night shift, Hubert?"

"I have offended someone higher up for sure. Though who and how remain a mystery to me. Perhaps you can solve it, Max." The sergeant laughed, perhaps at the thought of a private detective investigating the commanding ranks of the police.

"Too dark and deep for me, I'm afraid."

LePêcheur kept them waiting until the other two police wagons disembarked, the last containing Kiki and her companions. Once they were ushered to the cells for a "a night of reflection," he turned to the rest.

"You may return to your homes. In future, be more aware of your surroundings or more dire consequences may follow." He glanced darkly at the now closed gates. He touched Max on the shoulder as the others, only a few seemingly chastened, dispersed.

"Speaking of offending higher ups, I've heard some talk in the lunch room that your inquiries are beginning to ruffle some feathers. It didn't sound all bad to me but you never know. I'd hate to see you back here for real."

Max thanked him and began the long slow walk home in the soft drizzle of Paris at night, taking comfort in the foggy blanket of silencing grey and the light glimmering on the wet stone of the city streets.

Chapter 17 Friday-Saturday, October 16-17, 1921

By the time Max arrived back in his apartment it was well after midnight. Despite the excitement of the evening, or perhaps because of it, he was wide awake and thinking about tackling the mysterious codebook again. His plans were derailed when he discovered his door unlocked and Captain Marcel Fontaine sitting at his table, smoking one of his foul-smelling black cigarettes. At least he had had the good grace to open the window and, when Max entered, smash out the smoke in the dish that had become Max's unofficial ashtray.

"Good evening, Marcel. Couldn't sleep?"

"I could say the same thing about you. Too many parties will be the death of you."

"Undoubtedly, but I was working."

Fontaine looked dubious but nodded toward the other kitchen chair. Max went to the cupboard and took out a bottle of brandy and two more or less clean glasses. When Fontaine didn't object, he poured them both two fingers of the amber liquid.

"I'm sure you didn't drop by out of concern for my health."

"No, but I do worry about you. Having a Canadian killed on my watch would require a mountain of paperwork."

Max laughed despite himself; he was starting to enjoy these nighttime visits from his old nemesis.

"What are you working on, precisely?"

"The same as before. Two murders and a string of bombings."

Fontaine twirled the glass on the table top, the lights from the street below glinting through the liquid and drawing curious patterns of light across the man's face.

"You don't believe that anarchists are at the heart of these bombings."

"Everything I've found out—and there is precious little of it—says it was someone else. Perhaps it was even a plot to point the finger at followers of the black flag, to hide something else, something more nefarious, more dangerous."

"No one caught in a bomb blast would think there was anything more dangerous."

"I was caught in a bomb blast."

Fontaine looked down at the table. "I'm sorry. I try to forget about the war but I am constantly reminded." He looked up again, the lights of the street glistening in his eyes. "They wouldn't take me, you know. Something about an irregular heart beat. My youngest brother though. His heart was strong enough, until it wasn't."

Max raised his glass and held it in silence until Fontaine clinked his glass and drank. *The War has connected us all*, he thought, *bound us together in a web of grief and regret and self-recrimination.*

"I'm sure you would have made a fine soldier."

"Really? I thought you didn't think I made a good police officer." Fontaine smiled. "It's okay, sometimes I have doubts myself. And not just about my abilities. This whole anarchist thing doesn't add up. We rounded up the usual suspects and some pretty unusual ones, too, but our interrogations revealed nothing, no motive, no opportunity, not even any means. Now, our chemists are telling us, some of the evidence may have been planted, even fabricated.

"To tell you the truth, the theory would have fallen apart a long time ago if it weren't for the influence Gereau still wields with the higher-ups. That old man should take his pension and go back to Brittany. You know, he has even tried to set himself up as a private detective but hasn't the first idea how to go about it. He's forgotten it's the young constables who do the leg work, not old men with arthritic knees."

"It must irk you," said Max, "getting promoted and then not being allowed to run the show."

"Damn right it irks me. If I had my way, I'd put the old fool on the train myself. No matter. When I report our lack of findings—with solid police work to back it up—then we'll start to make progress."

"Why tell me?"

Fontaine hesitated. He had come here to tell Max something but now he seemed reluctant to speak his mind. Finally, he said, "I've come to think you're right, that these things, the two murders, the bombings are connected, though I can't see how."

Max had the impulse to tell Fontaine everything and he had to resist the urge to look at where he had hidden the two books. This was his responsibility somehow and, as much as he would like to be relieved of it, he had to carry on.

"Something bigger is going on than the usual political violence—the Camelots versus the syndicalists, the royalists against the republicans, right battling left while the centre looks on bemused," Fontaine continued. "I suspect foreign interference but I can't make the connection."

"A man named Giamatti is involved, I think," said Max. "He is here as an agent of Mussolini, the Italian rabble rouser, but I don't quite understand his purpose. To organize an international alliance of nationalist movements, the way the communists do, but without a central command?"

"Damn foreigners. France was better off when they stayed in their own country."

"When was that? France and Paris have been the heart of Europe for hundreds of years."

"Our blessing and our curse," said Fontaine. "Whatever else you think I am, I am a Frenchman first. I believe in the three colors of the revolution and the three principles for which they stand. I can't stand the politics of half my countrymen, but I can't stand the idea of Italians, Russians, or the goddamn Germans interfering in our affairs."

"You left out the Americans and the British. Not to mention the Canadians."

"Recent allies get a pass," said Fontaine, apparently forgetting whose side Italy was on in the war. "Look, Max, I think we can help each other. You can find out things I never could, talk to people who would slam the door in my face. If you find something out, bring it to me."

"What do I get out of it?"

"Justice for the dead. And the living. And, in the meantime, I can give you a certain amount of leeway, a bit of camouflage, to keep some of my colleagues off your back. Like what Gereau used to do for you."

Max's relations with the Prefecture had become more strained since Captain Gereau went into "retirement." Perhaps Fontaine could grease the wheels a bit and keep him from regular visits to the cells; he couldn't rely on the good will of LePêcheur forever. If only Fontaine hadn't always been so willing to accuse him of murder in the past. Max allowed himself a small smile. *Now I know how Bucard feels.*

He refilled their glasses and held his out in a toast. "Here's to our new partnership."

Fontaine clinked glasses and drank. "And a beautiful partnership it will be."

HE AND FONTAINE FINISHED half the bottle before the latter declared he had duties to attend to and staggered out the door for home.

Max slept until nearly noon and woke with the taste of dust in his mouth and a throbbing headache pounding through his temples. A cold shower and a couple of espressos later, he was fit enough to climb Rue Lepic and make his way to Le Coq Bleu where Henri and Josette were serving soup and sandwiches to the small lunchtime crowd, gathered close to the heater inside.

Time to give in to the reality of October and take the sidewalk tables in for the winter, Max thought. He busied himself with the task until the brief rush was over before settling in front of a bowl of hearty beef and onion soup and a thick wedge of rye bread. He ordered a pale lager to wash it down and his headache soon abated.

Max spent the day doing inventory, placing orders where they were short and restocking the shelves when some of the bar snacks and liquor arrived late in the day. He was little use for much else and the effort of moving boxes around in the cramped basement helped to clear his head. He decided to quickly drop by Chez Jake to see if they needed anything before retiring to his apartment to catch up on his reading and to make an early night of it.

When he arrived, he was pleasantly surprised to find Hugo Pomeroy, the orderly from Les Invalides, come to take him up on his offer of supper and an introduction to the finer points of "le jazz hot." The two musicians, Briggs and Bechet, were also there and Max made introductions to Jake Sullivan.

Jake accompanied Hugo and Max to Max's usual table, promising a waiter would be with them shortly and then went to introduce the two newcomers to the cluster of musicians near the stage. Briggs and Bechet were obviously known to the local musicians judging from the handshakes and backslaps and pretty soon a half a dozen of them were on the stage, trying out eight bars of this ragtime number and then sixteen more of a popular Dixieland number. None of the players used sheet music but just played the numbers they had stored in their head or that came to their fingers of its own volition.

"How do you like it so far?" asked Max at Hugo's wide-eyed expression.

"It's..." Hugo grasped for words before coming up with, "...befuddling. I mean I like it, but they just seem to jump around like water on a griddle."

Max took pity on the boy. "They're getting to know one another. Pretty soon they'll agree on a program and settle in for the night. Once some couples show up it will be all dance music all the time."

The waiter arrived and announced the carte for the night. The two menu choices centered around veal escalopes with onions or rabbit with mustard brandy sauce. Max chose the rabbit while Hugo went with the more familiar veal. They both started with barley soup with goose giblets and finished the evening with mousse á l'orange and, of course, generous glasses of pastis.

Max knew he should call it an early night but Hugo was so engrossed with the music, especially when a pretty blonde chanteuse took the stage to sing a half a dozen numbers, that he couldn't bring himself to call an end to the evening. By the time a third set began, the pastis had been replaced with a bottle of Armagnac and Jake had joined them at the table to help finish it. Jake was a player himself, "of modest ability," as he put it and knew more about what was happening on the stage than Max thought he ever would.

"You hear how they first play on the beat and then right before or right after, making the beat the central thing. It's that syncopated rhythm that makes you tap your feet, makes you want to dance."

Hugo nodded enthusiastically. "Why does it sound so familiar and yet so different from anything I ever heard?"

"Jazz players have educated ears. They've heard it all, from ragtime and blues, to marching bands and even symphonies and operas like they put on in the Palais Garnier. They take it all in and then they turn it into something else. See, listen, hear that melody, it's from a spiritual—a hymn that black folks sing—but sped up a little. Now listen, they're adding notes, bars, bits and pieces of what it could have been but isn't. They improvise around the melody but always come back to it."

Hugo was sitting, with eyes closed and Max thought if you could paint a picture of listening it would look a lot like that.

"Now, here's another thing. You hear the clarinet, playing a phrase, now the trumpet answers back with the same phrase but slightly different. Every instrument has a different voice and each voice is distinct, but together they form a chorus. And that's jazz."

By now, Hugo's whole body was swaying, intoxicated by both the brandy and the blues rolling from the stage. It took only a little encouragement from Jake to get him onto the dance floor with one of the girls that hung around the band. For his first time, he did alright, watching the other dancers and following their lead. He returned to the table flushed and breathless.

"It's like nothing I've ever heard or done before," he said. "Thank you both so much."

Then he threw up.

Jake and Max, with Smitty's help, carried Hugo upstairs to Max's office and stretched him out on the cot Max kept for such occasions. Max returned to the bar and ordered a strong coffee which he drank while the last of the late-night crowd dispersed.

When Smitty closed the door, only about twenty-five people remained, most of them musicians who had dropped in late after their own sessions were done in other venues. Jake put out a big platter of sandwiches and a case of cold beer and then got his own trumpet and joined the players on the stage. Over the next couple of hours, they all took a turn, trying out new numbers or riffing on familiar ones. Max listened for a while from one of the padded booths in the back until sleep overcame him.

When he woke, it was still dark though Jake told him it was approaching six a.m. Hugo was awake but looked like he'd rather be still asleep and was drinking milky coffee and eating toasted bread to settle his stomach. He was still thankful for the experience but considerably less exuberant as he and Max made their way through the glimmering pre-dawn streets, Max to his apartment and Hugo to the nearest Metro to take him to his home in the 17th arrondissement.

Chapter 18 Saturday, October 22

Max had barely fallen asleep in his own bed when he was roused by someone pounding on his door. He pulled on shorts and a shirt and staggered to the entryway. Latour was standing in the hall, sweat beaded on his forehead and his breath coming in short gasps.

"Dietrich has been killed, shot in the head with a heavy-caliber bullet, probably a .45 pistol or something similar."

Max owned a Webley .455 but as far as he knew it was still in the hidden compartment in his wardrobe. "Where was he killed?"

"He was found behind a restaurant on Rue Jacob. He could have been killed elsewhere and the body moved. My source says he was killed about six in the morning."

Rue Jacob was where Harvey and LeFoie had fought, probably near where the latter was later killed and then thrown in the Seine. Dietrich hadn't wound up in the river but the coincidence of place was too close for Max's liking. "I'll ask at the Prefecture; I have a few friends there."

"Maybe, but my sources tell me that Fontaine has obtained a warrant to bring you in for questioning."

So much for being given protection while he pursued his investigations.

"Thanks, Phillippe, I owe you one."

"On the house. Be careful out there. Whoever is behind this—if it is all connected—doesn't place a high value on human life. I'd go armed if I were you."

Latour looked like he had something more to say but, in the end, he turned away and left Max to pack a bag and retrieve his two pistols and the brass knuckles that were his weapon of choice.

If Fontaine was looking for him, Chez Jake and Le Coq Bleu were the first places he'd look. Jake and Henri wouldn't be considered reliable alibis, but Hugo Pomeroy might well be. They had been walking together at roughly six and had parted company a significant distance from where Dietrich's body had been found.

Combined with the testimony of the musicians and staff at Chez Jake, it should be sufficient to keep him out of police cells, though one never knew when Fontaine was involved. He needed to remain free, not only to solve the murders of LeFoie and Bilodeau but to ensure that Jacqui and Yesim won their own freedom as soon as possible.

It was doubtful that Hugo had a shift at Les Invalides on a Saturday, especially given his willingness to stay out so late the night before. Still, the doctor in charge might be willing to give Max the young man's address. If he had mentioned more than that he lived in a sixth floor flat in the 17th, Max didn't remember it.

He fell asleep to the gentle sway of the train car and overshot his stop by several stations, forcing him to double back to the hospital. The doctor was the same one who had been impressed at Max's efforts to reunite Andre Lambert with his family in Montresor and was happy to provide him with Hugo's address.

"I hope you catch him before he leaves the city. Yesterday was the start of his holidays and he talked of spending time with his family in the Loire valley. He told me once which village but my mind was on other things. Started with a Ch, I think."

Hugo lived on Rue de Senlis, an unremarkable neighbourhood except for the nearby triangular park, which held a small bandstand and had several restaurants on its borders. The concierge was closed mouth about the residents of her block of buildings but a ten franc note loosened her lips enough to confirm that Hugo lived alone in one of the small unheated flats on the top floor. She allowed Max to climb the stairs and knock on his door but all he got for his exertion was a cramp in his leg. She reluctantly—for another ten francs—checked her files and reported that he had put down his parents as next of kin. They were listed as living in the town of Chartres but no specific address was given.

Max had seldom left the confines of the twenty arrondissements and had never been to the Loire despite Jacqui's frequent suggestion that they spend a weekend in one of the beautiful castle towns that dotted the area. Perhaps, now, he would have to make that trip on his own. Though surely Hugo wouldn't have gone straight from the bar to his parents' home, thought Max, I'll wait a day or two before looking for him there.

The concierge, a grey-haired woman with a permanent scowl and the unlikely name of Pierrette, agreed to watch out for Hugo (for another twenty francs) and have him contact Max through Chez Jake if and when he returned to his lodgings.

Unable to return to his own bed and too fuzzy-headed to do anything else, Max checked into a cheap hotel in Montmartre and after, a quick and simple meal at a local bistro crawled between the thin sheets and fell into a deep but troubled sleep.

Chapter 19 Sunday to Thursday, October 23-27, 1921

E arly the next morning, he returned to Pomeroy's quarters but the young man was not there. Worried about his safety, he bribed the concierge to allow him access to the flat. It consisted of a single room with a sleeping area on one side and a few chairs surrounding a rickety table on the other. A gas burner, a small empty ice chest and a cabinet holding a few dishes and dry goods comprised the kitchen. A curtained off area held a sink and toilet which were spotless, undoubtedly reflecting Hugo's training at the hospital.

The wardrobe by the bed held some clothing, all clean and neatly folded or hung from a single bar and one pair of shoes that had recently been polished. There was no evidence of a valise and Max had to assume that Hugo probably had left for Chartres to visit his family. He was on leave from the hospital for two weeks but Max could hardly wait until then to clear his name.

He dropped by Alain's rooming house, checking carefully for police surveillance. The young man wasn't there and Max hoped he hadn't been brought in for questioning. He shoved a note under the door and asked Alain to meet him in the lobby of the hotel "where Giamatti was staying" at three that afternoon.

He would need to speak to his lawyer but he didn't know where Cleroux lived and he doubted he kept office hours on a Sunday. He walked by the building anyway but it was dark and the front door was locked. A man in a blue jacket and pants—some sort of guard—glared at him through the glass so Max tipped his hat, smiled and moved along.

He spent the rest of the morning wandering through Parc Monceau. He had visited it before, during a case that involved a number of the Russian exiles that lived close by, but it wasn't one of his usual haunts and the police were unlikely to be looking for him there. The park was an amusing place to spend a day, filled, even in late October, with couples strolling along the broad curving paths past a lily pond or children playing among the "follies" under the watchful eyes of doting parents. A miniature Egyptian pyramid was a particular favorite and the boys had to be constantly warned not to climb it. Max strolled past a row of Roman columns and found a wrought iron bench to sit on and consider the progress (or lack thereof) he had made on the case.

The bag slung over his shoulder was unpleasantly heavy and he wished he had left the pistols, or at least the Webley, in his apartment. He could not imagine using it but, as LaTour had pointed out, whoever was behind these events clearly didn't value human life. What would another murder mean to them? At one, his stomach began to grumble and he left the park in search of lunch. He had no destination in mind but wandered the attractive avenues and streets of the district until he came across the tiny Cave Pétrissans on Avenue Niel. Henri had mentioned the place several times, extolling the quality of its cellar but they had never visited it. He decided he would try it now and report back to Henri on the experience. If it proved as good as promised he would treat his old friend to lunch there one day soon. There was a small terrace but it was too cold to eat outdoors so Max went inside and sat on one the four stools against the oak bar.

The food was simple but very well-prepared. He chose a chicken in tarragon cream sauce paired with an outstanding chardonnay from the Burgundy region in the south of France. It was lightly oaked and had a bouquet of apple, pear and truffle with the flavours of toast and cinnamon and a crisp lemony finish. He would certainly be bringing Henri here, perhaps for his upcoming birthday. Max couldn't resist buying a bottle of the wine from the attached wine shop despite the added weight to his overburdened bag.

He entered the lobby of The Majestic and spotted Alain perched nervously on the edge of one of the leather-covered chairs. Max beckoned him to follow him outside and they walked slowly along Rue La Perouse while Max gave Alain instructions.

"Tell Henri to keep the bar open as best he can with your cousin's help. If you have time you can pitch in, too, but I have other things for you to do. After you talk to Henri, go to Chez Jake—I'll give you a note—and ask him to give you 10,000 francs and then bring it to me at Hotel L'Aquilon near Franz Liszt square." It was where he had first lived when he came to Paris and he still dropped by from time to time to chat with Jean-Marc, his former landlord. He was sure they would have a room for him. "I'll head there now. I'll give you further instructions when you get there. Also, remind both Henri and Jake that they have no idea where I've gone or when I'll be back."

Alain nodded and headed back the way they had come. Max followed at a distance and ducked back into the hotel to glance in the dining room, but there was no sign of Giamatti there or in the attached saloon. Perhaps, he had moved again—it seemed to be a habit with the man.

Jean-Marc greeted him warmly when he arrived at L'Aquilon. It had been his home for over a year and returning now brought back many memories, both good and ill.

"As it happens, your old room is currently free. The best room in the house, if you recall. By the way, what name do you wish to register under?"

Jean-Marc was right. The Prefecture kept addresses for all foreign nationals in the city. It was only a matter of time before they checked his file and found his stay at L'Aquilon. It was an obvious place to look though he thought it might take them a few days to think of it.

"Andre Lambert." He was now safely at home with his family in Montrésor and would not be easily connected to Max. Still, if the police came calling, he would have to move elsewhere to avoid surveillance. The false name would merely buy him time.

Max took the key and climbed the stairs to the familiar door. The room was much as he had left it. A single bed with a gleaming brass frame and a solid wooden headboard stood against one wall and a small armoire along the one opposite. A thick Persian rug covered most of the worn wooden floor. The only other furniture were a round-topped trunk at the foot of the bed and a narrow oak writing desk and straight-backed chair in front of the west-facing window. A small landscape painting hung over the bed. The only thing missing was the framed picture of the Eiffel Tower, which he had removed to hide an important clue in his first case.

Even the smell of baking bread was familiar; the large room was directly above the kitchen. Max washed his face and hands in the small sink; he would rise early when the water was still hot and take a bath in the room down the hall. He lifted the window and looked out on the small cast-iron balcony. The ceramic pot on one end held the last of the summer flowers bravely lifting their faces to the waning October sun.

He unpacked his few things, hiding the guns in a concealed compartment he had found at the back of the armoire when he first arrived in November of 1918. Finally, he went to the bed and sat down. It was here he had sat listening to Havel Barzani as he paced the room, trying to explain the intricacies of international politics to him. It was here he had lain the first time he made love to Minette, the first woman he had ever loved. As badly as all that had ended, he still clung to the bittersweet memory. But that was long ago—he had Jacqui now or, perhaps, she had him.

He was still sitting there half an hour later when Alain delivered the money he had obtained from Jake. "Mr. Sullivan said to let him know if you needed more. Fontaine has already been snooping around; Mr. Sullivan told him you had gone to La Havre to meet some jazz players arriving from New York. Henri told me he told Fontaine you were going to Marseilles. That should keep him running in circles."

Max felt a little bad given Fontaine's recent rapprochement but, then again, given their history, not too bad. He divided the money and gave half to Alain. "I need you to go to Chartres, find a young man named Hugo Pomeroy and bring him back here as soon as you can; he's my alibi for the time when Dietrich was killed."

"Surely, Fontaine doesn't really believe you had anything to do with that."

"Fontaine's beliefs are determined by what is advantageous to him. He'll listen to evidence but only reluctantly. I don't think he can make a case but he could make life difficult. Figuring this out is hard enough without having to do it from inside a jail cell."

Alain promised to be on the next train to the Loire Valley and begin his search for Pomeroy as soon as he got there. Max had no doubt Alain was up to the task; he was showing a remarkable ability to gather information and make use of it to good effect.

THE NEXT MORNING, MAX sent a message to Blaise Cleroux, asking the lawyer to meet him at a nearby café. Max wore a pair of fake glasses and a beret in an effort to disguise himself but Cleroux walked straight up to his table, sat down and, smiling broadly, said: "Don't try your hand on the stage; you have no talent for deception."

They ordered café au lait and a basket of pastries and, after they had broken their fast, Cleroux shoved a document across the table for Max to peruse. "It's a copy of the arrest warrant Fontaine obtained from a magistrate. You have been named a person of interest in the murder of Dietrich, less than a suspect, more than a witness. There is little I can do since you are not being charged. If you want my advice, turn yourself in. If you can answer their questions, you'll be out in a day or two."

"That's what you said about Yesim."

"Well, I was only off by a week or two. I have good news; Yesim was released this morning and should be back at his bar serving expensive drinks to Americans this evening."

"And Jacqui?"

"Good news there, too. I've arranged a hearing with a 'friendly' magistrate tomorrow. They really have no reason to hold her and if my instincts are even remotely correct, she should be a free woman by tomorrow evening."

"That is good news. Tell her to go to my place on Rue Lepic—"

"I'm not sure she will do that. She has been deeply frightened by her time behind bars. She may run."

"But to where?"

"You're her lover; you would know better than I."

She might go back to Marseilles. She had friends there, not all of whom were anarchists. Or she might hide in the banlieues. They contained plenty of anarchist safe houses.

"If you get arrested, you know how to reach me. I'll keep in touch with my contacts in the system. If I hear anything?"

"Leave a message at Chez Jake. I'll leave word with Smitty to seat you and a guest for dinner. It will seem less suspicious than if you simply drop off a note. I'm sure the place is being watched."

"This detective business has made you paranoid."

"I prefer to think of it as clear thinking."

MAX SPENT THE REST of the day in his room at L'Aquilon, pacing the floors and wondering if he could risk a return to his apartment on Rue Lepic. If he had to be holed up for a few days, the time could be well spent going through the coded journals left behind by the two dead reporters.

He finally judged it too risky and, instead, went to a local news stand to pick up a selection of papers. He perused the dozen or so journals the vendor carried and, as was his habit, selected one from the left, L'Humanité, two from the centre, Le Figaro and Les Temps and one from the right, Journal d'Action Française. He found it easier to separate fact from political opinion by cross referencing their stories.

The first had a short article speculating on the shooting of Dietrich in which the writer implied he had been gunned down by police working in cahoots with the Camelots, a somewhat ludicrous theory in Max's opinion. The last also covered the killing but ascribed it to a falling out among anarchist factions who "were always taking shots at each other." Max was no expert on anarchism in Paris but he knew enough to recognize this as a blatant falsehood; anarchists hadn't been engaged in wholesale violence for nearly twenty years and, even then, their targets had seldom been each other. It also mentioned an explosion that had taken place at a bandstand in the Bobigny which the writer tried to link to the shooting. None of the other papers mentioned it.

Le Figaro included the murder in a regular article on rising crime rates, which had been growing, along with the city's population, since the end of the war. "Our streets are remarkably safe when compared to America," the article concluded, "but the trends are worrisome." The so-called paper of record, Les Temps, had a three-line article on page fourteen, which quoted Fontaine as saying "the Prefecture is pursuing several lines of inquiry." Max was relieved that he wasn't mentioned by name as one of those lines.

The next day, Max loitered outside the Palais de Justice on Ile de la Cite, hoping to spot Jacqui if she indeed won her release that day. The weather had turned cold so he had an excuse to wear a hat low over his brow with a scarf concealing the bottom half of his face. Still, he had to quell the urge to bolt every time a policemen went by on a bicycle. He shifted his location regularly and took coffee in several of the cafes that served the area but, after an hour or so, felt he was beginning to attract unwanted attention. His chances had been small in any case, the building had many exits and it was by no means certain Jacqui would have come out the front door.

He boarded the Metro and took the train to the edge of the city proper before continuing on by autobus and foot to one of the safehouses used by Jacques Court, hoping he would have heard of Jacqui's plans. The building had been abandoned and, when Max approached another one a dozen blocks away, he was refused admission in no uncertain terms. If he was going to find Jacqui, it would be without the help of her former anarchist comrades.

He had few contacts in Marseilles and none he really trusted but he was desperate to locate his lover, a word that still made him uncomfortable. He sent a telegram to the most trustworthy of his southern associates and asked them to ask around about Jacques Grand, the only name that might be familiar to people in that city. She had adopted the name Jacqueline Grandet only after moving to Paris and leaving her partnership with Court. It pained him that he didn't know her real name but knew she would tell him when and if she were ready.

Returning to L'Aquilon, Max ordered his dinner from the kitchen, a hearty beef stew with a thick slab of dark bread, served with an adequate Burgundy. Chocolate pastilles and a mild orange liquor finished the meal and Max settled into bed with the latest book by Gaston Leroux, a crime writer Henri had recommended. He put it aside after a couple of chapters as it felt too much like work and went back to the previous day's papers. While reading a long article in Le Temps about the ocean liner, Paris, the largest French vessel afloat, which had departed a few days before carrying the former

French Chief of Staff, Marshal Ferdinand Foch, to an important conference in Washington on the aftermath of the war, he fell asleep and dreamt of sea voyages and secret plots.

After a fitful night, he awoke to a soft rapping at his door. One of the busboys at Chez Jake, Danny or Davey, was shuffling nervously from foot to foot, clutching a telegram in one hand. "Jake said you would want to see this, Mr. Anderson." He looked surprised when Max handed him a ten franc note but accepted it gratefully. "Hope to see you back home soon."

Max smiled at his retreating back. He supposed he spent enough time at the place, even sleeping there some nights, that the kitchen staff might think he lived there.

Alain was brief and to the point: **Hugo parents gone beach Saint Nazaire stop will follow Alain**. His exile would continue for a few more days at least. A number of villages had Saint Nazaire in their name, strung along a long stretch of beach where the Loire River emptied into the Atlantic, another place Jacqui had described to him. *When this is all over*, he thought, *I will see more of France than battlefield trenches and the City of Light.*

After a light breakfast in the common room downstairs, Max risked a trip across the Seine to seek out Erich Harvey. He had gotten him into this mess in the first place and Max figured the man owed him something, though what the old newsman could actually do was uncertain. He was not to be found in any of the Montparnasse cafés that were becoming popular with the ever-increasing number of American tourists. It appeared that Harvey had shifted his favours farther upstream and, it didn't take long to find him at one of the new restaurants that had appeared near the Eiffel Tower, though not La Fontaine de Mars but a cheaper one a few blocks away.

He was engrossed, scribbling notes in one of his pocket journals, while the coffee beside him grew cold. He jerked when Max spoke his name but kept writing for a few moments before looking up.

"You have to learn not to sneak up on people, Max. You could give me a heart attack."

"You need to learn to be more aware of your surroundings. This area is full of thieves; you could be robbed."

"A futile exercise," said Harvey, mournfully, making the gesture of snapping a twig.

"Broke, again, Erich?"

"Perpetually. A hundred Yanks arrive in the city everyday and every other one thinks he is a natural born journalist. Since they don't need the money, they work for peanuts."

Max nodded sympathetically. Undoubtedly, they all thought they could be detectives too but their lack of French limited their effectiveness. *Only a matter of time, I suppose.*

"Then let me buy you lunch." Max slid into the chair opposite Harvey.

Harvey glanced around the half-empty room and switched to English. "Do you think it's safe? You are a wanted man."

Speaking in English isn't a bad idea, thought Max. Like Americans with French, few Parisians were fluent in the tongue of their long-time British foes.

"I'm merely a person of interest. The police are too busy catching actual criminals to put a watch on every café in Paris."

"You know what they say, there's always a cop when you don't want one."

"I'll take my chances."

"Well, then, if I'd known you were coming, I'd have picked a nicer spot. Still, needs must." He gestured to the waiter who looked relieved that his table would be used for more than a place to cool coffee. Harvey ordered croque-monsieur and a glass of beer; Max took a quick look at the menu and chose a cassoulet with a large glass of Syrah. It was more than he needed but the food at L'Aquilon, while hearty, was frequently the same from day to day. He had grown used to variety since arriving in Paris.

"I assume this isn't a social call," said Harvey, when the drinks had been served.

"I was hoping you could tell me more about the circumstances around the death of Bernard Dietrich. The papers give contradictory accounts."

"That's because the Prefecture has been surprisingly cagey. These things are usually pretty cut and dried, you know. One *malfrat* kills another *malfrat*; round up the usual suspects. They are hiding something but it isn't clear what it is. In the absence of evidence, some journalists have the unfortunate habit of making things up in hopes the police will contradict them."

"Not you surely."

"As one ages, one learns to use whatever works. You'll see."

Max sometimes felt he had already aged well beyond his twenty-seven plus years; perhaps it was the trenches or, perhaps it was the murders he had forced himself into solving. He was already willing to use whatever worked.

"Has it helped?"

"Not so far. I think the police are somehow involved."

"*L'Humanite* said exactly the same thing."

"I read that." Max was forced to wait for Harvey's opinion as the food had arrived and the older man attacked his sandwich like he hadn't eaten in days — which perhaps he hadn't. When he had finished half of it, while Max had only taken a few bites of his own lunch, he continued. "I don't think it went that far. No officer was there when the trigger was pulled—not always the case by the way—but they are involved somehow. I was there for the official update yesterday. If I didn't know better, I would say Fontaine was embarrassed at the lack of detail."

"It takes a lot to embarrass Captain Fontaine."

"I think his new found responsibilities are beginning to weigh on him. And burdens make you stronger."

If they don't crush you, thought Max.

Harvey had little more to add and expressed reluctance at digging deeper into what the Prefecture might be hiding. "One visit to their cells is quite enough."

Harvey had gotten him involved in this case, a case that had expanded from trying to find an alibi for his sometime employee. Before parting, he decided the man owed him a final question.

"Would you be surprised to learn that LeFoie and Bilodeau were working together on something, something quite big I think?"

Harvey paused with his beer glass halfway to his mouth. His eyes slowly widened as the significance of Max's question sunk in. "Then they were probably killed by the same person. I had thought... well, that Bilodeau was somehow involved in Réjean's death and she had been killed by someone else by way of revenge."

It was the first time Harvey had referred to LeFoie by his first name alone. Max wondered at the significance of it; were the two men something other than professional and romantic rivals. Had they been friends?

"Look, Max," said Harvey. "This revelation is... disturbing. If someone is killing journalists—"

"I think they killed Dietrich, too."

"Small comfort. I appreciate the lunch Max and, really, all you've done for me over the years. But I'd prefer you don't seek me out again until this thing, whatever it is, is all over."

"Not even to give you a scoop?" Max said, half-jokingly.

"Who would I sell it to? Not all of these would-be journalists are talentless, and, as I say, they work cheap. I mostly make my money doing a little research these days. And informing on my enemies and acquaintances for cash."

It was Max's turn to look around the café this time. It had filled while they were speaking and the waiter was glaring at them as they lingered over their food. "Should I be worried?"

"I mostly inform to you," said Harvey with a wistful smile, "and I like to think we are more than acquaintances."

"I like to think that, too." Max gestured to the waiter for the bill. While he had his billfold out, he pulled out three five hundred-franc notes and passed them to Harvey, who hesitated but then took them and shoved them inside his jacket. "To tide you over until we can work together again."

"I shouldn't take it, then," said Harvey, though he made no move to retrieve the bills. "I have a brother in Chicago I haven't seen in thirty years. He's alone now and has offered me a place to stay. I'm thinking of going."

Max felt a real pang at the thought. "Then keep it as a going-away present."

Harvey nodded and reached out his hand. "Stay safe, my friend."

MAX'S NEXT STOP WAS the boarding house that Phillippe Latour used both as a residence and an office. He wasn't there and, according to the concierge, hadn't been for several days, meaning he had disappeared shortly after Dietrich's body was discovered. He checked in at several of the bars the man was known to frequent but got the same story—no Latour since Friday night. Max hoped that nothing had happened to him. He took a long walk along the Seine, hoping it would somehow all coalesce as it sometimes did while he moved, but nothing came of it but sore feet.

He arrived back at L'Aquilon as the hour approached midnight, entering by a side door to which Jean-Marc had given him a key. The hotel manager had clearly been on the watch for him because Max had only been in his room a few minutes when a sharp rap came at the door.

"The flics have been here twice today, asking about you. I showed them the register and swore I hadn't seen you but I'm sure there is one watching the front door." Jean-Marc looked down at his hands.

"I'll be out in an hour," said Max. "I don't want to get you into trouble on my account."

Jean-Marc looked relieved. "If there is anything I can do...?"

Max retrieved his Webley, wrapped in a thick cloth, from the compartment at the back of the wardrobe. "Could you keep this in your safe until I can come for it?"

"What is it?"

Max hesitated. "It's a pistol. It hasn't been fired recently, if you are worried about that."

Jean-Marc took the bundle. "You came here at the recommendation of Henri Compte; everything you have done has confirmed his faith in you."

Henri had rescued Max from robbery or worse the first day he arrived in Paris and brought him to this hotel. Had he been such an open book, or was Henri naïve in his judge of character? He suspected it was the former. He had, as Cleroux had said, little talent for deception.

True to his word, Max slipped out of the hotel and into the darkness. He stood in a doorway a block or so from the front entrance to L'Aquilon for several hours until he was sure Jean-Marc was right. The lone police agent was replaced by two new ones an hour before dawn, with the second slipping down the alley to watch the side entrance. *Too late*, thought Max, as he turned to go.

He walked up to the northern train station and contemplated his options. He had none. No, he thought, I have one, but he's not going to like it.

Chapter 20 Thursday to Saturday, October 27-29, 1921

M ax had the good grace to wait until light had started to appear in the eastern sky before knocking on Ginger Buchan's door. After the third try, the door cracked open and a bleary-eyed face appeared.

"Do you know what time it is?" Buchan asked.

"Ten to seven." Buchan's French was more than adequate but he preferred to speak in English so Max obliged him.

"That late? Good, I never need more than four hours sleep anyway." The door cracked open another few inches, revealing the ginger-haired diplomat in blue silk pajamas and a brocaded dressing gown. Pale ankles showed above a pair of black leather slippers.

"Aren't you in jail?" The door opened another few inches. The apartment beyond was immaculate save for a crumpled tuxedo draped over one of the living room wingback chairs.

"No."

"Well, you should be." Buchan opened the door wider. "Come on in. I'll call for breakfast. There is a place across the street who will bring it up to those of us too lazy to cook and too poor to have servants." He lifted the receiver from the telephone on the table next to the door while waving Max to take a seat in the living room.

He dropped his pack on the floor beside the door and subsided into the wingback chair not occupied with Buchan's evening wear. He was exhausted from his night of walking the back streets of Paris, avoiding those areas likely to be under police watch. He wanted nothing more than to sleep. Buchan busied himself setting out plates and cutlery on the small table in the dining alcove until a sharp rap on the door announced the arrival of breakfast. A waiter in a striped shirt and crisp white apron delivered a covered tray to the table and nodded his gratitude at the generous tip Buchan dropped in his palm.

Buchan poured coffee and offered to add a small dollop of brandy to the cup. Max declined and Buchan frowned before adding a half-ounce to his own. Breakfast consisted of an assortment of fruit—sliced pears, dark purple grapes, a few overripe figs and a jar of strawberry compote—a basket of fresh-baked croissants, brioche and cherry tarts and, as a sop to American tastes, a couple of soft-boiled eggs and a rasher of bacon. Buchan waited until Max had made his selections, a couple of the pastries, a pair of figs and a handful of grapes, before loading his own plate with most of the remaining food, only leaving the cherry tarts, one piece of brioche and some of the figs.

"Cherry doesn't agree with me," said Buchan by way of explanation. "And I thought you might like seconds."

Max nodded his appreciation, but only picked at his food. The stress of the last few days had blunted his usual hearty appetite. He finished his coffee and poured them both another cup. He offered Buchan the brandy but the diplomat shook his head.

"I only need a couple of hairs from the dog, not the whole pelt."

When Buchan had finished half his plate, he paused and looked searchingly at his dining companion. "Rousing a man from a deep sleep is hardly friendly. I might not have been alone."

Max raised an eyebrow at that. He had seen Buchan with a number of women but he sensed they came second to his work. "Don't you have a reputation to protect?"

"Quite right, Maxwell," Buchan drawled, displaying his southern roots. "Which is why having a wanted criminal appear at my door before the sun is up is quite...disturbing."

"I'm only a person of interest," Max protested. "But I have work to do which I can't do in the cells while Fontaine dithers about."

"So?"

"So, I was wondering if you could put me up for a couple of days..."

Buchan frowned again. "Hide you, you mean."

"I suppose..."

"How are you going to work any better hiding here than locked in the cells?"

It was a fair question but Max had had several hours to anticipate it and work out a plan. "I have several agents in the field. You could take instructions to work and leave them at the front desk of the embassy. They would drop reports the same way. It's not ideal but it could work to advance the case."

"A case that now includes three murders." Buchan didn't sound pleased and Max tried to think of where else he could go. There were plenty of hotels but he couldn't check into most of them without showing his papers.

"And several bombings, I think."

"I'm hiding you from both the police and some wild-eyed anarchists."

"I don't think anarchists are involved."

"Well, that's a relief." Buchan frowned for a few minutes and then suddenly broke into a broad smile. "It occurs to me that you will be deep in my debt if I agree to accommodate you. I may ask you to accommodate me in the future."

"Accomo—oh." Max had almost forgotten how often English words could mean two quite different things, an odd necessity in a language notorious for the expanse of its vocabulary. Buchan was more than a diplomat; he was a spy and maybe more. He might well ask Max to do something to advance American interests, a request it would be awkward now to refuse. *But what other choice do I have?*

"I will owe you favours, it's true…"

"Don't worry, Max, I won't ask you to assassinate anyone. That's outside my purview; I think the State department handles that." Buchan laughed and Max decided to take it as a joke.

As Buchan dressed for work, Max scribbled a note to Jake explaining the communication plan. He stuck it in an embassy envelope and addressed it to himself in block letters. Jake would expect it was something important and would open it and pass on the instructions. Buchan promised to mail it as soon as he got to the American embassy on rue de Chaillot. "There are a few sandwiches in the icebox that should be edible and help yourself to whatever you can find in the liquor cabinet – except for the 1900 Chateau Margaux, I'm saving it for a special occasion."

Max hated being inactive but Fontaine had left him little choice. Several times during the day he considered a quick visit to his apartment to retrieve the code books, though he suspected he had gained all he could from them. Deciphering the basic code was one thing, but determining who was represented by the various nicknames or what the references to dates signified was quite another. Still, at least he would be doing something. Shortly after lunch, Buchan called with the news that his apartment was under constant surveillance and police agents had been spotted at Chez Jake and Le Coq Bleu. "Apparently, you are an exceptionally interesting person."

After an afternoon of reading week-old American papers, Max was ready to tear the paint off the walls. This was almost as bad as days spent in the trenches waiting for the next German attack. At least the seating was more comfortable. He peered through the curtained windows but saw no signs of watchers outside the apartment building. When he finally saw Buchan approaching from the nearby Metro station, he breathed a sigh of relief.

"I can't stay. There is an embassy dinner for the Turkish Ambassador to celebrate the signing of the Treaty of Ankara. The Great War is finally officially over." He handed over a cloth bag. "I picked you up some beef stew. It should still be warm for a while yet. Dishes are in the mahogany cupboard next to the table."

Max put the bag on the dining room table and set a place for himself while Buchan changed into formal wear. "Here, help me with this bowtie, will you? I can never get the damn thing even."

Max doubted his skills were any better but Buchan seemed satisfied with his efforts. "I have some news before I go. My contacts at the Prefecture tell me the police have recovered the murder weapon but are reluctant to reveal that fact. It's a Lebel, similar to your Webley but with an 8mm cartridge. It's standard police issue, although the French Gendarmerie just took delivery of 2000 Mauser C96s – bigger bullet and larger magazine—so that will change."

"You're saying Dietrich was shot with a police revolver?"

"Not only that, but one whose serial number is registered with the Paris Prefecture."

"Then the flics were involved in his death."

"Not necessarily. My informant said the pistol was reported stolen about a week ago but that's all he had."

After Buchan had departed for his gala, Max sat staring at the phone by the door for several long minutes. Finally, he picked it up and asked to be connected to the Prefecture. He covered the mouth piece with his handkerchief to muffle his voice. He was surprised, but pleased, when Hubert Lepêcheur answered, his northern France accent quite distinctive. He had hoped to reach the Sergeant but hadn't expected him to be answering the main phone line.

"How can I direct your call?" There was a note of resignation in the man's voice.

"Hubert. It's Max Anderson."

"Where are you? You sound a million miles away. Have you left the country?"

Max removed the cloth from the mouthpiece. "I'm not so far." While the Embassy was technically considered American soil, he didn't suppose the same applied to Buchan's apartment. "Are they short-staffed at the Prefecture? Or do Sergeants' job descriptions include reception duties?"

"They don't." Lepêcheur hesitated. "I've temporarily been reduced in rank. I'm lucky I'm not back directing traffic."

"Then, it was your gun that was stolen." Max took a shot in the dark and hit a bullseye.

"Is it common knowledge then that even private detectives on the run know of my misfortune?" The man sounded genuinely despondent.

"Lucky guess, Hubert. I heard about the gun and when a good cop gets demoted... well, it was a logical conclusion."

"I suppose."

"Any details you can share?"

"It was taken from a locked cabinet in the armory. It had to have been someone who had access."

"An inside job, then."

"It must be. Fontaine has questioned everyone who has been on duty from the time I last saw the pistol until the night of Dietrich's murder but so far, no one will admit to the theft. I shouldn't be telling you this, but I've become a pariah. If I could discover who..."

"If I find out, you'll be the first one I tell."

Lepêcheur sighed. "That might help get my career back on track. I... well, thanks, Max." Another call came in and the former-sergeant had to disconnect.

Max felt sorry for the man; he was a good cop and didn't deserve to be treated like a criminal though he supposed his superiors had little choice but to make an example of him.

Max slept better that night, even on Buchan's too small chesterfield, knowing that the noose was loosening. Even Fontaine wouldn't imagine how Max could have stolen a pistol from a locked room in the Prefecture itself. He wondered if Gereau had any idea who might have taken the gun; he seemed to know everything that happened within the stone walls of police headquarters, though that might have changed since his recent retirement.

He didn't hear Buchan return but heard him gently snoring through the thin door of his bedroom when he made his way to the bathroom in the morning. Despite Buchan's claim to be too lazy to cook, his larder had the makings of an adequate breakfast. Max had coffee made and bacon and eggs frying on the hotplate and bread warming in the small oven, when Buchan stumbled from his bedroom, still in his pajamas.

"Am I in heaven?" he asked, sniffing the air.

"Yeah, and I'm your guardian angel."

"More like my resident devil." Buchan took a cup of coffee and headed back to his room, returning a few minutes later in business attire. He held out his cup for a refill and took his place at the table as Max served him a plate of bacon, eggs, toast and a few leftover figs from the day before.

"You seem in a better mood this morning," said Buchan, said between bites.

"The stolen gun belonged to a friend of mine who is keen to clear his name. It was obviously an inside job and inquiries are being made but no clues yet as to the culprit." Something niggled at the back of his mind but he couldn't quite pin it down. "If I can find out who took the gun, the rest should all fall into place."

"Maybe," said Buchan, 'but tracing its journey from a weapons locker to Dietrich's murder could be more complicated than you think. Jacques stole it for money and sold it to Jean who passed it on to Michel—you get my drift."

Buchan could be right but Max didn't think so. Someone stole the pistol for the purpose of killing Dietrich and, either did it themselves or placed it in the hand of the person who pulled the trigger. For the first time since he'd been wakened by Erich Harvey's call, he felt he was on the right track. The sooner he could get back on the streets, the better.

"By the way," said Buchan, "I've asked Gustav Reinhardt to drop by and talk to you. I pay him a retainer but a little extra cash might loosen his tongue. He's surprisingly informative when he's in the right mood.

AS PROMISED, REINHARDT showed up shortly after four that afternoon. Max had spent most of the day, going over what he knew and, more importantly what he needed to know, to question his informant effectively. He had gotten word to Jake via Buchan that he needed a few thousand francs in fifties and hundreds and a messenger had arrived at Buchan's apartment just before lunch. Finding little to eat in the larder, Max had risked a quick jaunt across the street to pick up a sandwich, plus a basket of pastries in case Reinhardt were hungry. A full stomach was often conducive to an open mouth.

More than anything else, he wanted to discover two things. Were the three murders linked as he suspected and were they also connected to the series of bombings (there had been another newsstand blown up the night before) that were plaguing the city? No lives had been lost in the last few attacks and the newspapers had been deliberately downplaying them so as not to encourage the bombers but it was clear that journalists and police were on edge.

Reinhardt was dressed in the latest fashion, a light brown pinstripe three-piece suit with cuffed trousers and wide lapels over a pale-yellow silk shirt with a pleated front and a matching collar.

Two-tone Oxfords and a straw boater hat finished the ensemble. He carried a long black overcoat on one arm and a matching pair of leather gloves in the other hand.

"You're Max Anderson?" Reinhardt asked, as Max took his overcoat and gloves and put them in the hall vestibule. He gave Max a long appraising look, as if sizing him up for a fight. Max returned the favour. Reinhardt might be dressed as a dandy, with his carefully pomaded hair and gold watchchain across his vest, but his hands were big with scars on the knuckles. His face, too, had the marks of brawling though not enough to ruin his rough good looks.

"Mr. Reinhardt, can I offer you something to eat or a drink?" Reinhardt had crossed the room to one of the wingback chairs, the one facing away from the window where afternoon sun played on the closed curtain. He dropped his hat on the side table and crossed his feet at the ankles.

"I'll have some of that American whiskey Buchan is so fond of. Neat, if you don't mind."

Max found a bottle of Kentucky bourbon in the liquor cabinet and poured a generous two fingers into a tumbler. He opted for a small serving of pastis, adding a considerable dollop of water to dilute the potent liquid. If Reinhardt was going to seize the advantage of the sun's glare, he would take the one afforded by a clearer head.

Reinhardt checked his pocket watch, gold or a good simulation. "Let's get to the point; I've an early dinner date and it's on the other side of the city. You have questions, I might have answers. Depending..." He rubbed his thumb and forefinger together.

"I pay a hundred francs for every useful piece of information; I get to judge what's useful." It was twice his usual rate but Reinhardt clearly had expensive tastes.

Reinhardt nodded his agreement and leaned back in the chair with his fingers steepled in front of his face, further obscuring his expression.

"You knew Réjean LeFoie and Nicole Bilodeau from your time with the AF."

"Sure, I saw them both around from time to time though never together, which was odd since they were supposed to be engaged. LeFoie soon wore out his welcome but Bilodeau was tight with a lot of the main players, and a few, like Bucard, who operated on the fringe of the movement."

Max put a hundred franc note on the table next to him, more to encourage Reinhardt than because he had told him something new, though the fact the two reporters kept their distance was interesting.

"Is there a pattern to the series of bombings? I think there have been seven so far. If there is, I can't see it."

"That's because you're looking too hard for a pattern, instead of considering them one by one. Only three are linked, the first, the third and the one last night. The other four: a cover-up, insurance fraud, petty revenge on a journalist who was sleeping with the wrong married woman, boys being boys playing with toys—one lost his hand and the other two are under arrest. The target, the technique, time of day and location are all over the place. The police are keeping quiet about it because they don't like what the three important ones look like."

Max put another hundred-franc note down. The first and the third were newspaper offices, but so was the second one; the one last night had been a bookstore that specialized in anti-Dreyfusard tracts, even publishing some of them on site. "Why isn't the second one part of the pattern? It was a newspaper office, too. And a conservative one."

"A clever accountant had been draining some friends of mine dry; he used a bomb to cover his tracks, hoping the police would lump it in with the first explosion. Unfortunately, he wasn't as clever as he thought. I recovered the cash, gave him a beating, and sent him back to where he came from. Madrid."

"Three bombings of conservative—or at least not Liberal—publishers. A plot to cast suspicion on people on the left—"

"Or anarchists."

"You were seen on the night of the first bombing at The Real Truth news office. You were with Nicole Bilodeau. You both went inside. A couple of hours later the place blew up, killing the editor."

"I don't deny being there," said Reinhardt. "The publisher—there are such things as conservative Jews, you know—was sympathetic to the cause and there had been threats. I was sent to make sure there was nothing to them. Bilodeau was curious as to how I work. We went inside and made sure the door locks were working and nothing was amiss, No sign of a bomb. That came later. It was... embarrassing."

"When the police hauled you in, you accused Phillippe LaTour of being the mastermind behind the attack."

"I don't know who told you that but he was lying. Sure, I saw LaTour there—"

"He was working for me, following Bilodeau."

"Then he's in the clear. However, I may be a lot of things but I don't shop on people, even if they deserve it."

Max put two more bills on the pile; one for the explanation of Bilodeau's presence at the bomb site and another for revealing that LaTour had lied to him about Reinhardt's accusation. He didn't know what that meant but he knew it meant something.

"I know the connection between LeFoie and Bilodeau—"

"Something more than their reputed engagement?"

"A lot more. But what was their connection to Dietrich?"

"You've probably heard I'm all wrapped up in the Camelots, tight with the people they work for, right?"

"But you're not. Otherwise, you wouldn't be here right now in an American diplomat's apartment."

"A *Jewish* American *spy's* apartment."

Max raised his eyebrow at that. Buchan didn't hide his religion but he didn't actively advertise it either. He had told Max once that he was from the Reform branch of the faith and eschewed outward symbols of his religion so as not to interfere with his work. He was surprised he would have revealed himself to a man like Reinhardt.

"Dietrich was sort of like me but coming from the other side of the street. He was an anarchist, sure, but one willing to work for whoever paid him. I even saw him at an AF meeting once, discussing something with Bucard. The latter didn't look happy, but then he seldom does. I suspect Dietrich was telling tales and the journalists were paying him."

That makes a kind of sense, thought Max. If he had been one of their prime informants, he might well know the inside story, might well become a target for their killer if he threatened to reveal it. Max added another bill to the total.

Rienhardt checked his watch again and rose to leave. As he reached for the money, Max dropped another couple hundred francs on the pile. "In case you remember some detail that might be useful."

The former Camelot tucked the cash into his inside jacket pocket and flashed Max a generous smile. "I'll be in touch. No need to get up. I know my way."

After the man had left, Max sat in the wingback chair for some time, considering what Reinhardt had told him. Maybe Bilodeau had gone to the newspaper office for her own reasons as part of the investigation she and LeFoie had been undertaking. It made sense that she would try to discover LeFoie's killer. They weren't lovers—that was simply a cover to allow them to see each other without arousing suspicion—but had a close working relationship. Harvey had blown their cover; if he had told on LeFoie to Bilodeau, he certainly was capable of repeating it to someone else.

Harvey probably wouldn't remember who might have overheard his drunken ramblings but Max was pretty sure that someone had gotten wind of LeFoie and Bilodeau's real connection, though maybe not until LeFoie had already been killed for betraying those behind the plot,—whatever that plot might have been. He needed to talk to Harvey again and he needed to get back to the code books to finally put it all together.

He was tempted to sneak back to his apartment under the cover of darkness but could not risk incarceration when he was getting so close to the truth. He dined on the remains of his sandwich, the basket of pastries and a half bottle of sauterne before curling up on Buchan's sofa for a fitful night's rest.

Max woke to a glare of watery October sun on his face and the smell of coffee wafting from the dining room. He ran his hand through his hair and staggered down the hall to the bathroom before joining Buchan and his guests at the table. Alain and Hugo were already helping themselves to pastries and compote.

"Alain! Hugo! You're back."

"Barely," said Alain around a mouthful of croissant. "We just got off the train from Chartres. Luckily, Henri was at the station having coffee with some of his old cronies and he directed us here. Mr. Buchan said to let you sleep and then ordered in some breakfast."

"Hugo must have sent you on a wild goose chase," Max said, laughing.

The two young men exchanged glances. "I'll let Hugo tell his own story."

"As you know, I went to visit my parents in Chartres. I was there a few days and the weather was so nice that my mother suggested we spend a day or two at Saint Nazaire. I have an uncle there so we could stay for nothing. The first morning, I was feeling a little restless so I went for a walk along the boulevard that fronts the beach. I hadn't gone more than a block or two, when a black car pulled up beside me. A large man—he must have weighed 100 kilograms—wearing a black hood over his head leapt out and grabbed me. A smaller man was behind the wheel of the car. I struggled but the big man put a cloth over my mouth. I knew at once it was chloroform; I had smelled it often enough at the hospital.

"The next thing I knew, I was the one wearing a hood, this one without eyeholes so I couldn't tell if it was night or day. I was tied to a chair. I could hear the men moving. There was just the two of them as far as I could tell. Once they knew I was awake, they took turns questioning me. The hood muffled the sound so I don't know if I could recognize them if I heard them again, but I thought they were from the north.

"They seemed to know a lot about you and a little about me. Somehow, they knew I had been in your office and wanted to know what I had seen there. I told them I'd been drinking and really didn't remember much but they wouldn't let up. One of them was getting pretty mad and I was afraid they might get violent. At first, they seemed to want me to describe everything but eventually they gave that up and asked me if I had seen any odd books or journals. I think they had something specific in mind but all I could remember were a few novels and a ledger of some kind. At last, one of them said: 'He must have hidden them somewhere else. We'll have to wait until the prefecture stops watching his apartment and bars.' After that they dumped me back in the car and we drove around for a while. Then they untied me and pushed me onto the road, with the hood still over my head. By the time I'd got it loose, they had driven off. I hurried home—I'd been gone an entire day and night—to find my parents in a panic and Alain waiting to take me back to Paris. What was it all about?"

Max knew exactly what it was all about: the secret coded journals that were still hidden on Rue Lepic. They had failed to get them when they killed LeFoie and had their search interrupted when they killed Bilodeau. Two men, one large and one small, had grabbed Hugo. They could have killed him. Max wondered why they hadn't. Unless they were trying to send a message to him, that they could lay their hands on anyone, do what they willed to them, and would if he didn't stay out of their way.

Chapter 21 Saturday October 29th, 1921

Buchan took Hugo to the Prefecture after breakfast and returned to report that Max was no longer wanted for questioning, although Fontaine, who had been called in specially to hear the alibi Hugo provided, said he would be interested in an informal chat "at Max's convenience," perhaps later that evening at Le Coq Bleu. He had no comment (or perhaps no clue) as to who might have abducted Hugo. "He acted like he didn't believe me," said Hugo before gathering his things and heading back to his rooms. Alain had already departed but promised to check in with Max on Monday.

Max thanked Buchan for his help and hospitality to which Buchan replied: "You owe me." With those words jangling in his ears, he determined to head for Le Coq Bleu to check in on his friends but, more importantly, to discover if they had any idea if Jacqui had been released and where he might find her.

He took the Metro at Place Monge, changing at Chatelet to arrive at Gare Nord some twenty minutes later. From there he could walk to Hotel L'Aquilon to recover his Webley from Jean-Marc's safe. and another twenty minutes at a brisk pace would take him to Le Coq Bleu half way up the hill at Montmartre. After so many days stuck inside, he was looking forward to the exercise.

After leaving Rue Nord, he spotted Alphonse Gereau coming out of a small café on Rue de Compeigne with a younger man of medium height. Max didn't recognize him, though he seemed vaguely familiar. They shook hands and the younger man continued down the street while Gereau turned and headed back toward the train station. Max crossed the street to intercept him. The former police Captain didn't seem all that pleased to see him.

"I take it Fontaine is no longer planning to arrest you. Or should I be escorting you to the Prefecture?" Gereau had continued to stride toward the station and Max had to hurry to keep up.

"I was hoping to ask you a few questions."

"I am already late for an appointment," Gereau said, not looking in Max's direction. "It will have to wait."

"It won't take long. I could ride the Metro with—"

Gereau stopped and turned suddenly, his hand shooting out to grab Max's arm. The expression on his face was unreadable, as if he were feeling several emotions at once—anger, sadness, fear—and couldn't decide which one he preferred. "Where I'm going, Max, you cannot follow."

"Is there something wrong? Is there something I can do—"

Gereau cut him off again. "No." He released Max's arm and rubbed his hand across his face. "Have you ever started out for someplace, sure you knew the way, but then found yourself walking down an unfamiliar path?"

"I suppose..."

"When that happens, Max, there is only one thing to do. You have to forge ahead, confident your feet will find the way." Gereau chuckled humourlessly. "You see, in Paris, everything always comes back to the beginning. Remember that and you can never be lost. Now I must go and so must you. I'm sure your friends are waiting to see you."

Gereau knew about the release of Yesim and the other anarchist suspects. It was as if he somehow blamed Max for the outcome.

"Maybe we can talk again, when you are not so occupied."

"Perhaps..." said Gereau, but he was already walking away. Max watched him until he disappeared into the cavernous entrance to Gare Nord. *Something is troubling Gereau,* Max thought, *and he doesn't trust me enough to tell me what.* Max felt a brief wave of sadness, the same one that came over him whenever he thought of Havel Barzani or his father.

When Max finally reached Le Coq Bleu, Yesim was busily rearranging the glasses behind the tin bar while Henri muttered over a glass of brandy. "Just when Josette and I had everything perfectly organized."

Yesim grunted and slid a glass and the brandy bottle in Max's direction. It was barely time for lunch but he poured himself a small glass and raised it to toast Yesim's return. Yesim grunted again and kept rearranging the glassware.

"I thought you'd be happy to be out of jail and back where you belong."

"I'm happy. Can't you tell I'm happy?"

"So that's what you look like when you're happy," said Max. "What do you have for lunch?"

"I don't know. Ask the maître d'." Yesim gestured at Henri.

"What's going on?"

"The first thing he did when he got back was to fire Josette. I told him if she went so would I and he said that was fine; he had managed without us before."

Then, there's nothing for lunch?" Max glanced from Henri to Yesim and back again.

"Quite the contrary," said Henri. "We have pork chops in rhubarb sauce and green beans almandine. If you prefer fish, we have some Greek-style mackerel with black olives and au gratin potatoes and sweet pepper salad."

Max raised his eyebrows. "Did you install a full kitchen while I was away?"

"Josette's uncle is the chef at Lux-Bar on Rue Lepic," said Henri. "On Saturdays and Sundays, he provides us with half a dozen plates of whatever two meals are on special there at a discount. Josette brings them over in a covered basket. When they're gone, we have a hearty beef soup and sandwiches that Josette and I make in the back. We give Yesim a cut and split the rest. That way I can work part-time behind the bar and Josette is not Yesim's problem."

Max tried not to laugh; it was exactly the kind of cock-eyed scheme the two old friends would come up with so they could both get their way. "And how is it working out?"

"I think we are about to find out," said Henri as three couples of bluff-looking Americans pushed through the door and took seats at the two tables closest to the street. Henri bustled over and described the menu in a mixture of simple French and train-station English. One of the men answered in French and Henri was soon scribbling orders on a small notepad.

Josette had appeared as if by magic and was soon delivering plates of food, carafes of red and white wine and mugs of beer to the tables.

"They took three of each," said Henri, rubbing his hands together and looking out the window, "and looks like four more customers are on the way. If you want one of the specials, you better order it now."

"Save it for the paying customers," said Max. "I'll have soup and a sandwich and a small lager."

Yesim poured the beer and leaned across the bar and whispered in a low voice. "I haven't seen Henri this happy in years."

"You don't mind then?"

Yesim's mouth tightened in a supressed smile as he glanced at Josette, laughing at something one of the customers had said. "A young woman isn't exactly bad for business—and she's a hard worker, too. If this works out... the cafe next door is up for sale, you know."

"I do now," said Max. "It will be expensive but I think I can find the money."

Yesim let his smile free. "I have a little saved, too. I had set it aside for Minette's dowry but..."

Max laid his hand on Yesim's arm. It was the first time he had mentioned his niece since she had died in the flu epidemic. "Let's all talk about it after closing tonight."

The smile had left Yesim's face and his attention was riveted on the face of a man peering through the side window. Max started to turn but Yesim shook his head.

"Someone you know?" asked Max.

"No, and that's the problem. If he wants a drink or is expecting to meet someone, why doesn't he come inside, instead of gawping like a yokel at the zoo?"

"Maybe he's curious about—"

"No, he's a police agent."

Max doubted the police were spying on Le Coq Bleu, though you could never tell with the Prefecture. Yesim was clearly more shaken by his time in the cells than he was letting on. It might be a while before he was comfortable with strangers in his bar which made this evening's proposed conversation complicated.

"Let him look—there's nothing to see here, right? Cleroux told me the magistrate didn't just drop all charges but apologized for the excessive zeal of the officers involved."

"Hah! A lot of red faces watched as we marched out of court singing the Black Internationale. It brought tears to my eyes."

The man in question had apparently satisfied his curiosity and drifted down the stairs that led to Rue Chappe. Before Yesim could pick out another target for his suspicions—several more men had entered the bar in singles and pairs and were ordering food from Josette—Max asked if he had heard from Jacqui.

"Briefly," said Yesim, as he busied himself pouring the drinks for his new customers. Max signaled for another lager himself, mostly to keep the conversation going. "She was pretty shaken. It was her first time in jail, believe it or not, and I don't think she ever wants to go back.

"Don't worry. She's still in Paris but has taken a room under an assumed name. And, before you ask, I don't know what it is; I didn't want to know. She said she will send for you when she feels it is safe."

Frustration knotted his stomach but there was little he could do. Jacqui would call for him when she felt it was safe for her to do so. Why couldn't she see that the safest place she could be was with him? *No.* he thought, *that isn't fair. I didn't keep her out of jail in the first place; why should she think I could do it now?*

He knew the only way to make Jacqui feel safe under the present circumstances was to solve these crimes and bring the perpetrators to justice. But how?

Latour had lied to him and was now avoiding him. He was a small man. One of the killers was a small man. It wasn't much but it was what he had. Finding Latour had to be the first order of business.

Max was finishing his last sip of beer when a real police agent came through the door. Captain Fontaine was out of uniform again but his swagger as he entered the bar drew every eye to him. Several men, nursing drinks at one of the tables at the back of the room shifted uneasily but Fontaine ignored them and walked over to Max, taking the stool next to him.

"Is there somewhere we can talk in private, away from prying ears?" He gazed pointedly at Yesim and Henri.

"I'll only tell them what you said after you leave."

"Then it will be hearsay, inadmissible in court." Fontaine laughed. "Seriously, some of what I tell you, you may not want to share."

"You can use my quarters," said Yesim. "If you don't mind the mess."

Max led the way behind the bar and up the narrow stair to the second level where Yesim kept a small apartment, nothing more than two tiny bedrooms, a sitting area and a toilet and wash basin. He used the sparsely equipped kitchen off the bar to make his meals. *That will need expanding*, thought Max, *if we are going to go from a bar that serves food to a restaurant that serves drinks.*

Yesim normally kept the place remarkably tidy but now books were scattered over most surfaces—Henri's doing he supposed—and a large black flag was tacked to one wall.

"Yesim had almost forgotten his anarchist past, until you had him arrested."

"That wasn't my idea, you know." Fontaine cleared the most comfortable chair of books and took a seat.

"I thought Gereau was retired."

"Not retired enough for my liking. He still has his sycophants in the Prefecture."

Max felt a certain sympathy. He had spent his teen years dominated by an overbearing uncle and only the war had allowed him to escape. It must be hard for Fontaine to work in the shadow of Gereau. Max spotted a half-empty bottle of brandy on a sideboard along with a few mostly-clean glasses. He poured them both a couple of fingers and handed a glass to Fontaine, who looked at it dubiously before taking a sip.

"That's better than the stuff he serves downstairs."

"Better than the stuff he serves to you," said Max.

"The policeman's lot is not a happy one," Fontaine sang in barely-accented English. "Don't look so surprised. I'm much more sophisticated that most people think."

More sophisticated than me, thought Max, who didn't recognize the lyric. "You wanted to talk?"

"It wasn't easy to persuade the magistrate to cancel the warrant for your arrest. I think he was under pressure from the Prefect himself."

"What does he have against me?"

"Not you in particular. M. Leullier dislikes all foreigners, especially Americans."

"I'm Canadian."

"Unlike me, the Prefect does not make fine distinctions. He's very strict about keeping track of foreign nationals in Paris. He tried to extend his grasp over legitimate residents by introducing a new identity card, you know, this one with fingerprints. When they told Leullier it was an insult to honest Frenchmen, well, I thought he was going to have a stroke."

"I'm glad you were able to overcome his resistance."

Fontaine finished his drink and held out the tumbler for more. "Don't look shocked; I'm officially off duty."

Max poured Fontaine another drink but sat his own glass on the table beside his chair.

"You are not exactly off the hook. The Prefect still thinks you are involved, not quite a suspect, mind you, but close enough that a wrong foot will land you in the cells. The one thing Leullier dislikes more than Americans are private detectives."

"I'll keep that in mind."

"The important thing is that I don't think of you as a suspect." That sounded like the old Fontaine, sure of himself no matter what the circumstances.

"That's a great relief to me, Captain."

"Please, call me Marcel. But only when I'm off duty."

"Of course."

Fontaine stood up abruptly and walked over to the wall displaying the black flag. He lifted it to look at the peeling wallpaper underneath. "This place needs a woman's touch."

Max was surprised at the sudden turn in the conversation.

"My own wife left me last year. She said I was too tied up in my work. Can you imagine?"

"Why tell me?"

"I have more work now but feel less tied up. I'm able to make my own decisions and make my own mistakes. It is strangely liberating. I sometimes think I'd like to get Jeanette back but then, I suspect, without real evidence, other factors were at play. Jealousy is a terrible thing, you know."

"Yes," said Max. "yes, it is."

"I'm sorry, I get like this when I'm off duty, maudlin." Fontaine picked a book off a precariously leaning pile. "Proust. I tried reading him but... well, even my sophistication has its limits."

"I'm sure you didn't come here to discuss books or relationships."

Fontaine returned to his chair and put his untouched drink on the table beside Max's glass. "I think you are right. The three murders and the bombings, at least some of them, are connected, though I don't grasp the underlying plot."

"Neither do I, at least not yet, but I know the motivation is somehow political."

"What isn't, these days? That's the problem for me. Politics and political crimes disturb me. I told you; I think of myself as a patriot. I voted for the Bloc because I thought they were best suited to protect France's interests, to guarantee our security in a turbulent world. If I stop thinking that I might vote for the Socialists or even the anarchists—"

"I don't think they run for public office."

"Hah! You are likely right but you see what I want to say. I'm uncomfortable questioning politicians, even if I knew which ones to question or where to find them. You on the other hand..."

"Fools rush in where the wise call stop. I hope I'm less impulsive than that."

"You *have* been shot at a number of times since the war ended."

Fontaine was right. He had been shot at several times and had guns pointed at him more often than he liked to remember. There were reasons he seldom went out without his five-shot Kolb tucked inside his coat. Other than one notable exception, he had avoided actually shooting someone.

"I could go with you..."

Fontaine made a face and picked up his drink again. "All I'm saying is that you should follow any leads you have, wherever they take you. I'm happy to keep the Prefecture off your back and do what I can to investigate your theories. When you have a suspect and enough evidence to go to court, I'll swoop in and make the arrest. I'm only a phone call away. In the meantime, I will keep an eye out for Gustav Reinhardt and Phillipe Latour and any of the anarchists that got away, just in case."

Reinhardt and Latour mentioned in the same breath by a police captain. It sent a shiver up Max's back. What or who did they have in common?

THE CUSTOMERS KEPT coming well into the night so the business conversation was put off to another time. Returning home at long last, Max was relieved to see no obvious police agents watching his door, unless one of the gaudily-painted prostitutes on the corner was a swallow in disguise. He stashed his Webley in the usual hiding place, took out the two journals and began to copy information and formulate questions in his own leather covered notebook. Someone would be able to identify the men (or women) referred to only by nickname and he had a pretty good idea whom he might ask. He always knew where to find Colonel Ledux but he wondered if Joseph Asper, a reliable if reluctant informant, was back in town. He would set Alain to searching for him tomorrow.

The nicknames had grown in number: Ironhead, Dunce, Weasel and Sailor Boy were joined by Chateau, The Fist, Tiger, Stinker and The Lieutenant. The dates continued to confuse "my brother's birthday," "the day you stumbled," plus "the convention of fools," and "the Tuesday before we broke up." Cleroux might help with the last one if it referred to the breaking off of their engagement. Tiger might refer to Clemenceau, the wartime leader who had recently returned to active politics.

The rest of the text was all over the place—exactly what you might expect from an ongoing investigation where new facts turned up and old theories were refuted. Max decided to mostly ignore the early pages and focus on the last dozen or so entries. What had at first seemed to the journalists like a widespread plot to overthrow the French state now appeared to be narrower in focus. Instead of a broad conspiracy, they became convinced that it was a fairly small group, half a dozen at most, whose motives were obscure but whose plans were increasingly apparent.

They would stir up public sentiment against specific left-wing groups, notably anarchists, to provide cover for the assassination of one specific man, someone whose death would both lead to a crackdown on the left but also jeopardize the unstable peace with Germany. Whoever it was had to be involved somehow in the payment of reparations, either from inside government or as a vocal critique of the process. There was no shortage of those on both the left and right, though both LeFoie and Bilodeau seemed convinced the target was someone on the right, possibly on the right wing of the governing Bloc National or one of the disgruntled far-right organizations who felt ignored and excluded from power.

Of course, all these conclusions were reached before the string of bombings. Bilodeau must have suspected something like that was afoot, which would explain her visit to the newspaper that was the first target. She had been murdered two nights before the third blast. Had she known about the target? Had she identified the conspirators? Was that why she wanted to see him and why she had been murdered minutes before he got there?

Once again, he felt he knew enough that the evidence was serving up the answer like a bowl of savory stew to a hungry man, but, for some reason, his mind turned away from it as if it were rancid meat. Perhaps the days of fitful sleep in an unfamiliar and uncomfortable bed had caught up with him. Perhaps every thing would be clearer in the morning.

In a topsy-turvy world, anything was possible.

Chapter 22 Sunday-Monday, October 30th-31st

Max was enjoying a leisurely breakfast in the café across the street from his apartment when he spotted Alain turning the corner onto Rue Lepic. He beckoned him over and waited until he had settled and been served food and coffee before asking: "What brings you around so early on a Sunday?"

"Three things," said Alain. "I have some updates on the cases you gave me, including receipts from the search for Hugo. I'm afraid I spent all the money you gave me and a little beside."

"Don't worry. I'll make you whole. Why else are you here?"

"I thought you might have some more work for me to do. Things must have piled up while you were in hiding. Also, I can tell you where Mme Jacqueline is staying. I heard you mention to M. Buchan that you were worried about her."

Max's heart pounded against his ribs. He longed to hear what Alain had to say, longed to rush to her and take her in his arms. But, no, Jacqui had made it clear to him that she needed to be in control of the things in her life, needed to make her own decisions on her own timetable. He would not rush in "when the wise call stop." He needed the one thing he had always lacked: patience.

"I... I don't want her address," he said, "though I'm curious how you found it."

Alain looked perplexed at Max's decision but shrugged and said: "Pure luck, I'm afraid. I was returning from south of the city and spotted her getting off the Metro at Place d'Italie. I followed her and wrote down the address of the rooming house where she stopped. Are you sure you don't want it?"

"I'm sure," said Max. "What else do you have to tell me?"

Alain had tracked down the last of the missing persons who unfortunately had died in hospital nearly two years before. He had been in the south of the city to confirm the burial site at a graveyard beyond the city proper. "I wanted to tie up every loose end before reporting to you."

Alain went on to report that Giamatti was still in the city though he had shifted his accommodation again, this time to the Ritz. It would seem his pockets were deep indeed. "I know the head waiter in The Little Bar—he says Giamatti comes in everyday at about five, sometimes alone, sometimes with a woman, sometimes with a whole crowd."

Good, thought Max. I need to talk to Giamatti again. This time I'll try to be a little more persuasive. Max reimbursed Alain for the balance of the expenses for the trip to Chartres as well as his regular pay that was past due. He described Joseph Asper—short, slim, with dark hair and sharp features—and suggested places he might be found if he indeed was in the city. Alain promised to track him down and report, one way or another, late on Monday if not before.

RETURNING TO HIS FLAT, Max put in a call to Colonel Ledux's residence. His manservant informed Max that Ledux was visiting a friend in the country for the weekend—a notable departure for the reclusive ex-spy. However, he had left standing orders to invite Max to visit if he were in touch. Max made arrangements to drop by at three the next afternoon.

He spent a few minutes jotting down the list of people he wanted to question: Giamatti, Bucard, the newspaper editor Braque,

Reinhardt and Latour if he could track them down, Asper if he was in the city, Harvey for no other reason than the man often knew things he didn't know he knew. Harvey had asked to be left out of it but, to quote the journalist's own words: Needs must. If he required anything from the Prefecture, he could try Fontaine or, better yet, LePêcheur. And, of course, Gereau. He looked at the list and decided it would have to do. He would have liked to see Simonne LeFoie as well if only to see how she and her children were doing but any questions about her husband's private life could probably be answered by Braque.

Satisfied that his next few days would either solve the case or leave it for God to sort out, Max hid one of the coded journals and took the other, LeFoie's, with him. He had to go to Chez Jake anyway and it was as good a place as any to keep the book, especially if he hid it somewhere other than his office. He was sure Jake Sullivan would have someplace secure.

Jake, Smitty and a few of the regulars were hanging around, drifting on and off the stage to take their turns in an improvised jazz festival. He was surprised to discover that Smitty, the large and sometimes fearsome bouncer, had a sweet tenor voice and knew his way around a number of songs, both traditional and popular. They all paused when he arrived to shout their greeting but Max waved them on and pretty soon, he and Jake were seated near the back of the restaurant, listening to a lively bit of ragtime.

"They're pretty good," said Max.

"They are, they are," Jake nodded in time to the music. "But the competition is getting hot both here in Montmartre, but also across the river in Montparnasse. That's the place to be, ever since Picasso and that artist crowd moved out of the Agile Rabbit to new digs in the Latin Quarter."

Le Lapin Agile had been a cabaret and artist haunt since before Max had been born. He'd only visited it once or twice even though it was only a few blocks away. The habitués had seemed weird even by Max's newly broadened sensibilities.

"Anyway, I'm thinking of building on another room on the vacant lot next door. The owner is willing to sell cheap. What do you think?"

"It's your bar."

"Mostly, true. But you're still my partner."

Max had inherited ten percent of the place from Havel Barzani but had made further investments over the years which had doubled his stake. If he wound up as part owner of one more bar, he'd have to give up detective work altogether. He made a note to avoid investment opportunities.

"Do you need money?"

"Probably a little, say another five percent?"

Apparently, they were unavoidable. Both bars are profitable, he thought, which was more than he could say for his day job. "Sure, when do you need it?"

"I'd like to finish the expansion before New Year's."

"Why not?"

They retired to his office, where Max wrote a cheque on his personal account and handed it along with the codebook to Jake. "Hide that but don't tell me where. If anyone asks, you never heard of it."

MAX SAT IN THE LITTLE Bar, a misnomer if there ever was one, with his back to the entrance, when Giamatti entered precisely at five as promised. The Italian had an attractive woman on his arm, the same Max had briefly met the last time he encountered Giamatti. Madame Novak. He watched them in the mirror behind the bar as they were escorted by the head waiter, Alain's friend, to a booth near the back.

Max let them get settled with drinks in front of them before gliding across the bar and sliding into the booth beside Novak.

"Cazzo! You are following me!" Giamatti appeared more surprised than angry.

"You've become a very well-known man about town. You can't stay at the finest hotels in Paris without being noticed."

"I'll keep that in mind. Maybe I'll try the Hotel L'Aquilon. I hear it's nice and cozy."

Max must have looked suitably shocked. Giamatti laughed. "You're not the only one with contacts in Paris, Max."

"I won't keep you from your drinks. I only have a couple of questions."

"And if I don't feel like answering them?"

"Don't be a spoilsport, Jaco," said Novak. "M. Anderson took the trouble to find you, so why not answer his questions? It's not like you have something to hide." She placed the back of her hand against his cheek and moved closer; Giamatti blushed and flashed her a boyish smile.

"You have a fan," said Giamatti. "Go ahead, ask away. I can't guarantee I have any answers but we'll see."

"Do you know anything about a man called Bernard Dietrich?"

"The anarchist the police shot? Only what I read in the papers."

"You should read better papers. He was shot with a police revolver but the Prefecture has determined it was stolen. But I think you know that."

"Why would you think that?"

"Like you say – you have contacts. Dietrich was seen at Action Français meetings on more than one occasion. An odd place for an anarchist perhaps but not for someone more interested in filling his pockets than in fighting for a cause."

"Maybe he was interested in following Valois's lead." Valois was a prominent figure in the AF, running their publishing house and often appearing beside Charles Maurras, the AF's leader at rallies.

"In what way?"

"Valois was an anarchist himself during his youth before he saw the error of his ways. Now, his national syndicalist ideas are starting to permeate through Europe. Benito encourages us all to read his work. A bit dry for my tastes but then I've always considered myself a man of action rather than ideas."

"Oh, you get plenty of ideas," said Novak, stroking Giamatti's face again and bringing on another blush.

"Maybe I have seen this guy a time or two, but Bucard could probably tell you more about him than I could. It was rumored that Dietrich was doing some 'errands' for the old man. "

"I thought you said Bucard is a spent force."

"That may have been premature. He's back in fashion now that his nephew, Marcel, is on the scene. Nothing like a war-hero to burnish a fading reputation."

This was the first that Max had heard of the younger Bucard, though he supposed it made sense. Andre Bucard valued loyalty above all else yet he had often been betrayed by the veniality of his followers. He might well feel more comfortable with followers whose loyalty was based in family.

"Maybe I should talk to the nephew."

"Maybe you should but he's in Rome right now."

Yet another connection between the rising Italian leader and the right in France. The war that was supposed to end all wars had done nothing but sow division and desperation among the peoples of Europe. Russia had fallen to the Bolsheviks and their mirror images on the right were putting down roots across the continent. Max wondered if he would ever know peace—real peace—again in his lifetime.

The bar was slowly filling up, mostly with American tourists, whose dollars stretched far in post-war France and whose sole goal in life seemed to be to get drunk and run wild. Their loud voices and boisterous laughter made quiet conversation difficult and Max leaned in to ask his final question.

"I'm looking for a man called Phillipe LaTour. He's a private detective like me but specializes in being invisible. If he followed you, you'd never spot him. He moves easily among groups of all political stripes though I'm not sure he has any firm beliefs of his own."

Giamatti shook his head, frowning, as if trying to recall where he had heard the name.

"Is Latour quite short but tough looking, clean-shaven with dark hair? With a purple mark on his face." asked Madame Novak. Max nodded. "We do know him, Jaco. Remember when I was having trouble with the Viscount last winter?"

"I remember." Giamatti leaned back in the leather booth, his eyes half closed. Whatever the trouble had been, he seemed unwilling to elaborate.

"The Viscount followed me from my native Hungary. A troublesome, avaricious man who had obtained certain documents that would have made staying in Paris difficult for me."

"He was blackmailing you?"

Novak continued speaking is if Max had not interrupted her. "We—I engaged this Latour as a go-between. One of Jaco's friends recommended him, remember it was—"

Giamatti closed his hand over her wrist. "I remember."

"The outcome doesn't matter," she said. "It was more than satisfactory."

"Have you seen him since then?" Max knew that Latour was somehow the key to this whole thing.

"Yes, a week or so ago. I had gone with Jaco to one of those interminable rallies he loves so much. I was waiting in a café across the street for it to end when Latour came in. I was going to call to him and thank him again for his services but he was clearly there for a purpose. He joined another man at a table against the far wall. They spoke for a few minutes and then left together. I thought it funny to see them walk off—Latour so small and the other man, practically a giant by comparison."

Two men, one large, the other small. "Could you describe the big man?"

"Not really, the lights were low and his back was mostly to me. He was wearing a slouch hat and an old suit. There was something about the way he moved that, I don't know, gave me the impression he was an older man, but one who was used to wielding power. Latour certainly seemed cowed by him."

Bucard would look like a giant compared to Latour and he certainly fit the description of an older man of power. Yet, there was something off about it too. Bucard never got his own hands dirty. Why would he make an exception now?

WHEN MAX RETURNED TO his apartment, a folded message had been slipped under the door. "Come now. J." followed by an address on Rue de Tolbiac in the 13th arrondissement. He took the Metro to Place d'Italie and walked ten minutes to find the boarding house where Alain had followed Jacqui. The concierge was expecting him and directed him to a small apartment on the third floor. The door was ajar so he pushed it open and entered.

Jacqui was sitting on a small chaise longue, reading a book. She looked up as he entered, the light of the single floor lamp illuminating her pale oval face. She carefully placed a strip of dark leather in the book and sat it on the table beside her as she rose. Max closed the distance between them in a few strides; she leapt to meet him and he caught her in his arms and held her tight against his chest. He kissed her tentatively, then harder as she responded to him. She was as light as a spring breeze, as heavy as a mid-winter gale. He rocked from the force of her presence in his arms, burned from the heat of having her slim body pressed against him.

After, they lay together on her narrow bed, sharing shy glances as if it were their first time together. Max opened his mouth to speak but Jacqui put her fingers against his lips. He kissed her fingers than her wrist and along her arm to her shoulder, her neck, her mouth. His hand drifted across the softness of her breast, her belly and her thigh. He pulled her on top of him and they made love again, slowly, tenderly, like old lovers returning to an accustomed place. Max reveled in the familiarity, the newness of her body against his.

They slept and when he woke, she was in a chair across from the bed, her body draped in a simple robe, as she gazed at him. He rolled on his side, pulling the thin sheet across his legs, a faint flush of embarrassment at the scars that marked his skin.

"It's alright, Max. I've traced every inch of you in my memory. There is nothing you need to hide from me."

Max thought of the tears he had shed in the presence of Simonne LeFoie and knew Jacqui was right. He had hidden his pain for so long he had begun to pretend it didn't exist. That was over now. He would never keep anything from this woman, this woman he loved more than he knew how to express. But he would find a way.

"I've missed you, Jacqui."

"I've missed you too. But..." Jacqui hesitated and then dropped her eyes to the floor. "I need to confess something."

Max's chest squeezed until he could barely draw a breath. "Yes?" His voice rasped and Jacqui looked up and smiled.

"Not that. Never that. Not now."

The release of tension made his head spin. He pushed himself into a sitting position.

"I am not Jacques Grand. Nor even Jacqueline Grandet. My real name is Joelle Meunier. My mother changed it after my father was sentenced to life at hard labour in 1894 for his role in a series of bombings in Paris. I was a mere babe in arms when he was sent to the penal colony in Cayenne, where he died fourteen years later. Though she was an anarchist herself, she abhorred what he had done and didn't want my life to be tainted by his name. I never met my father and only discovered the truth when my mother confessed it to me on her deathbed.

"By then, I was part of the movement—a movement that had long since rejected 'propaganda of the deed.' It now seems I am ready to abandon every other principle of anarchism. For you. If you will have me."

Max rose from the bed, the sheet falling to the floor, and took a step toward Jacqui, holding out his hand to her. She took it and pulled herself to her feet, letting the robe fall from off her shoulders, so they stood facing each other, naked, without passion but filled with emotion.

"I would never ask you to give up your beliefs. I know they are part of who you are."

"Don't you want to marry me?" Her voice trembled.

"I do. But I think there is another way. My ancestors were Scots; there was an ancient tradition called handfasting – a way of two people to declare their love and their intent to live together. It wasn't even permanent unless they wanted it to be. I want it to be but I'm willing to take the chance that you will too."

Jacqui—he knew he would always think of her that way—stepped into his arms. "I do,"

It was enough for him.

Chapter 23 Monday, October 31st 1921

He and Jacqui lingered in her rooms until noon and then enjoyed a leisurely lunch at a nearby café. Max left for his appointment with Ledux while she returned to her rooms to gather her things. She would take them to his place on Rue Lepic and they would meet at Le Coq Bleu later that day.

Ledux was waiting for him in his quarters in the 13th arrondissement. As usual, he was impeccably dressed and Max was glad that the man could not see his own clothing, which had rested in a pile on the floor in Jacqui's bedroom for the night. After the pleasantries, Max settled into a wingback chair with a small glass of Armagnac.

Ledux lit a cigarette, the smoke curling from his mouth and around his face. "You have made progress in your inquiries?"

"Some," said Max. He briefly described how he had discovered that the murders—Ledux was aware of all three—were linked to some of the bombings and that the whole thing was apparently going to culminate in the assassination of a French politician, though Max was still uncertain who it might be. After he finished his summary, Ledux leaned back in his chair, crossed his long legs and lit another cigarette.

"Coded journals that can only be read together. Clever. I had some experience in cryptography. The best techniques always required a key but this was a double key. I won't ask to see them; obviously that would be useless. So, what did you want to ask me about?"

Max pulled a sheet of paper from his jacket pocket, with the list of nicknames and coded dates. He read them off, trusting Ledux's prodigious memory to retain them. "I'm wondering if any of these meant anything to you."

"It's possible. Some may have been jokes between LeFoie and Bilodeau but others I've heard—sometimes publicly but generally behind the recipient's back. Tiger, of course, refers to Clemenceau, a name he relished so much that he recently went to India to hunt his namesake. He's come back full of oriental fire, determined to dabble in French politics behind the scenes. You would think at eighty he would have had enough but then, he was prepared to carry on as President a year ago if the Deputies had been more effusive in their support.

"As for the rest, I've heard Georges Valois called a weasel, mostly by anarchists who resent his shift from their camp to the far right, though I've never thought that was much of a leap. The Fist may refer to the former head of the Black Fist, whom you know well, or it might refer to his nephew, Marcel, a young man known for his ready use of violence. Chateau is sometimes used in a derogatory fashion for Aristide Briand, our current prime minister, though I've never really got the joke."

"Overrated and overdone, perhaps." Max said. He remembered now that Henri had referred to him that way, when he became prime minister for the seventh time earlier in the year.

Ledux laughed. "Perhaps. Stinker is almost certainly Coty, the perfumier who is using his considerable wealth to promote right wing ideas. He recently bought stock in Le Figaro, a respectable conservative paper. I wonder if it will remain so. The Lieutenant could refer to any number of people—even you Max—but since we are looking at French politicians, it is likely Andre Tardieu, who served as Clemenceau's chief advisor, his lieutenant, during the negotiations of the Treaty of Versailles, which by the way was referred to in certain circles as 'the convention of fools.' So that would be January 18th, 1919, though it might refer to the date of the signing or it's coming into force."

"That seems like ancient history."

"To the young, last week seems buried in the past, but it could be short form for any January 18th, a few months from now for example."

"I suppose."

"I'm afraid I can't help you with the rest though 'my brother's birthday' must refer to Mlle Bilodeau's brother Ferdinand who was killed in the war; LeFoie was an only child, I believe."

Ledux gestured to the counter holding the bottle of Armagnac, indicating he had something more to say. Max refilled their glasses, pouring a scant ounce in his own but giving the Colonel a more substantial portion.

"Mlle Bilodeau came from an interesting family. Did you know her mother was English?"

"She mentioned that."

"Did she also mention that her mother—Madeline Atterton—worked for Section 6, the Secret Service Bureau? She was a junior, of course, but I had some dealings with her on the India file. Extremely clever woman who should have risen higher than she did. But she met and married Jacques Bilodeau and settled down to raise their two children. Jacques was a colleague, not particularly bright but with a strong curiosity about things that made him useful. Very good looking though. Marie got his looks and her mother's brains."

"And the father's curiosity to be a good journalist."

"She wasn't just that, you know. There is a fledgling organization, formed during the darkest days of the war, made up of agents from the secret services of several western countries. Your friend, Buchan, knows about it but this is more secret than top secret so I doubt if he would tell you."

"Then why are you?"

"Because I don't give a wank about it anymore. Anyway, Marie worked for that bunch and her main assignment was to hunt down discontents in the Prefecture. If you ask me, that's what got her killed, not some stupid plot."

"Then I'm completely wrong..."

"Not necessarily. Discontent takes many forms."

AFTER LEAVING LEDUX with a promise to let him know how it turned out, Max headed for the offices of Le Grand Parisien to see if its editor, Tristan Braque, might be able to help with the remaining nicknames and the coded dates. The rumble of the train car seemed to stimulate his thoughts as bits of his conversation with Ledux replayed in his head.

Who was Bilodeau investigating in the Prefecture? The Prefect himself was certainly discontented with the results of his attempt to introduce identity cards but he was relatively new to the Paris office and to Paris itself and was unlikely to have deep roots in the local community.

His mind kept drifting back to Captain Fontaine. Since the first time he had run into him more than two years ago, the man had constantly complained about how his work was underappreciated. He lived, still lived, in the shadow of Gereau who had frequently shown himself to be a better detective and a better man. Gereau was now retired, but he retained considerable influence on Île de la Cité, and Fontaine still found his decisions being second guessed. Perhaps, his discontent, and his dislike for politicians, had twisted him. That might explain his sudden friendliness towards Max. What was the old saying? "Keep your friends close, but your enemies closer." Fontaine would certainly have had access to the weapons locker that held LePêcheur's revolver, but who had he persuaded to pull the trigger?

Someone had ordered Fontaine to round up the usual anarchist suspects. Their release and the criticism from the magistrate who had let them go would make it harder to pin the blame on them for subsequent events. He was missing something. He almost had it, but then the train pulled into the station and the jostling of the crowd as it pushed out of the packed car drove the thought from his mind. He stepped out into a light drizzle and hurried the half block to the newspaper offices.

Braque had just finished putting the final touches to the evening edition when Max arrived. He ushered him into his office.

"I can't give you long," he said. "My wife's brother is coming to dinner and there will be hell to pay if I'm late. Again. But I'm glad you dropped by. It saves me the trouble of tracking you down."

"You have something for me?"

"From Simmone LeFoie."

Braque pulled a small envelope from his top desk drawer and passed it across to Max. It was addressed simply to Max Anderson in delicate hand. It was sealed with a dob of wax. When Max pulled it open, he smelled a faint whiff of rose-scented perfume. The note inside was written in the same hand.

M. Anderson,

A man appeared at my parent's house in Strasbourg. He was a small man but had an aura of danger, of violence, about him. He gave his name as Pilier but I think he was lying. He claimed to represent one of Réjean's colleagues who was following up on the story my husband was working on when he died. He asked if I had any of Réjean's notebooks. I'm afraid I let it slip that I had given the only one in my possession to you. He thanked me but the expression on his face, it was like that of a devil. I am afraid he will come back so I am taking my children and family to a cousin. You may still contact me at the post office here.

Simmone LeFoie.

Max folded the note and put it back in the envelope and slipped both into his coat pocket. Pilier was French for "pillar;" LaTour meant "tower." Max had little doubt as to the identity of Simmone's visitor. The detective was at the heart of this matter but for whom was he working?

Braque probably longed to know the contents of the message. After all, he was a journalist and LeFoie had worked for him; he would be curious to know what the man's widow was writing to someone like Max. Max shook his head slightly as he secreted the note. Braque shrugged and said nothing.

"I'll give you the first interview if I solve this thing," said Max.

Braque laughed. "Am I that obvious? Well, you must have come here for a reason."

"I'm trying to identify some people that LeFoie referred to only by nicknames." He considered telling Braque about the partnership between LeFoie and Bilodeau but the fewer who knew the details of that, the better. It was enough that the conspirators knew; that knowledge might yet draw them into the open.

"Réjean was a great one for nicknames. He used to call me Braqueur because, he claimed, I was always trying to steal his scoops. Whom are you trying to identify?"

"Ironhead, Dunce and Sailor Boy." Max was satisfied with Ledux's suggestions for the other ones.

"Dunce was Louis Loucheur, even though he was anything but. Quite a brilliant man, now in charge of repairing the devastation in north-eastern France, a job for a generation. But his name is slang for cross-eyed so, to LeFoie, he was Dunce. Sailor Boy, I don't know. I never heard Réjean use it but Ironhead was a favorite of his. It didn't refer to anyone in particular but was reserved for people—mostly officers in the prefecture but others as well—who, once they had an idea fixed in their heads, couldn't be moved from it."

"Like Alphonse Gereau's fixation on anarchists," said Max, half to himself.

"You know ex-Captain Gereau, then? I'm sure he must be in his heaven, with all these bombings. He would see anarchists behind every bush. It must be frustrating for him not to have a flock of swallows at his beck and call, ready to round up the unavoidables."

"It must be. I won't keep you from your dinner."

"Too bad. I was looking for an excuse. Stephane is a terrible bore. Now, don't forget about that interview."

MAX FOUND JACQUI SITTING at the bar, chatting and laughing with Henri, Yesim and Josette. The few customers on a wet Monday evening were scattered in ones and twos along the wall of windows across from the bar. One of them lifted his hand as Max entered and Josette was by his table before Yesim could even react.

Jacqui turned as he approached and graced him with a broad smile. "Max, I've missed you!"

"It's only been six hours but...I missed you, too."

"Stop it," said Yesim, "you know too much sugar upsets my digestion."

"I can always use a little sugar," said Henri. "What, Max, you think I don't listen to what those singers at your other club are always crooning about?"

Max glanced at the cluster of glasses on the bar. "It looks like you started the party without me."

"Don't worry. I've seen you catch up." Yesim poured some brandy in a snifter and pushed across the tin bar.

"Have you solved the case yet?" asked Josette as she returned to the bar with several orders. "My cousin, Alain, says it is only a matter of time before you 'crack it wide open.'"

Max glanced at Henri who smiled back. The old man had shared his love of crime novels to yet another impressionable youth.

"I'm glad someone still has confidence in me…"

"False modesty is as bad as unwarranted pride," said Henri. "Havel had faith in your abilities and you proved yourself to Mme St. John. You have never failed, so why would anyone think you will this time?"

Max wasn't sure what he had done to win such accolades, such loyalty, but he was glad of it just the same. He raised his glass and all the rest, even some of the regulars along the window, raised theirs in turn.

"I do think I'm close. I understand what it's all about and why it happened. I'm sure I know who one of the two miscreants behind all this are but the other still eludes me."

"Whom do you suspect?" asked Yesim leaning across the bar.

"Not yet," said Max. "All the pieces are balanced in my head and I'm afraid if I speak too soon it will all come tumbling down. But tomorrow is another day."

With that he took Jacqui by the arm and led her down the hill to the apartment on Rue Lepic.

Chapter 24 Tuesday, November 1st, 1921

After a leisurely breakfast with Jacqui at the café across the street, Max returned to the apartment and placed a call to the Prefecture. Lepêcheur was still on telephone duty.

"Hello, Hubert, I see you yet lack the odor of holiness."

"Your nose continues to work. How can I help you, M. Anderson?"

Lepêcheur was usually not so formal; there must be a superior officer hanging around his desk. "I'm looking for Captain Fontaine. Is he in?"

"He was. There was another bombing this morning and he was sent to investigate. The reporting officer said it was nothing much but they sent him anyway. Everyone is getting jumpy when it comes to explosions. You can find him in front of Hotel Meurice on Rue de Rivoli."

"That's where Andre Bucard holds court. Was he the target?"

"Not likely since the blast was in a mailbox across the street. In any case it's where he *used* to hold court. His nephew has more modern tastes, and a more modest budget, and prefers to be in the centre of the action. Since he has brought new glory to the family name, old Bucard follows his lead. They usually lunch in one of the Chartier brothers' places in the Latin Quarter, most often La Bistro de la Gare. Shall I tell Fontaine you were looking for him?"

Max hesitated. The police captain had become one of his prime suspects, yet he still had his doubts. He would see him soon enough, either to confront him or to hand over the real culprits.

"Thanks, but it wasn't important. I'll find him later."

He hung up the phone and considered his next move. He had no sure way to reach Reinhardt except through Buchan. He knew where Gereau lived but didn't feel comfortable showing up unannounced, especially after their strange conversation outside the Gare du Nord, though he supposed he would do so if it came to that. He valued the older man's advice despite his obsessions.

As he was putting on his jacket, with the Kolb tucked into a holster under his arm, a soft tap at the apartment door signalled the arrival of Alain Laurent.

"Sorry, to disturb you. Josette said you were having a 'reunion.'" The tips of the young man's ears had flushed a bright red and Max wondered what his cousin had actually told him.

"It's alright. Jacqui stepped out to replenish our larder." Max waved his hand towards the small kitchen whose cupboards, during Jacqui's and, later, his absence, had been reduced to a few small bottles of condiments and some wizened carrots. "What do you have for me?"

"There is a stack of mail at Chez Jake, some of which looks urgent."

The month end bills, no doubt, thought Max, they can wait for another day. "You didn't come here to tell me that."

"I've tracked down Joseph Asper. I only managed to speak to him late last night so I left it for this morning. He said he'd be happy to meet with you if the usual arrangements—I guessed he meant money—were agreeable. He'll be taking an early supper in the Russian district. He said you would know where."

It was starting to look like a busy day. Before he got out the door, the phone rang. It was Reinhardt.

"I said I'd get in touch if I found out anything else I thought would be useful to you. I found the chemist that has been making the bombs. He was recently fired from the Société Générale de la

Dynamite and blames the current government for his misfortune. He has a workshop on the far side of Montmartre at Rue Champoinnet. He is operating under the name of Andre Gagnon but he will answer, most reluctantly, to Pepin. He's from Toulon but is staying in rooms above the shop so you should be able to find him anytime. Consider us even after this."

Max thanked Reinhardt and cradled the phone. There was no guarantee the bomb maker could identify the men he was making explosives for but it was the best lead Max had received since the case began. He knew he should contact Fontaine but he was now suspicious of the man and, besides, this had become personal. He would track down Bucard, drop in, despite his misgivings, on Gereau and then meet with Asper. Knocking on Gagnon's door after the sun was down was likely to frighten the man, maybe enough to reveal who the killers were.

As promised, Bucard was dining with his nephew, looking decidedly uncomfortable in the art deco designed restaurant, with glass and steel and laminated wood rather than the aged oak and leather to which he was accustomed. He spotted Max immediately and waved him over.

"This is the man I was telling you about, Marcel. The detective who constantly accuses me of murder. How many times has it been, Max, three, four?"

"I only recall two." Max slid into one of chrome chairs at the table, finding it surprisingly comfortable. *Maybe I should talk to Jake about updating the bar.*

"Americans should mind their own business," said the young man slouching in the chair opposite. Max had the feeling he had seen him before, recently too, but couldn't place him. Marcel Bucard was square-jawed and fit, though not as large as his uncle. Max judged him to be in his early twenties, though his hard, dark eyes made him look older.

"Max is Canadian," said Bucard. The younger man shrugged, clearly unimpressed by the distinction. "Do you know my nephew?"

"Only be reputation. People say he's part of the coming thing."

Marcel smirked at Bucard and straightened in his chair. "See, what did I tell you, uncle? The old approaches will no longer work. Even the Americans, pardon, *Canadians*, know that."

"I'm sure you are right, Marcel," said Bucard, though he didn't seem happy to admit it.

The younger Bucard abruptly stood up, throwing back his shoulders and puffing out his chest, like a bantam rooster trying to impress his larger rivals. "I have business to attend to," he said. "Meet me here again on Friday, uncle. I may have something for you."

He strutted across the room to the door, without a glance back. Being neither large, nor particularly small, Max ruled him out of involvement in the current plot. That required something more than the "coming thing;" it called for a man of gravitas and connection. Still, Max watched him as he exited the restaurant and strode quickly toward the train station. They would meet again, of that Max was certain.

"Will this be the third time that pays for all, Max?" Bucard smiled, but his eyes looked sad, like a man whom history was passing by.

"I don't think you're involved in my current case, but you may know something that will help solve it, the murders and the bombings both."

"Even if I did know, why would I tell you?"

Max considered that. Bucard had played a role—not always an agreeable one—in solving several murders. Every time he did it was both because his honour demanded it and because he had something to gain by doing it. What did his honour demand now and what did he have to gain?

"These bombings—"

Bucard held up his hand. "I can read the papers and can make my own conclusions. Most of these bombings have no purpose. It may be that the bombers have deliberately included random targets or it may be they are crimes of opportunity or spite. I suspect the latter. Every crime leaves a trace; this kind of campaign would prefer to leave as few clues as possible. After all, people have died; if they are caught, the guillotine awaits."

"I'm sure you are right." He repeated Reinhardt's theory that only some of the bombings mattered and his own that it was meant to cover a larger crime, an assassination that could be blamed on anarchists.

Bucard nodded. "I've heard rumours. They flow through this city like sewage going down a drain. But, again, why should I tell them to you?"

"Because France isn't ready."

"Ready for what?"

"Ready for the revolution your nephew is preparing himself for. Strike too soon and the state—and the people—will turn on him and his compatriots."

"Now you are an expert on how the drive of the French people will manifest?"

"I can read the papers and I can draw my own conclusions." Bucard glared at him but Max continued. "The AF ran candidates in the last election and didn't elect a single deputy. They have influence, yes, on the mainstream right, but the Bloc will turn on them in a moment if they even suspect them of killing one of their own. Your nephew and all your colleagues will be sailing for Devil's Island before their victim is in the ground. You know as well as I do, that every movement has its moment; is this their moment?"

"I thought these crimes would be blamed on anarchists," said Bucard.

"I believe that was the original intent; it is still the intent of the main actors in this campaign. But an assassination has secondary impacts. Choose the right target and the consequence is not outrage, it is war. The treaty was nothing more than an armistice. There are those who would see it fail."

"You are right; France is not ready for the revolution that will, that must come. I blame the education system. It will be the first thing we reform."

Max had no interest in Bucard's plans to reform the school system or anything else for that matter. All he wanted was justice for the dead and security for the living, for Jacqui and Yesim and Jake.

"Then your honor demands that you do not let it be stillborn. What do you know?"

Bucard stiffened in his chair. "You push me too hard."

"Look around," said Max, waving his hand at the modern décor with the stained-glass designs of geometric shapes in black or white or brilliant colors, the chrome and composite wood furniture and dramatic arches creating space where little space existed. "The world is changing. Your sense of duty has to change, too."

"Does it? My sense of duty could get us both killed."

"I got used to the idea of dying." *Is that still true*, he wondered, *now that I have something to live for.*

"At my age, I should have such courage. Very well." Bucard closed his eyes, either as an aid to memory or because he couldn't bear to watch Max as he revealed secrets he should protect. "Bear with me.

"This struggle has been going on since they deposed the emperor, since they turned on the generals who sent that dirty Jew to prison, since they demanded the legal separation of church and state. At every step they drove us back, even though God himself was on our side. Some of us lost faith; some decided to bide our time.

"The anarchists have nothing to do with the bombings but they are not the only ones who can form cells, remain hidden until they are ready to strike. The Black Fist was meant to be such a thing but I was betrayed by jealous and greedy men. Now, a new generation must take up the cause. But they are not ready—my nephew still thinks the Action Française is the answer but his thinking will mature.

"This plot was dreamed up inside one of these cells. Don't ask me which because I don't know. They needed a dupe and they found one. Now, even they don't know how it will end. The dupe is far smarter than he looks."

"Then you know who is behind this?"

"I'm not certain and I won't take the risk of being wrong. If you go after the wrong man, it will come back on me. But I can tell you two things. Several names have been floated as possible targets for this final murder: Tardieu. Valois, even Briand himself but my money would be on Louis Loucheur. He seems like a minor figure but he is deeply involved in the issue of reparations."

"And the other thing?"

"Stop looking away from hard truths. Stop judging with your heart. Assess with your head. Now, I, too, have business elsewhere. Pick up the bill, won't you?" Bucard stood and walked slowly, with dignity, to the door. Max noted he turned in the opposite direction to his nephew.

He pulled the bill across the table. It wasn't much and he dropped some francs on the table. He stared at the geometric design behind the bar, feeling his eyes pulled one way, then another. Stop looking away from hard truths. Then he knew and his heart sank. It couldn't be but he knew it had to be. *I must be wrong*, he thought. *I must be.*

But before he went to the Prefecture, he had to have hard evidence. He had to see if Asper had anything to add and talk to the bomb maker. And, of course, speak to Gereau and track down Latour.

GEREAU WASN'T AT HIS apartment. In fact, it wasn't even his home anymore. The concierge told him that she heard him arguing with someone—she didn't know who—and the next morning a van came and took his things away. There had been no sign of Gereau.

"Too bad," she said. "He was a good tenant, never heard a peep until last night. He's even paid up to the end of the month. I don't suppose you're looking for a place?"

Max shook his head and asked if she knew where he might have gone or who he had been arguing with.

"Sorry, no on both counts."

Max walked slowly away, wondering what could have caused Gereau to move. Had he been threatened or warned off and, if so, by whom? Could it be as simple as family trouble back home? Max knew he had nieces in the north; perhaps they had needed his help urgently. But then what was the argument about and who had it been with? The answer was right in front of him but the proof seemed elusive still.

It would be easier if he could have talked to Gereau first but, no matter, his absence was almost as informative as his presence would have been.

He found a phone, perhaps the one Gereau had been using and left messages for Alain to meet him at Chez Jake.

ASPER WAS BENT OVER a plate of dumplings that were the specialty of the house at Restaurant Petrograd. Several newspapers were spread across the table and his attention shifted from his food to the papers and back again. He stopped for a moment to take a slurp from a large glass of red wine as Max approached. He struggled to stand but Max waved him back into his seat.

"No need for formalities among old friends, Joseph."

"Is that what we are, friends?" Asper looked doubtful. "I haven't seen you in months."

"I'm from Canada. The place is so big you sometimes don't see your friends in years."

Asper laughed. "Sounds lonely."

"It's why I live in Paris."

"Are you eating? I'm told the veal Orloff is very good today. Out of my price range I'm afraid."

"I've arranged to eat later. I won't keep you long. The usual arrangement. Fifty francs for each bit of useful information."

"I heard it was 100 now."

"News travels fast."

"The world of professional information traders is a small one, Max."

"Snitches are a dime a dozen."

"Is that anyway to talk to a friend?" Asper didn't manage to look hurt. "I've come up in the world since I got my degree."

Max raised an eyebrow at that. Asper had been a starving student since the day he met him. "Congratulations."

The waiter approached with a menu and a glass of water. "I'll have a small glass of white wine and bring my friend the veal Orloff. Not a payment, Joseph, a graduation present."

"I'm touched. No, I really am. Now, I'll give you a present. Philippe Latour shot Dietrich. I don't know why, but I know he did."

"Can you prove it?"

"There was a witness. A pierette was on her way to meet a client. As she turned the corner into the alley, Dietrich cried out and then there was a shot. She ducked into the shadows but she got a good look at the shooter, small dapper man with a purple birthmark on his face. I don't know him well but it sounds like Latour."

"How did you find out?"

"She's a compatriot down on her luck. She came to me for money—I think she hit up every Croatian she could find—and I said I'd loan her some if she told me why she needed it. It was not what I expected. Anyway, I took her name and the address in Lyon where she was going." Asper slid a slip of paper across the table. Max glanced at and put it into his pocket.

"How did Latour get the gun? It was stolen from police headquarters."

"I had heard that. Don't look so surprised—nobody loves to gossip more than a cop on the beat. I make it a point to chat with a swallow every day. Any idea who took it?"

"The pistol was assigned to LePêcheur—an up-and-coming sergeant who is being punished for the loss. But I don't think he would steal his own gun."

"Then who did?"

The waiter arrived with the veal Orloff. The smell of roasted meat mingled with the earthy aroma of mushrooms made Max's mouth water and he regretted not ordering food for himself. Asper moaned softly in satisfaction as he tasted the dish. Max let him eat for a few minutes before answering his question.

"It was an inside job. At first, I suspected Fontaine—"

"The old Fontaine, maybe, but not the new one," said Asper around a mouthful of béchamel-covered veal.

"The new Fontaine?" Max had thought that Fontaine's changed behavior was only directed at him.

"I was robbed recently, not much of course, but it mattered to me. Fontaine himself took charge and caught the miscreant. He even got back some of my money."

"Fontaine investigated a petty theft?"

"He said he felt duty bound to help, given how he had treated me in the past. I asked around—he's making amends to all kinds of people. Did he give up drinking or something?"

"His wife left him."

Asper looked thoughtful. "I suppose that might make a man reassess his life."

"In any case, I'm not sure anymore if Fontaine is involved. If not Fontaine, then who?"

"I'm afraid I can't help you there," said Asper. "But I know someone who might. Do you know David Roget?"

"I know a Pierre Roget."

"Same guy, I think. Word is, if you want a gun, he can get it for you. No questions asked."

And there was the final link. His head had been right after all. Max dropped three hundred francs on the table then added another hundred to cover the meal. "Thanks, Joseph. I'll see you again soon."

Asper nodded, signalled the waiter for another glass of wine and turned his attention back to his food.

THE WORKSHOP WAS RIGHT where Reinhardt said it would be. Lights glimmered in both the lower floor and in the apartment above. Max touched the gun under his left armpit but left it in its holster. The front door to the workshop was open—it looked as if it had been forced—and a faint chemical smell drifted on the cool evening air. He looked through the doorway but saw no-one.

The interior was jammed with boxes, cupboards and equipment. A burner was on under a nearly empty flask on one black tabletop. A scatter of wires, clockwork and metal boxes covered another. Behind the table with the burner, a stool had been knocked over and there was a scatter of broken glass on the floor.

At the back of the workshop a narrow stair led up to a door, that was also ajar. A man's voice, high pitched and trembling, floated down the stair.

"I swear that's everything. Those papers are the only evidence of what we were doing here. All the rest I kept in my head. I swear. I swear." The man was almost blubbering.

Another man answered. Max couldn't make out the words but he recognized the timbre and cadence. It was Latour.

"No, don't! I have a wife. Children." The voice cut off in a cry of agony.

Max took the steps two at a time, throwing his weight against the door at the top. It slammed in to a something heavy. Max stumbled and almost fell.

The room was dim; only a single light illuminated the scene. A man. Gagnon, he presumed, was slumped on the floor, holding his stomach and moaning. It was his body the door had hit.

Latour, a bloody knife clutched in his left hand, stepped back in surprise at Max's appearance. Now, he stepped forward.

"I don't want to kill you, Max, but I will." He waved the knife in a slow circle, and took another step closer.

Max gauged the distance between them. If he went for his gun, Latour would be on him before he could draw it. He stepped around Gagnon, avoiding the puddle of blood pooling on the floor. He closed to within two arms lengths. Better for Latour to make the first move.

Kid O'Brien had lectured him over and over how to fight a southpaw and had even found a few for him to practice with. He had learned how to focus on the left hand, turning his head and shifting to the right before countering. More often than not he had taken a hard left cross that left his knees shaking and his vision blurred. He had gotten better but he had never truly mastered the skill.

And he'd never fought a southpaw who had a knife in his fist.

Latour circled to the left, drawing closer, keeping his knife-hand low and ready to strike. Max followed his lead, gliding along the wall, and keeping his distance. He occupied the centre of the room, flickering his eyes to get a sense of the space while never letting his attention drift from Latour's deadly left hand.

The room was mostly bare, as one might expect for a temporary residence. A narrow cot stood against the far wall, a table holding the single light beside it. A small carpet was on the floor next to the bed. Max took several quick steps, bent, and scooped it up.

Latour charged after him, knife extended. Max jerked the carpet up to block the thrust. The knife slipped through the thin cloth and then his jacket.

A searing pain along his right arm pulled a gasp from his mouth. He turned away, lifting his arm as he did so. The pain was excruciating.

Latour swore. "Putain!" His wrist twisted, forcing him closer. Max's left hand jerked up from his belt. Latour's head snapped back as Max's fist clipped his jaw. He jerked back. The knife pulled free but clattered to the floor.

"Baise ça!" Latour reached inside his jacket. Max dropped the carpet and grabbed at his pistol. Latour fired first but the shot went wide. Max gritted his teeth to control the pain. His first bullet caught Latour in the left shoulder; the second hit him in the ribs on the right side.

He was still holding his revolver. Max kicked it from his hand and heard it clatter down the stairs.

"Where is he?"

"Eat shit!" Latour was tough, Max gave him that.

"I have three bullets left in this gun."

"You won't kill me; you need me to testify."

"I don't. The chemist is still alive and the papers you came for are sitting on that table over there. I have an eyewitness to the murder of Dietrich and I know who gave you the gun. And I know who Roget is working for."

"Look, Max, the money was too—"

"I don't care. I won't kill you but I can leave you so you never walk again. Where is he?"

"At your apartment with your girl."

Whistles were sounding in the street. Max left Latour and Gagnon to the tender mercies of the swallows.

MAX TIED UP HIS ARM while he walked. The wound was long but shallow. Another scar to add to the collection. Chez Jake was on his route home. Alain was waiting out front.

"Walk with me."

In the few minutes it took to get to Rue Lepic, he handed over the address of the witness and the chemist's papers. He outlined his conclusions and then told Alain to hurry to the prefecture. "Tell Lepêcheur if you can find him. If not, tell Captain Fontaine or someone who works closely with him."

"Are you sure you don't want to wait?"

"I'm sure. After you've dropped off the evidence go to Le Grand Parisien and talk to the editor Braque. If he's not there, have them call his home. Tell him it's the scoop I promised him."

Alain nodded. Max watched him until he stepped into the Blanche Metro station and then climbed the stairs to his second-floor apartment. When he pushed the door open, his revolver in his hand, Jacqui was sitting at the table. Beside her was Alphonse Gereau.

Gereau stood, pulling Jacqui up and in front of him. She was tiny against Gereau's broad chest, her head just at the level of his heart. Gereau had Max's Webley in his hand.

"The police are on their way," said Max' lowering his pistol.

"No matter. I won't go to prison."

"I was thinking the guillotine."

"No. I have friends. I would be spared that. But this is over now and it can only end one way."

"Gereau."

"Captain Gereau, if you don't mind. I have failed. Failed to start the revolution. Failed even to take my vengeance on the goddamn anarchists. There are forces bigger than us. Bigger than France. Change is coming. For all of us."

Gereau pushed Jacqui away and raised the revolver. He fired before Max could move. The room filled with sound but Max still could hear the bullet whizz past his left ear. How can he miss from eight feet away. A second bullet passed by his right ear. The acrid smoke billowed.

Gereau was saying something but Max couldn't hear but he could read the lips beneath the bristling mustache. "Tirez! Shoot!"

Max placed the three remaining bullets in a circle on the left side of Gereau's chest. Blood gurgled from the big man's mouth. Then he fell on his face.

He was still there, standing over his friend's body, Jacqui cradled in his arms, when Fontaine and Lepêcheur arrived.

Chapter 25 Friday, November 4th, 1921

Max was waiting at Le Coq Bleu, dressed in his best suit. His right arm was held in a black sling. His ears were still ringing but he could hear the voices of his friends well enough.

Yesim had hung a "Closed for Private Event" sign on the door and then stood guard to let the guests trickle in. Candles on the table and the glowing parrot were the only lights. A black flag hung behind the bar.

Hugo had been the first to arrive though Harvey, who never missed the chance for a free meal, showed a few minutes later. Jake and Smitty, each with a pretty woman on his arm, were representing Chez Jake. Alain was there with his cousin Josette. Colonel Ledux sent his regrets along with a bottle of well-aged Armagnac. Buchan came alone, carrying two enormous bouquets of flowers.

Captain Fontaine arrived in full dress uniform with a squad of swallows, although LePêcheur, restored to sergeant's rank, was the only one of them permitted to enter. LePêcheur had brought his wife. Asper had promised to be there before eight. Giamatti and Mlle. Novak stood by the bar; the Italian kept glancing nervously at Fontaine.

Bucard had declined the invitation but Jacques Court had shown up, dressed in an outrageous outfit that looked more like silk pajamas than a suit. He had brought a man and two women, Jacqui's closest friends from the movement. Braque was sitting at a table along the wall, notebook in hand. The story had been a sensation and now he wanted to do a follow-up for the weekend edition.

Reinhardt arrived with Delacroix and two beautiful women. Max barely noticed them as he glanced at his watch again. Still twenty before the hour, when Jacqui was due to walk down the stairs from Yesim's apartment.

"Stop looking at your watch," said Henri, who had bought a new suit for the occasion and was freshly barbered and smelling of cologne. "She's not going to flee down the fire escape."

"You never know. She is a free spirit."

Henri laughed. "No doubt about that. She's exactly what a stodgy Canadian needs to keep him alive."

"I'm not stodgy. I own part of a jazz bar."

"The stodgy part. Yesim and I have come to an arrangement. I'm to give up working as a porter and become a part time bartender. Josette and I will continue to provide food from the Luxe until the workers finish the renovations. To make ends meet, I will become an informant. You'll need someone who knows the city now that Erich Harvey is returning to America."

"I only pay for useful information."

"All my information is useful."

Asper showed up at a few minutes before the hour. He had bought a fresh shirt in the latest style but the rest of his outfit was somewhat shabby.

Yesim locked the door and went to stand beside the stair. He would walk with Jacqui—they had decided that Joelle could stay in the past—to meet Max in the centre of the room. He would then stand with Henri to be the primary witnesses.

There would be no music, no religious or even civil ceremony, no officials and no record other than in the memories of those present.

Jacqui appeared at the foot of the stairs. She was dressed in a simple white silk dress, that reached to her ankles. There was lace at the throat and the wrists and white flowers were twined in her hair.

She had explained that white was the color, not of purity, but of new beginnings. A clean slate they would write their future on.

They met at the centre of the room and clasped left hands. Jacqui wound a soft blue cord around their hands. "I pledge my body and heart to you. I will walk with you along a path of our mutual choosing. If that path should diverge, I will part from you with a full heart and wishes for your happiness."

Max's throat tightened at the thought of his love ending but they were the words they had agreed on. Henri stepped forward and wrapped a red cord on Max's behalf. Max's mouth opened and the words tumbled out. When he had said them, tears began to run down his face.

"I love you, Jacqui."

"I love you, too, Max."

He leaned in and kissed her. Yesim unwound the cords and handed the blue one to Max and the red to Jacqui. "I witness this love freely given."

"I witness this love freely received," said Henri.

"No bonds will ever tie you," said Yesim.

"Save the bonds of love." Henri's eyes glistened as he spoke the final words of the ritual.

Max and Jacqui kissed again while their friends cheered them on.

Later, after most of the guests had retired to Chez Jake in a parade of taxis, Max sat with Henri, Yesim and Jacqui and shared a bottle of the best champagne from the cellar.

"I was surprised to see Fontaine here," said Yesim, glumly. "Is that going to be a regular thing?"

"Probably. He backed my plea of self-defence and kept me out of court. He may prove useful now he's been promoted."

"I would never have suspected Gereau was behind it all," said Henri.

"That was the problem. I couldn't suspect him either. I had a blind spot as bad as Gereau's one about anarchists."

"How did he go so wrong?" Jacqui asked. "Everyone said he was honourable."

"I think he was," said Max. "He truly believed he was acting in the interests of France, stopping the destruction of the state by the Black Flag, but I think he felt lost after he was pushed out of the Prefecture. He was looking for something to believe in and it found him.

"Gereau was recruited, by a small far-right cell, if what Bucard told me was true, to arrange the diversion campaign, a series of bombings that would look to implicate anarchists while providing cover for the assassination. Before the first blast, he discovered that Lefoie—who was never one of his sources—had discovered the plot and planned to out the conspirators. Gereau recruited Latour, whom he had known for years, to help intimidate LeFoie. Things got out of hand and Lefoie wound up in the Seine. After that, Gereau knew he had gone wrong but had no way to turn aside. I think he was trying to tell me that but his pride wouldn't let him.

"They weren't the cleverest of operatives. Gereau needed the structure of the Prefecture and better help than LaTour could give him, so it was no great feat for Bilodeau, using some of LeFoie's notebooks he had left at her house, to figure out what had happened. I don't know how they got the gun and scarf they planted at the scene, maybe from Deitrich though more likely from Roget, who had infiltrated an anarchist cell. It was clear they meant to implicate Jacqui, one of their hated anarchists. It may have been to distract me and keep me from discovering the truth as well. Gereau and Letour were inept conspirators but efficient, if reluctant, murderers."

"Reluctant seems an odd description," said Yesim.

"They could have killed Hugo but they didn't. That says something."

"I suppose," said Henri. "But who recruited Gereau?"

"I don't know. The only trace of them are several large deposits into Gereau's account. There was nothing in any of his papers that suggests who was behind all this. We don't even know if they were French." The thought that the originators of the plot that had first corrupted and then destroyed an honest officer and, yes, a friend, might escape troubled Max deeply. They must have left a clue somewhere and he would find it and them, that he promised himself and Gereau.

"But it's all done now," asked Jacqui.

"There will be no assassination attempt. The Prefecture has decided not to even tell Loucheur he was in danger, though they will be keeping an eye on him and some of the others mentioned in the secret journals. So, yes, it is all done now."

"Hah!" said Henri. "Nothing is ever finished in this place. You may call it the city of lights; I call it the city of plots."

"You may be right," said Max. "But it's done for now."

"Yes," said Jacqui. "Let's forget our troubles for tonight. There's a party waiting."

Max took her hand in his. He could already hear the music.

The end

Don't miss out!

Visit the website below and you can sign up to receive emails whenever Hayden Trenholm publishes a new book. There's no charge and no obligation.

https://books2read.com/r/B-A-ZSKO-CBVLC

BOOKS 2 READ

Connecting independent readers to independent writers.

Did you love *The Glare of Truth*? Then you should read *By Dawn's Early Light*[1] by Hayden Trenholm!

[2]

When a naked corpse is found in the Luxembourg Gardens, Captain Gereau approaches Max Anderson to take on the case "to aid a fellow Canadian." Sarah St. John, the wife of the deceased, is the primary suspect but Max has his doubts. Mark St. John was in Paris, supposedly to visit his mistress, Irina Pavlovna, but he clearly had other reasons to be there -- politics, arms smuggling and stolen Italian money. Max soon finds himself embroiled in the violent world of French and Russian politics and the even more uncertain world of *les liaisons dangereuses*.

Read more at https://www.haydentrenholm.com/.

---

1. https://books2read.com/u/mq15Bv

2. https://books2read.com/u/mq15Bv

Also by Hayden Trenholm

Max Anderson Mysteries
In the Shadow of Versailles
By Dawn's Early Light
The Glare of Truth

Standalone
Let Me Gather My Thoughts

Watch for more at https://www.haydentrenholm.com/.

About the Author

Hayden Trenholm is an award-winning playwright, novelist and short story writer. His short fiction has appeared in many magazines, including Analog Science Fiction and Fact, and anthologies such as The Sum of Us and Strangers Among Us, and on CBC radio. His first novel, A Circle of Birds, won the 3-Day Novel Writing competition in 1993; it was recently translated and published in French. His trilogy, *The Steele Chronicles*, were each nominated for an Aurora Award. Stealing Home, the third book, was a finalist for the Sunburst Award. Hayden has won five Aurora Awards – three times for short fiction and twice for editing anthologies. He purchased Bundoran Press in 2012 and was its managing editor until the press closed in 2020. He lives with his wife and fellow writer, Liz Westbrook-Trenholm, in Ottawa, having retired in 2017 after 15 years as a policy adviser to the Senator for the Northwest Territories.

Read more at https://www.haydentrenholm.com/.

About the Publisher

House of Straw is an Ottawa based publisher of mysteries and other genre books.